Praise for Marianne K. Martin

"Marianne Martin is a wonderful stor[y] with a light, witty touch with langu[age] emotions of people in love. There is [...] to her characterizations that ma[ke] beguiling." —Ann Bannon

"*Under the Witness Tree* is a multi-dimensional love story woven with rich themes of family and the search for roots. This is a novel of discovery that reaches into the deeply personal and well beyond—into our community and its emerging history. Marianne Martin achieves new heights with this lovingly researched and intelligent novel." —Katherine V. Forrest

"[*Under the Witness Tree*] was entertaining, and the way the pieces all came together was ultimately quite satisfying. Read it for the tight plot, for the mystery, for the romance, and don't miss this engaging story." —*Midwest Book Review*

"Marianne Martin is a skilled writer who fully develops her characters and pulls the best from them. . . . *Under the Witness Tree* is a novel rich in character and storyline."
—*Mega Scene Book Review*

"*Mirrors* is a very fine novel, well worth your time and treasure."
—*The Bay Area Reporter*

"Not only does [*Love in the Balance*] have love and excitement, but it has issues very close to all of us."
—*The Alabama Forum Gaiety*

"[*Legacy of Love*] is undoubtedly one of the finest . . . worth reading." —*Our Own Community Press*

"[*Dawn of the Dance*] is a beautifully written love story, filled with gentleness and drama." —*Mega Scene Book Review*

Also by Marianne K. Martin

FOR NOW, FOR ALWAYS

MARIANNE K. MARTIN

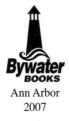

Ann Arbor
2007

Bywater Books, Inc.
PO Box 3671
Ann Arbor MI 48106-3671

Printed in the United States of America on acid-free paper.

Bywater Books First Edition: October 2007

Cover designer: Bonnie Liss (Phoenix Graphics)

ISBN 978-1-932859-43-0

This novel is a work of fiction. All persons, places, and events were created by the imagination of the author.

Mixed Sources
Product group from well-managed forests and other controlled sources
www.fsc.org Cert no. SW-COC-002283
© 1996 Forest Stewardship Council

For Jo

ACKNOWLEDGMENTS

The author would like to offer her gratitude and thanks to the following for their invaluable help in the production of this book:

Publisher and editor Kelly Smith, whose attention to detail and wonderful ability to analyze plot and character is invaluable.

Editor Mandy Woods, whose keen eye and expertise is so important to the finished quality of this book.

Mr. Eric Skrumbellos, who provided much-needed information on the workings of the Child Protective Service system and Probate Court.

Marcy Tyson for sharing her time and her Above and Beyond Childcare children.

Joan Opyr for the time from her busy schedule to do child-proofing.

Best friend and partner Jo, whose support and loyalty is immeasurable.

Prologue

It hardly looked like a place where lives could be transformed so drastically. The little third-story room with large windows and pew-like seating seemed too bright, too everyday. Renee Parker couldn't believe this was the setting where children could be uprooted from their homes and separated from their families forever. The destiny of five lives was going to be decided here. There should be dramatic lighting and foreboding strains of music to match the turmoil Renee felt inside. Instead, there was only innocuous chitchat and easy laughter.

One-year-old Rory moved in her arms to nuzzle against her chin, but did not wake. So unaware. His innocence truly a blessing. *Will it be five years, or ten, before he realizes what today meant?* She kissed the warm, smooth skin of his forehead. *Will he know, will they all know, that I did everything I could to keep us together?*

Renee looked up as Shayna Bradley rejoined her at the table. "Jean will take him right after she testifies. You doing okay?"

Renee nodded.

"We need to think positively here," she said, meeting Renee's eyes directly. "The judge will be looking for a confident, competent guardian. And that's you."

It is. It will be. Merely Shayna's presence was enough to quell at least her biggest fear. If the best child advocacy attorney in the state couldn't make the case to keep them together, then she knew there was nothing more she could have done. And the other fears, scratching her like an old wool sweater, she'd shed in time.

"We aren't setting precedence here," Shayna continued. "That was done a few years ago, and the girl was a year younger than you are."

Renee nodded again. "And you like this judge?"

"I do," replied Shayna. "But she relies heavily on CPS case-worker recommendations—the very thing that usually helps my cases is what makes our job harder today."

Concern creased a hard line between Renee's brows as she rested her cheek against Rory's forehead.

"Hey, I said it made it harder," Shayna said, "not impossible. I'm at my best when my guard's up. And believe me, your case worker had my guard up the minute I met her. We're ready for her," she promised as the bailiff entered the courtroom. "You just be you."

They stood as a younger than expected and bespectacled Judge Taylor was announced. They sat as she did. Rory woke only to look around, and then settled back against Renee's chest to suck his thumb.

"Good morning, everyone," Judge Taylor began. "We're here this morning to decide guardianship of the five minor Parker children: Renee, seventeen, Jaylin-John, six, Jennifer, five, Rachael, three, and Rory, one." She glanced up from the file to acknowledge those sitting at both tables and continued, "I understand from your report, Mrs. Gordon, that Child Protective Services is recommending foster care for all five?"

"Yes, Your Honor," Millie Gordon replied.

She had risen to address the judge, standing military straight in her gray wool suit, and Renee thought how effectively a suit and pulled-up hair had transformed the matronly figure of their interviews.

"I see that the mother is incarcerated," the judge continued. "Where is the father?"

"The biological father of the four younger children is deceased," replied Mrs. Gordon. "Renee Parker's biological father is unknown."

"Are there no other family members capable of helping with this situation, even to take a couple of the children?"

"No, Your Honor. There is one living grandparent on one side who is suffering from Parkinson's disease, and one living grandparent on the other side who is, well, less than responsive. The only other relative is an uncle who is single and frequently out of the country with his job."

Judge Taylor nodded as she studied the report. "And you are opposed to the request for guardianship by Renee Parker of her four siblings."

"Yes, Your Honor, I think that we would be expecting more from a seventeen-year-old than she could handle. The children are very young. They will need full-time care. Renee, as their guardian, would not be free to pursue a career, or even more than limited hours of work. It would be impossible for her to have the normal life of a teenager. As much as I dislike splitting up siblings, I do believe foster homes would provide these children with the best chance at normalcy. There was a time when women just naturally had their children at a very young age. Families were larger and there was an extended support system around them and there wasn't the concern that they couldn't manage. But we don't live in those times any more. We don't live in Mayberry or on Walton's Mountain and our concerns for children must reflect that."

The judge looked thoughtful as she leaned forward on her forearms.

The fear that had waned with Shayna's confidence now trembled awake in the pit of Renee's stomach. If only the judge would let Shayna talk, let her tell everyone how we've thought about everything. And how no consequence could be greater than what she saw in Jaylin's eyes when he realized that his mother was not coming home. Is it even possible for someone else to understand what I feel, to know that I would do anything to keep it from happening again?

Shayna knew, not because she had been told how it felt, but because she knew how it felt in her heart to lose someone. That, Renee decided, was what created the edge in her voice, the

3

urgency that sounded as though someone's life depended on her conviction. It made people listen. Renee anxiously awaited Shayna's chance.

Shayna stood beside her, solid and sure, ready to present the case that would decide the future of five lives.

"Ms. Bradley," the judge addressed, "I'm well aware that we will not be breaking new ground with my decision today, so I don't need to hear that argument. I do, however, need to be convinced that Renee Parker has the maturity and ability to care for her brothers and sisters and that giving that care would be in her best interest as well."

"We're prepared to do that, Your Honor. You were given affidavits from four of Renee's teachers, in which they all speak to her academic discipline and her maturity. And another of her teachers, Jean Carson, is here today to give you a more personal picture of Renee and her family."

Renee watched gratefully as Ms. Carson, her confidante of three years, took a seat beside the judge's bench. There was no better listener, no better advisor, no one she trusted more to speak for her than this woman. She smiled for the first time today.

"Thank you for coming in this morning, Ms. Carson," Judge Taylor began. "What can you tell me about this young lady that will help me make a very difficult decision?"

"First, let me say that students like Renee are why teachers continue to teach." Jean sent Renee a reassuring smile before continuing, "Over the past four years I've watched her grow from a young girl into a young woman. I've acted as her teacher and her advisor, and she has trusted me with her concerns and her fears and hopes. And I've seen her adapt as those fears and hopes have changed, in a way that few adults are capable of doing."

"Such as?"

"She made the starting line-up on the varsity softball team as a sophomore, which at our school is quite an accomplishment. But when her stepfather lost his job she quit the team in order to babysit latchkey kids and contribute some money toward the family bills."

4

The judge's attention, which had been fixed on Jean, shifted momentarily to the sandy-haired young woman in question.

Jean continued. "Renee is a good student, and going on to college was something that she had been excited about and planning for three years. She queried many of the teachers about the schools they had attended, then wrote to colleges and universities to learn as much as she could about each one. I helped her understand the types of financial aid available through grants and loans and work-study programs, because I knew how important being able to go was to her. So, after her stepfather's death, when she left the applications on my desk unsigned, I knew that she had made a very personal and difficult decision—one for which she did not want or need my advice."

"Did you support that decision?"

"I supported the love that brought her to it."

Judge Taylor offered a polite smile. "That was nicely put. I suspect support like that is held in high regard by your students, and deservingly so. Thank you, Ms. Carson, you've provided me some much-appreciated information."

Jean stepped down from her seat and crossed the room to lift Rory from Renee's lap.

"Renee," the judge began, as Jean left the courtroom. "I'd like to hear what *you* have to say ... just stay right there," she said as Renee rose, "and tell me why you want this responsibility."

"Yes, maam." Her voice was soft and somewhat unsure. "Your Honor."

Judge Taylor held up her hand. "I have an idea." She stepped down from behind the bench, down two steps, and stopped a few feet in front of the table. "Now, try to explain it to me as if you were talking with Ms. Carson. Okay?"

Renee nodded. She wished she could close her eyes and open them again and be sitting in Ms. Carson's office, looking into the eyes she knew and trusted. But she wasn't. She was looking into a stranger's eyes, empty eyes, waiting for her to fill them with recognition of the real Renee Parker. And they were giving her only one chance. "I ..." One chance to say it right. "I want to keep our family together; that's the most important thing to me. I'm

5

quite a bit older than my brothers and sisters, so my parents counted on me to help. I babysat a lot while they worked. There were often times when either my mother or stepfather was out of work, but we never knew when that was going to happen. I was the one the kids could count on most to be there. I don't know ..." Her voice had begun to waver. She cleared her throat and glanced quickly at Shayna, standing next to her, and tried again. "It was really hard when my stepfather died ... and when my mother went away. I don't think I could stand to see how scared they would be if I ..." The tears had begun and Renee's best efforts at control only resulted in a puff of her cheeks and a look of anguish.

"Ohh," Judge Taylor uttered, opening her arms. "Come here and let me give you a hug."

Renee complied, leaving her place behind the table and accepting the judge's offer. "I'm sorry," she said softly. Sorry for being weak, and so sorry for blowing the one chance she had. "I don't usually cry like this."

"But we all need to cry now and then. It's perfectly all right." The judge gently tightened her arms and then released her embrace. "There. A hug sometimes helps more than anything else." She smiled as Renee returned to her place, and added, "I want what's best for you, Renee, for all of you."

When she returned to the bench she redirected her attention. "Ms. Bradley," she said, leaning forward and looking intently at Shayna, "give me something concrete here, otherwise I'm not going to be able to do what I really want to do."

Renee closed her eyes. Two down in the bottom of the ninth and we're losing. The acids roiled in her stomach and threatened to rise to her throat. Suddenly the fear was more real than it had ever been. How do I explain it to them? They'll think that I don't want them, that I don't love them enough. How could they possibly understand?

She opened her eyes again as Shayna began to speak. Maybe if she could stay focused on Shayna—on the eyes nearly matching the cocoa-brown skin, and the voice so clear and sure—maybe the fear would stop.

"Aside from the usual available assistance," Shayna was saying, "on which we plan to work closely with CPS," a quick glance of acknowledgment to the other table, "Mrs. Gordon, we have taken great care in assuring that every aspect of the Parker children's lives has been considered. There is a subsidized apartment available within the school district which will avoid uprooting the children from their friends and classmates, and we've found a daycare willing to take an additional state-assisted child. As far as employment, Renee will be able to work morning hours at a bookstore and stay within the hourly limits to qualify for food stamps." She held up a folder in each hand. "I have commitment letters from all three establishments for both you and Mrs. Gordon. Plus there's an additional commitment letter included in there from an auto mechanic."

The bailiff retrieved and delivered the folders as Shayna continued. "A five-year-old mini van has been donated to the family, and the mechanic who has committed to keeping it in good repair at no cost for the next three years is my brother, so I can vouch for his integrity."

Shayna paused to allow the judge to examine each letter, and continued when she once again had her full attention. "Finally, two of Renee's teachers, Ms. Carson and Ms. Talbert, have volunteered to be on an emergency contact list, along with myself and my parents, in case any situation arises where Renee needs a little extra help."

Judge Taylor removed her reading glasses and fixed her gaze silently on Shayna.

Renee couldn't pull her eyes from the judge's face. Was she thinking? Hesitating to say what she really did not want to say? The constriction in Renee's chest would not allow a normal breath. Fear winning out over hope.

At last the judge spoke. "You know, a lot of people, including myself, have off-handedly used the phrase 'It takes a village.' I think we even believed that we understood it, that we used it with humility ... I venture to say that we did not." Her focus shifted to Millie Gordon. "Our responsibility, all of us vested in civil service, is to be part, an integral part, of that community. I think in our ignorance, or our arrogance, we have come to believe that our

7

responsibility is to *define* the borders of that community. It is not."

She returned her attention once again to Shayna. "I don't know, Ms. Bradley, if guardianship, even with all that you have done to assure the help that she needs, is the best thing for Renee. I do believe it is the best thing for the younger Parker children."

Renee held her breath, her eyes wide with the hope that she understood what was being said.

Judge Taylor met her eyes. "Because I haven't been able to tell what is best for you, Renee, I have to do what your teacher and your attorney have done, and that is to trust that indeed *you* know." She straightened her posture and picked up the gavel. "Guardianship of her four younger siblings is hereby granted to Renee Parker." And with a thwack she added, "I wish you luck, Renee."

Chapter 1

Renee sat quietly with her brothers and sisters around the table in the prison visiting room, waiting for the inevitable. It began the moment Sylvia Parker entered the room.

Tears, predictable and disheartening, welled in Sylvia's eyes as she rushed to hug each of her children. Always Rory first. For three of his four years, twice a month was all she had had to get to know her youngest.

"My precious boy," she said, kissing the top of his head. "Have you been good for Renee?" He nodded his head vigorously, then planted an obligatory kiss on his mother's cheek. "That's my good boy." Sylvia looked up at Renee. "Two seizures this week?"

A full year after the diagnosis of epilepsy and eight seizure-free months had eased the concern considerably, but this week he had Renee worried. "I'll make sure he gets more rest next week. I think maybe he overdid it."

Six-year-old Rachael jumped from her chair and wrapped her arms around her mother's shoulders. "And my sweet Rachael," Sylvia said, adding a smile. "I miss you all so much."

"Rory wasn't good all the time"—information from Jenny that garnered a "that's enough" look from Renee. Eight-year-old reasoning, however, doesn't always see the need for compliance. "He broke my butterfly lamp."

9

This time Renee said it aloud. "That's enough, Jenny."

"He didn't mean to," Rachael said, standing defiantly next to her little brother.

"But he lied about it," Jenny defended, bringing Rory to tears. "And now he thinks they're going to lock him up, too."

Renee rose and shot a look of anger-tinged disapproval at Jenny. "I wonder why he thinks that," she said, continuing around the table.

"They wouldn't lock up a sweet little boy," Sylvia said, kneeling to again hold Rory. "Especially one *this* sweet." She wiped his tears and kissed his cheek.

"I've got him, Mom. Go sit and visit. He'll be all right. I'm sure Jenny can find happier things to tell you about."

Sylvia rose and feigned a smile at the others. She pulled a chair around to sit between Jenny and J.J. "Jenny, I would much rather hear about what you're doing in school. And Jaylin, I want to hear all about baseball."

"My name's J.J.," he said as he pushed his chair back noisily and left the table.

"He hates to be called Jaylin," Jenny explained.

Sylvia started to get up, but Renee interceded. "I'll take care of it. You stay here and visit. She approached J.J. on the other side of the room. "Come on, J.J., be nice while you're here. You and I'll talk about it when we get home. Okay?"

"I hate coming here!" he said, contorting his normally genteel features. Then, loud enough for the whole room to hear, he added, "And I hate *her*!"

"Enough," she said firmly. Renee stepped in front of him to look him directly in the eyes. "I thought we had a deal. You promised me you wouldn't do this."

He had no chance to respond before Sylvia appeared at his side. "Honey, I'm sorry. I promise I'll remember to call you J.J. Come on and talk with me, please, honey." She reached out to take his hand, but he jerked it away. Hugs had been routinely denied to her, but today even a touch wouldn't be allowed.

"Leave me alone," he shouted. "I hate you."

Renee stepped between them. "Stop it, J.J.! You don't hate

anyone. Now go sit over there by the door." She turned to her mother to see the watery blue eyes now spilling their contents down her cheeks.

"I'm sorry, Mom. Maybe I should have let him stay home like he wanted; it would have made it easier on all of us."

"He's only nine."

"He would have stayed at a friend's house, Mom. I wouldn't have left him alone."

"I know, Renee. I meant he's too young for all that anger." Her hand shook as she tried to wipe her cheeks dry. "What have I done to him? What have I done to you?"

"Don't, Mom. It won't do any good. It never does any good ... It won't change things."

"I would, Renee. You know I would change it if I could. I'm working real hard in here, so maybe they'll let me out early. You know that," Sylvia touched a still shaky hand to Renee's cheek, "don't you, baby?"

"I know, Mom; you don't have to tell me. But there's nothing you can do about it now. You just have to trust me to take care of things." For five more years, or seven, for as long as it takes.

"So much responsibility," Sylvia replied, concern clearly pressed into the lines of her face. "You were too young to have to shoulder keeping a family together. And you've done such a good job. I'm so proud of you—so proud that I tell everyone who will listen. I talk about it like I'm any normal mother bragging on her children's accomplishments." She turned her gaze to the younger children entertaining themselves at the table with paper and crayons. "Then I lie awake in my cell at night, and all I feel is shame." She folded her arms across her chest and dropped her gaze. "I have no right to be proud of anything—even you. All I can do in good conscience is worry."

Renee was shaking her head before her mother finished. "No. I don't want you to worry. It does no good. Study the books I bring you; concentrate on helping some of the women. Help where you can; don't worry about where you can't."

"I am, honey, I am. It does help me to be useful, and I am making a difference. Did I tell you how good Danny's doing? She read the comic from the newspaper today. I couldn't believe that someone my age couldn't read at all. You know who I mean, don't you? The one whose girlfriend works in the laundry?"

Renee looked away to scan the room. "Yeah, Mom, I remember."

After a few seconds of awkward silence, Sylvia asked, "You're not bringing girls to the apartment, are you? If social services found out—"

"No, Mom. I don't even have time for friends."

"Honey, maybe you should try, you know, to find a nice boy." She took Renee's hands and tried to make eye contact. "It would make things so much easier, and you wouldn't have to worry—"

"No, *you* wouldn't have to worry." She reluctantly met her mother's eyes. "Look, it wouldn't matter; I don't have time for that either."

"Then how do you know that it wouldn't be the right thing for you—some day?" She pulled her daughter's hands up to hold them tightly against the front of her uniform. "All I'm saying is that one experience doesn't make you ..." Her eyes remained fixed. "You're too young to say that you never want to be with a man. You don't have to decide things like that now."

"It's not a decision at all," she said, slipping her hands from her mother's grasp. Despite her better intention, the tone of her voice dipped into cynicism. "Just like the rest of my life, it's not a decision at all." As quickly as she said the words, she regretted them. She needed to have better control—she usually did. There was no excuse, not frustration or exhaustion or even anger, for hurting her mother further. Incarceration was enough hurt, painfully obvious in her mother's eyes—always so close to tears. And now, words spoken without restraint had brought the tears spilling down her mother's cheeks again.

"I'm sorry," she said, wrapping her arms around her mother's shoulders. "I don't mean to hurt you. Sometimes I'm not as grown-up as I think I am. I love you, and so does J.J. What he hates is that you're not home. He just can't sort out the difference right now."

Sylvia eased from their embrace and wiped her tears with the sleeve of her uniform. "You're more grown-up than you think you are. I only hope that someday you'll be able to forgive me for making such a mess of things."

"The little ones don't know there's anything to forgive. You'll just have to be patient with J.J."

"And you?"

She looked away from her mother's eyes and lied, "Already forgiven."

Chapter 2

Renee moved about the tiny kitchen with a prowess born of practice. She simultaneously planted a kiss atop Rachael's head and placed a bowl of cereal in front of four-year-old Rory. "Hey, sports fan," she called toward the hallway. "Are you planning to watch the game with me tonight?"

J.J.'s sleepy voice answered from the bedroom, "Yeah."

"You know the deal. Out the door in fifteen minutes or bedtime at eight, no matter what the score is."

"I'm up," came the reply.

Renee snatched two pieces of toast from the toaster and quickly buttered them. On route to the table, she dropped one piece on Jenny's plate and took a bite out of the other.

"Why does J.J. get to stay up for the game?" Jenny asked, taking her seat next to her little sister.

"First, a thank-you," Renee directed, delivering two glasses of milk to the table.

"Thank you," Jenny said as she jabbed the corner of her toast into the center of her egg. "Can't I stay up, too?"

"Is your geography project done?"

"Uh huh," she managed around a mouthful of toast.

"Swallow first." Renee hesitated, hands on her hips. "He *is* a whole year older, you know. And I'm remembering that nine was the perfect 'stayin' up for special stuff' age for me." She paused

14

again, turning as if the conversation was over. "But, I'll tell you what," she said, turning back. "A bath and your pajamas, a pillow and blanket for the couch, and you can join us tonight." She noted Jenny's excited smile and squeezed around the table to look into Rachael's frowning face. "Don't I even get a 'good morning'?"

"She doesn't see why she has to go to daycare today," Jenny informed her, "with the *baby*."

"Ohh," Renee said with a raise of her eyebrows.

Rachael scowled at the informant and took another bite of cereal.

"Yeah," Renee muttered, "six is so grown-up." Such mutterings she knew should remain thoughts only, but it had become a habit hard to break. "You know they can't have school if there's no water. Where would all those kids go to the bathroom?"

Rachael silently concentrated on her breakfast.

"She's mad because me and J.J. get to go to the coach's house."

Renee fought a smile as Rachael sneaked a quick peak for a reaction. "Mrs. Gregory's going to be home with her three kids, so I think asking her to watch two more is enough to ask. Besides, you're very lucky," Renee continued, "that one of the kids is home sick today and Stacy has room for you at daycare. Otherwise, you'd be stuck carrying my books all over campus and sitting through all my classes with not a thing to do except listen to boring teachers talk." Surely that sounded bad enough to a six-year-old—it was certainly enough to turn off people three times her age.

Rachael's silent treatment continued.

Jenny, however, was in full know-it-all mode. "She's not going to talk, she's mad."

Renee cocked her head toward Jenny. "And you're quite sure that I haven't gotten that yet. Is that why you had to tell me?"

Jenny shrugged her shoulders and offered an impish grin as she rose to clear her dishes to the sink.

"How about letting your brother know that he has five minutes to eat something before we leave." A task Jenny was well suited for. She marched determinedly from the room.

"Okay," Renee began as she swept toast crumbs from the table with one hand into an empty cereal bowl in the other. "I have an idea." Now she had Rachael's full attention, the hard line of her frown softened quickly into her normal serious look. "If you help Stacy at lunch time, cleaning up the table and whatever she needs you to do, I'll ask her if you can use the computer during naptime."

The line between Rachael's brow disappeared completely. She jumped down from her chair and gathered her dishes. "Okay," she said with a tone as light and positive as if the whole thing had been her idea.

Renee smiled at the back of the little blond bob. Of all her siblings, it was Rachael, quirky and introspective, with whom she felt most closely related. With different fathers it had to be something they shared from their mother, or even further back in the lineage, that created such a similarity of spirit. It was nothing she could readily identify, only a sense, a feeling, but there was something there very close to her younger self. And knowing it was there made it hard not to favor her. Not a major sin if you're just a big sister. But if you're doubling as a parent, it just won't do.

She wiped the leftover breakfast from Rory's face and hands and smoothed down the static light brown hair. "Okay, big guy, let's go to Stacy's."

The Little Only Once daycare occupied the basement and first floor of a cottage-style home in a modest little neighborhood near the edge of town. Its location was nearly perfect, just a long walk or a short bus ride to campus. Today was a bus day, which left a little extra time to visit with Stacy.

Of course, carrying on a conversation with her during business hours meant fitting sentences over and around every manner of interruption. But Stacy was a godsend and it was worth the effort.

Rachael led the way in the back door and through the mud room where Stacy was depositing a youngster's bag in the proper cubbyhole.

"Hi," Rachael greeted cheerfully as she hung her most likely unneeded sweatshirt on a peg and marched on through the kitchen. Stacy turned a quick glance at the retreating figure, then directed a half smile at Renee. "Are we expecting a thunderstorm?" she asked, in clear reference to the bright red rubber boots still on Rachael's feet.

"A fashion accessory," Renee replied. "Not to be confused with an actual need to wade through puddles."

Stacy chuckled.

"A staple," continued Renee, "that seems to go just as well with jeans, skirts, and pajamas." She placed Rory's bag in his cubby-hole and watched him run to join the others in the play room. "I can't talk her out of them."

"Don't waste your breath," Stacy said, relieving an arriving mother of a diaper bag. "It's a battle that wouldn't count in the big war. Besides," she added, "they're stunning."

Renee smiled at the thirty-something woman in her Mickey Mouse sweats and blond spiked hair. "You would think so."

"Here's her veggie treat," a mother injected, handing Stacy a sandwich bag and placing her toddler on the floor. "I wish I had time to sit with her and get her interested in something before I leave."

"It worked yesterday. She didn't even know when you left," Stacy added.

"My sister, Rachael, is the fashion-plate in the red boots—just ask her to help you out."

She offered a grateful smile, took her toddler's hand and made her way to the play room.

Before Renee could get a question in, however, a little dark-haired boy grabbed Stacy's hand and her attention.

"Poo poo, Stacy," he said, looking up with wide brown eyes.

Stacy leaned down and pulled back the waistband of his pants and diaper. "Whew," she exclaimed. "Damon, you're supposed to tell me *when* you have to go, not *after*. We want the poopie in the toilet, not in your pants."

Renee smiled. "He's got half of it. His timing's just off."

With Damon on his way with her assistant for a diaper change, Stacy turned her attention back to Renee. "Yep, and so is yours."

17

A typical Stacy grab-it-from-nowhere-and-throw-it-at-you comment. No time between interruptions to put it in context.

"What are you doing for you?" she continued. "Kids will take every minute you give 'em. Don't lose *yourself* in all of this."

"I do what I can," Renee admitted with a frown. "But it means time away from the kids, and I can't expect them to understand that."

Stacy waved at a parent as he stuck his head in the door and dropped off the last of the kids for the day. "They don't have to," she continued. "They know your decisions have kept them all together as a family—give them a chance to trust your other decisions, too."

"They get kind of jealous when I spend time with someone else and they're not included."

"Goes with the territory of a single parent, and face it, that's what you are." She finally made direct eye contact. "You're doing a good job, Renee, but it's not being selfish to take some time for yourself."

"There isn't much time. It always gets pushed down on the priority list."

"Well, move it up. It's important. Do something special for you."

"I am," came the quick return, "I'm finally going to college. That's high on the priority list if I'm going to get out of the system before my assistance runs out. And speaking of special, can Rachael help you at lunch for some computer time?"

Stacy grinned. "In those red boots, special's the word of the day."

Chapter 3

Lies. They make your nose grow longer, set your pants on fire, and weave a tangled web. A moral lesson in whatever form taught to her mother, learned from childhood, and taught in turn to her siblings.

Renee pulled the strap of her backpack over one shoulder and left her last class of the day to head for the bus stop. The fact that she had once again chosen to defy that moral lesson by lying to her mother still bothered her days after—so much so that she had missed part of the discussion of *Pride and Prejudice* while deep in her own thoughts.

It *is* hypocritical to expect honesty from others when you aren't willing to give it yourself. And I had no right to get upset with Jenny. As irritating and self-righteous as she can be, she was right; Rory had lied, and even at four he needed to understand that there were consequences. Not a Pinocchio nose or jail time, but consequences nonetheless.

As for the hypocrite? What are *my* consequences? Renee dropped her backpack on the ground next to the Transit Authority sign and sat on it. Maybe it's sufficient consequence that it takes days of rationalization to justify a lie. That the justification that allows a lie in the first place is always challenged. At least it's never easy. Even when it's practically necessary, like with Mom. What good would have come from the truth anyway? Some grand insight or lesson that Mother hadn't yet learned? Like what? Crime pays until you get caught? The means do *not* justify the end? Leaving your children, no matter what the reason, is not easily forgiven? J.J. had already made that point abundantly clear. I couldn't in good conscience unload my own poundage on her guilt. That would have felt worse than lying about it.

The city's mid-size bus serving the campus area rolled to a stop and Renee paid her fare, greeted the driver and took her usual seat up front. On days when she was the only rider, she passed the time with the driver in casual conversation. Today, though with three other passengers carrying on an animated conversation nearby, Renee was free to stare silently out the window and continue her thoughts. Rare time alone to think during the day. Maybe this meant a full six hours of sleep tonight.

The stops came and went without notice, and along the route other passengers entered and left the bus. Their voices, rising and falling in pitch and tone, accompanied the hypnotic hum of the big tires.

She had made a pretty good case for the lie over the past few days, good enough to be able to let go of it. The hypocrisy, however, still needed some work. Can I, with good conscience, expect something out of others that I can't do myself? Can I expect J.J. to forgive when I can't? How do I justify that?

The bus swung through the wide turn of an intersection. Just over a mile left for self-therapy. Hardly enough time for a revelation, but plenty of time to pile on the unanswerables, for pondering the purpose of denying forgiveness to someone when they don't know it's been denied to them. Mother wants forgiveness probably more than she wants her freedom, and I let her think that she has it. Who is that hurting? At least J.J .is honest. He hasn't forgiven her and she knows it. But the older he gets the more obvious it is that something has to replace his anger. Isn't forgiveness supposed to do that?

The bus stood idling at her stop while the little voice in her head once again brought the quandary full circle. He's too angry to forgive.

"Look, Nay," Rory said, proudly offering Renee a tiny clay pot sprouting an even tinier green sprig. "It's growing. I planted it. It's gonna have tomatoes."

Stacy draped his bag over Rory's shoulder. "He can leave it here if you'd rather not take it home."

"Can you water it by yourself, buddy?" Renee asked.

He nodded his head in return. "Stacy showed us."

"Okay, ask Rachael to hold it in the car. You two take your stuff on out and I'll be there in a minute."

As soon as the door closed behind him Renee turned to Stacy. "I'm angry, aren't I?"

Stacy merely smiled in return.

"Have you known that I've been angry for a long time?"

"Have I known for a long time that you were angry, or—"

"Both," Renee replied.

"Yeah," Stacy shrugged with her reply, "to both. But who wouldn't be in your place?"

"It's been that clear to you and God knows how many others and it takes me this long to see how angry I am?"

"You have a lot to be angry about. You have a right. What's the big revelation?"

"But I can't get rid of it. I can't forgive."

"You will. I don't know of any rule that says you have to be able to forgive in a certain amount of time or you're crap. You got past the first hump, you got guardianship. And getting everything arranged so that you can go to school, that's a hell of a hump. You'll feel better about your life as it smoothes out. It's a lot to deal with. Give yourself time."

"I've got to give *J.J.* time. I can't make his anger go away any faster than I can my own. He's a good kid. I've got to stop trying to make the visits with Mom comfortable, and stop denying that her absence affects him—and all of us."

Stacy nodded. "If that's what it is—stop trying to make it into something that it isn't. Each of you has to deal with it in your own way, and that includes your mother. She should know how it's affecting each of you."

An impatient Rory opened the back door to peer in and Stacy added, "Just take care of now."

Chapter 4

The sign at the top of her monitor promised "*No child left behind—not a poor one, or an abandoned one, or an abused one*" and Millie Gordon was totally dedicated to the fulfillment of that promise. Today was no different from the three-hundred-and-sixty-five before it, or the year before that, or the one before that. Her caseload was beyond the human capabilities of one social worker and it made her tired and irritable, but it had not made her quit.

She glanced at her watch, then quickly retrieved the cell phone from the brocade bag hanging from the back of her chair. "Ron," she said, activating her husband's number. "Hi," she said with an apologetic tone. "No, I'm still at work. I'm sorry. Will you go ahead on to Sharon and Glenn's and tell the girls that Grandma's coming. She's just going to be late. Thank you, dear—I have to make a home visit on that Porter case. Oh, and I told Sharon we'd be bringing dessert: would you pick up something for us? Yes. I'll be there as soon as I can."

Millie sat in the parking lot of the apartment complex. Low income, government subsidized. Adequate in the short term, unfortunate for the long term. No parks or play areas for the kids. Minimal housing, and minimal, if any, incentive for improvement. She watched a group of five teenagers hanging around an older car, music pounding from its enhanced speaker system. Two younger boys approached the group and begged cigarettes. She recognized a couple of the boys, an older one and a younger brother. Not bad kids, just products of poverty and three generations in the system. Allowing them to live with their mother had been a tough decision. Making sure the father stayed away from them and the mother stayed off drugs was even tougher. Too few days and too many cases meant just getting them into what looked to be the best situation possible and hoping for the best, except for cases like the Parkers. Despite four years of her best efforts, the Parker children were still living here, soft petals trying to withstand a hard driving rain, instead of safely tucked into foster homes.

"And I won't sleep a good night through until they are," she said, tucking her bag under her arm and exiting the car.

Unscheduled visits are the only ones worth the time. I don't want to hear the practiced answers and inspect a polished-up apartment. Let me see what's really going on. Millie knocked at the apartment door, identical to nine others that lined the stretch of sidewalk outlining the parking lot.

Jenny Parker answered on the third knock. She opened the door as far as the chain lock would allow and peered through the opening. "It's Mrs. Gordon," she yelled, closing the door and releasing the chain. When she re-opened the door she said, "Come in. You can sit over there in the comfortable chair. I'll get Renee. She's studying for a test."

Millie took the time instead to take a quick look through the kitchen where J.J. was helping himself to a glass of milk. "Hello, Jaylin. How is your baseball team doing?"

She looked right past him as he replied "Okay" to notice that the refrigerator contained only two covered dishes beyond the expected staples. "That's good," she answered absently, as she noted the clean sink and the little counter and table free of crumbs. "How is school going?" she asked, finally turning her attention to the boy. A pair of jeans and a T-shirt, she noted, clean.

"Okay, I guess," was his reply.

"Just okay?"

Her question went unanswered as Rory raced into the kitchen and stretched his hands up for J.J.'s glass. "Some," he said, dancing on his tiptoes.

J.J. held the glass just out of reach until Rory began to whine and Renee entered the room and took it away from him.

"Hello, Mrs. Gordon," she said, handing the glass to Rory. "J.J., will you show Mrs. Gordon around while I get Rachael out of the bathroom? Show her the girls' room and yours. I hope you put your clothes away."

The look on J.J.'s face told her that he had not. "They're clean," she directed toward Millie Gordon, "just not put away."

"Don't worry about that, dear," she replied with a motherly pat to Renee's arm. "I raised two boys of my own. Come on, Jaylin, tell me about school."

They sat like four stepping stones on Renee's couch/bed in the living room, mannerly and as cute as children can be. And Millie knew that a strained and guarded conversation with Renee would never yield the information she could glean from these little ones. Art Linkletter had proven years ago that children were as brutally honest as they were cute. In the last ten minutes she had already learned that Jaylin revered his baseball coach, hated his teacher because she wore the same perfume as his mother, and was especially proud of his baseball card collection. She had the perfect foster parents in mind. They may even be willing to take Rory, too, if she could convince them that his medical condition was under control. It would be nice to keep the boys together, but ...

"Jenny, how do you like school this year?" Millie asked, turning to an empty page in the notebook on her lap.

"I was teacher's helper four times and I only got one 'B'." In typical fashion she added, "Renee got *two* 'B's," emphasizing her point with two fingers in the air. "She has to study more so I let her use my room."

Rachael sported her usual frown. "It's my room, too. I can go in there if I want to."

"Of course you can," Renee said. "Just not while I'm studying."

"But you're always in there," she replied, adding a pout to her frown.

"Come here," Renee said. "What's this all about?"

Rachael slid from the couch, her red rubber boots still her most important accessory, and snuggled in next to Renee on the beanbag. Millie Gordon jotted notes in her notebook.

Jenny, of course, was ready with an answer. "She's just mad because you didn't read that stupid story to her last night."

"It's not stupid," protested Rachael.

"It is, too," Jenny countered.

"Enough now," Renee demanded. "Mrs. Gordon doesn't want to hear you arguing."

J.J. flopped back against the back of the couch in apparent boredom. "I'm hungry."

"Pizza, pizza," Rory declared, pumping his hands in the air.

"Yes, pizza," replied Renee. "I'll order it as soon as Mrs. Gordon leaves. You can wait and be patient a little while longer."

"You said you were going to order it before you studied," J.J. added.

"Well," Millie injected, "I won't be much longer. I've got to get to dinner, too. I just have a couple of questions." She directed her attention fully on Renee. "You're working mornings at the bookstore and taking three classes a week?"

"Yes, one three-hour class and two two-hour classes."

"How much time each night are you finding you need to devote to your studies?"

"Usually about two hours a night."

"But you're finding that that isn't enough."

"Not if I have a paper due or a test."

"And what seems to be adequate at those times?"

Renee shrugged her shoulders. "It depends. Three. I try to make up the rest on the weekends."

"What are the children doing while you're studying?"

"That's their time to do their school work."

"And Rory?"

"Oh, I let him watch his favorite video until Jenny is done.

She's always the first to finish her school work, and then she plays a game with him."

"How about Rachael?"

"She's very good at entertaining herself. Since I use her room to study and Jenny and J.J. have the kitchen table, Rachael sort of made this little room out of the coat closet where she can draw."

"She pretends she has a friend in there," Jenny offered.

Rachael returned an instant scowl. "I do have a friend."

"You do not. You made her up," replied Jenny.

"That's enough," Renee said. "Jenny, move over so Rory can lie down before we eat. He's getting tired."

"Yes," Millie said, "I should let you get dinner now. I'm sure everyone is hungry. I have some other questions, but they can wait until a later time. I'd particularly like to talk with J.J. again." Millie tucked her notebook neatly in her bag and rose with a smile.

Jenny, ever diligent of her self-appointed hostess duties, ushered her to the door. "If you tell us that you're coming over next time, you can have pizza with us."

"What a nice thought, Jenny. We'll talk again soon," she said with a cordial wave to Renee.

"They're precious," she said later that night as she watched her husband perform the same nightly routine he'd practiced for nearly thirty-four years.

"Who's precious, Millie?" he asked, tucking his slippers under the side of the bed and adjusting his reading light.

"The Parker children," she replied. "They're delightful, and well-mannered."

"Then the older sister is doing a good job with them. You could have been wrong about this one. It has been known to happen," he said with a sly glimpse over his glasses.

"Well, of course I've been wrong before. I'm not applying for sainthood. But there's more to it than politeness and manners. Those kids have emotional issues that need to be dealt with, and the youngest one has physical issues. It's more than she can deal with, and now going to school ..." Millie shook her head, pulled the cover back on her side of the bed and slipped in. "Even if I could get a couple of them placed I'd feel better about it."

"This from a woman who has touted her belief in keeping the family unit intact whenever possible. When will the mother be released?"

"Maybe another five years with good behavior."

"With a good chance at regaining custody?"

"It didn't seem that her parenting skills were in question, just her monetary judgments."

"As difficult as it is to get kids out of the foster system once they're in, wouldn't it be wiser to let the sister care for them until the mother can take them?"

"A lot can happen to those kids in five years. I just don't have a good feeling about this one. There's something about Renee that doesn't feel right to me."

"Careful," he warned. "The emotional side of that scale sounds like it's outweighing the factual side."

"What does a graphs and figures guy know about the emotional side of anything?"

He dropped his magazine to his lap. "I'm just not seeing what you see that makes you think those kids are getting any worse an upbringing than any number of other families that have *issues* to deal with."

Millie fluffed her second pillow upright and leaned back.

When he received no response, Ron added, "Are they fed, clothed, and loved? With a roof over their heads?"

"Her attorney is Shayna Bradley."

He turned palms up and stared at her.

"What if Renee's a lesbian?" she asked.

"Okay," he said with a nod, "I've had years of practice and I admit that I should be better at following your logic here."

"Shayna Bradley is a known lesbian."

"And I'm sure that she has clients who are not," he replied.

"But think about it. How is it that a young woman in Renee's position even has an attorney, let alone one of Shayna Bradley's stature, taking on her case pro bono?" She placed her hand on her husband's arm. "What if she is?"

He picked up his magazine and replied, "Then you'll prepare your argument against lesbians raising children."

Chapter 5

Renee's heart jolted into double-time as her cell phone vibrated against her waist. She grabbed it quickly and slipped from the back of the classroom into the hallway.

She checked the number. Just as she feared. "Stacy, what's wrong?"

"I debated whether to call, but, Rory had a seizure and he's not resting normally afterward. It could be because I've got two crying babies right now, I don't know. I just think he'd be better off at home."

"I'm on my way."

Renee carried an exhausted Rory, arms hanging loosely over her shoulders, to his bedroom and settled him on the bed. "Here you go, buddy. Your own bed, comfy and quiet." She removed his shoes and pulled the bedspread over his legs.

Rory pulled the edge of the pillowcase over his face and Renee moved to close the window shade and darken the room.

"Nay?"

"Right here, buddy," she said, moving the pillowcase and kissing his forehead.

"You take a nap, too."

"Okay." She stretched on her side against him and draped her arm over his waist. "That's a good idea. I am kind of tired."

He turned and snuggled in against her. His voice was very soft. "Does Spiderman take naps?"

"All important people take naps, especially Spiderman. How do you think he—" But no further explanation was needed. Rory was asleep.

Renee rested there with him until she was sure that moving wouldn't wake him. He'd been more restless lately, waking often during the night, making her question whether not sleeping well was causing the increased number of seizures, or if the restlessness meant that his medication wasn't effective anymore. It was so hard to determine what was normal—what was just being four and a boy and pushing himself beyond his limit. If only she weren't so intimidated by the doctor. After all, getting the questions answered was far more important than worrying about looking too young and naïve. She struggled with her perceived image; being a convincingly confident guardian was paramount. She couldn't afford any challenges there. It was a matter of walking the tightrope and holding the pole just right.

The slow squeaking of the bus brakes stopping on the street indicated that the kids were home from school. Renee met them at the door, and put her finger to her lips. "I brought Rory home early. He had a seizure at Stacy's. J.J., put your things on the couch for now, and let him sleep, okay?"

"Can I get my Jeter card? Bobby doesn't believe it's autographed."

"All right, but don't open the door so wide that it squeaks."

"I won't." He disappeared around the corner, but a moment later he was calling for Renee.

His tone was urgent and Renee ran to the bedroom where Rory was in full seizure. His legs were tangled in the blanket still clinging to the bed, his head cradled in J.J.'s hands just as he had been taught.

Quickly she pulled him free of the blanket and away from the bed and the dresser. "That's good, J.J. You did it just right—kept him from hitting his head." She looked into J.J.'s wide eyes. It didn't matter how many times he'd seen it before, each time was still clearly upsetting. "He'll be okay, J.J.," she said reassuringly. "It's almost over."

The violent jerking movements lessened in severity and then stopped. Only then did Jenny, standing with her sister in the doorway, speak up. "Are we going to take him to Dr. Becker's?"

"Yes, Jenny, take the keys and my backpack out to the car. J.J., stay with Rory while I call the doctor's office."

"I'll stay, too," Rachael said, kneeling beside her little brother and stroking his hair. "Nay said you're going to be okay, Rory."

Renee fought through her concern and kept her voice calm and steady. She described the situation to Dr. Becker's receptionist, and was told that he was on afternoon rounds. They could meet him at the hospital.

The emergency room was about half full. People with a variety of needs waited, and coughed, and slept while the children watched videos and Renee watched Rory closely. He appeared to be watching, but didn't react at all when the others did. He was in that strange zone, the one just before or after a seizure, where he was unable to focus. It touched every sensitive part of her to see him like this. She searched for something that she could control, something she could do better that would stop the seizures. Had she followed everything the doctor told her to do? Rory should have gotten more rest. She could do a better job of making Jenny understand about stress—somehow convert that uncanny knack of pushing guilt buttons into a positive motivator. It was moments like this when she felt the most unprepared, unqualified. Could someone else have given him better care? Was she truly doing what was right for Rory?

"So, Rory's been having a rough time, has he?" Dr. Becker's voice rang out beside her.

"Yes, Doctor." Her adrenaline level spiked as quickly as Renee rose from the chair. "I'm glad that you could see him today."

"Well, let's see," he said, squatting before Rory and looking into his eyes. "How about you come with me, big guy." He stood and held out his hand to Rory.

He didn't indicate that she should follow them, but the feeling that Dr. Becker didn't care one way or another didn't stop her. Renee followed and thought, as she watched his examination, that possibly the doctor just wasn't as good at communicating with adults as he was with children. No intimidation intended at all. Maybe the problem wasn't that he was treating her as a child, maybe it was that he was treating her as an adult. Not that it made dealing with him any easier, but it was a nice realization.

She realized that he always tried to remain at eye-level with Rory—sitting, bending, squatting—and gave a soft-toned monologue of little explanations and reassurances. Rory was totally at ease. Ultimately, isn't that what is most important?

"Has he missed taking his medication?" The doctor's question was asked, as usual, without benefit of eye contact.

"No," Renee replied. "I give it to him every day."

Dr. Becker retrieved his clipboard from the counter and focused his attention on that. "Kids can be tricky."

His inference was not missed. "I make absolutely sure that he takes his medication every day, on time. That's at the top of my priority list."

"Mm, huh, okay," he replied absently. "How's his environment been?"

"As stress-free as I can make it. The other kids are very protective of him most of the time. They know what the rules are."

"And daycare? Any unusual situations there?" He finally looked up when Renee hesitated to answer. "Kids picking on him, not getting his naps, erratic routine?"

"No, none of those things that I'm aware of. There've been several times when I've stayed to help out for a little while, and everything seems to run pretty smoothly. Stacy handles arguments right away and follows a daily routine. I don't believe there are any unusually stressful things going on there. Stacy's care is unquestionable in my opinion."

"Any falls where he hit his head?"

"None that he's told me about. He wears his helmet when he plays on the climber and swings at Stacy's, and even on the little bikes. And Stacy documents and reports every scratch ... Rory, did you fall and hurt your head and not tell Stacy or me?"

He shook his head "no," then pointed to his knee.

"Okay, just your knee," she confirmed. "He skinned his knee last week."

Dr. Becker rose abruptly from the stool. "I'm going to admit Rory. I want to observe him for twenty-four hours."

"Well, I," Renee also stood quickly. "Can I stay in the room with him?"

"There's really no need; we have a good staff of pediatric nurses. They'll take good care of him. You take the other kids home and we'll see you tomorrow."

And that was it. He was out the door before Renee could ask a question. The next forty-plus minutes became a tangle of forms and personnel and shuffling children from one place to the next and all the while trying to provide a calm, reassuring explanation for Rory. It wasn't until she stood next to the hospital bed, with a dazed Rory and his sisters piling on next to him, that Renee realized that she hadn't yet called Jean. The decision to stay with Rory had been made the second Dr. Becker left the examining room. The arrangement for the other kids was another thing altogether. Short notice was only rude when it was avoidable, she reminded herself as she dialed Jean's number. When was the last time they'd needed her help? The afternoon she registered for classes? No. A ride home from baseball for J.J.

"Jean," she replied, startled from her thoughts, "this is Renee. You're probably still at school. I hope it's okay that I called."

"No, actually, I'm at Meijer's picking up Shayna's list of ingredients for dinner this weekend. We're having her parents over. How are you doing?"

"I'm fine, but Rory's been admitted to the hospital for observation. I can't leave him here alone, Jean—"

"Of course you can't. The kids with you or Stacy?"

"They're here with me. I hate to ask—"

"You don't have to. I'll be there in twenty minutes."

Twenty minutes to her word, Jean Carson breezed into the hospital room and greeted everyone as though she was about to embark on an exciting excursion. She was, Renee decided, a beautiful lesbian saint.

"Shayna's going to stop by and check on you on her way home, and pick up the groceries from me."

"There are clean sheets in the laundry basket in the front closet," Renee explained. "I'm sorry you have to sleep on that pull-out."

"I've slept on the ground in a sleeping bag for a week at a time at summer camp. Pull-outs are only tough on wusses."

"What's a sleeping bag?" Rachael asked.

"Well," Jean thought for a moment, "think of folding your quilt in half and crawling into it."

"On the ground?" frowned Rachael.

"I've got a great idea," Jean said with a raise of her eyebrows. "I'll teach you how to make bedrolls just like sleeping bags and we'll have a camp out in the living room tonight."

Rachael's face brightened with nearly as much excitement as Jenny and J.J. were showing. She slid from the edge of the bed and grabbed Jean's hand. "Okay, let's go," she said, starting for the door.

Jean sent a look of mock surprise over her shoulder, then laughed and followed her campers out of the room.

Olivia Dumont entered the room of her newest patient and offered a cordial smile to the young woman standing uncomfortably beside the bed.

"Hello," she greeted cheerfully, lifting the chart from its holder. "Rory, is it?" She leaned on her forearms across the foot rail and looked intently at her young patient. "That's a great name. It makes me think of cowboys herding cattle and sleeping by campfires at night."

He raised his hand and slapped it on the bed like she had just guessed the million-dollar question. "I've got a cowboy hat," he said with a grin. "It's at Stacy's."

"I *knew* it!" Olivia replied with a sharp nod of her head. "I know my names."

She directed a wink in the young woman's direction, a natural-born reaction intended to put her patients and parents at ease. Something about this woman's smile, though, made her question its effectiveness today. That same something made Olivia want to try a little harder to ease her apprehensions.

"What does your mom's name make you think of?"

"Sister," Renee corrected. "I'm his sister ... well, his guardian, too."

"That's Nay," he added.

"Renee."

Olivia smiled and returned her attention to Rory. "So, what does Nay make you think of?"

"A pretty horse, 'cause she has a ponytail. Sometimes Jenny braids it like the horses in the show."

"He saw a horse show on television."

"You know," Olivia said, "you're pretty good with names yourself, Rory."

He gave her his closed-lipped smile and nodded.

"Well, *my* name's Olivia and I'll be taking care of you tonight."

"Can I play with that?" He pointed to a bright yellow truck on the table by the window.

"I thought you might like that." She dropped the chart back in its place and retrieved the truck. "I'll let you check this out while Renee and I talk, okay?"

With Rory's attention quickly focused on the truck, Olivia motioned for Renee to join her on the chairs in the corner of the room.

"Did I overhear you say that you plan to spend the night here with Rory?"

"Yes, is that going to be a problem?"

Now it was clear, the something that had eluded Olivia earlier. Right there in Renee's eyes. Frightened eyes. Blue and dark and frightened. They betrayed her, flashed insolently against the confident set of her shoulders, the hold of her head. And they were watching her, waiting on her.

"Not at all," replied Olivia. "I encourage parents—or guardians—to stay when they can. A hospital is a scary enough place, but a little one alone—"

"Thank you."

Olivia returned a questioning frown.

36

"I've felt like—well, Dr Becker told me to take the other kids home and he'd see me tomorrow. But Rory's never had to stay overnight before. Maybe he didn't remember that."

"He's a hard one to figure. He's a good doctor, and he has kids of his own, but his communication skills sometimes leave me scratching my head."

Once again the smile she received came up short of relief. *What is it you need? What can I do to lighten the dark eyes, to put a real smile on such a nice face?*

"You're doing exactly the right thing, Renee. You should trust your instinct."

"I need more than instinct. I need answers. There's so much I need to know."

"If you have questions about Rory's health or his care, you ask me, Renee. I promise to answer them honestly and as completely as I can."

"I don't want to be annoying, and I don't want to sound stupid, but I need to be as sure as I can that I'm making good decisions. I have four children counting on me, *depending* on me."

Four children. What has happened in your life? So young, so worried.

"That's something I understand very well. And I know how it feels to have kids depending on you when you don't always have the answer. So, you just keep asking, and I'll do my best to give you what you need."

Renee turned to check on Rory, and found him asleep with the truck still on his lap. "I've read all I can get my hands on about epilepsy. The Epilepsy Society also sent me a lot of things to read, and I've e-mailed them questions."

"And what has you most concerned?"

Renee stopped the nervous scraping of the ridges of her fingernails, and glanced quickly at a still-sleeping Rory. "That I don't understand his condition well enough and that we'll keep changing medications and they'll keep failing."

"Okay, let's see if I can ease your mind some here. Medication, especially with children growing and changing so fast, isn't a one-size-fits-all. Treatment is a matter of tailoring the combination and dosage to the child. It's an ongoing thing and it's to be expected. You're not even close to running out of options."

"So why didn't Dr. Becker tell me that?"

"I don't know him well enough to be able to answer that. In many respects you can be a good doctor without good communication skills, but probably not the most popular one."

"Which makes you, Olivia ..." she looked to the last name on the uniform badge.

"Dumont."

"... very popular with us."

"So I *have* set your mind at ease."

This time a convincing smile—wide and open and radiating relief. "You have."

"Good. Rory is going to be all right. We're going to take very good care of him. *And* you," she said as she stood. "I'll bring back some blankets and a pillow, and show you how that chair folds out for tonight."

"Thank you, Ms. Dumont."

"My patients call me Nurse Olivia, and parents just seem to follow suit ... Oh," she said with a turn of her head, "and that's the last time you need to thank me."

Chapter 6

Nurse Olivia was true to her word, taking good care of both of them. She brought blankets and pillows to settle Renee in on the pull-out chair for the night, and she even brought a toothbrush. And she monitored Rory closely, so closely that she was in the room for his third seizure in twenty-hours. Just over a minute in duration, but scary nonetheless. Renee lay next to him and held him when it was over. He was more frightened and disoriented than usual, Renee more worried. Putting her concern aside, she calmed him, stroked his head and reassured him until the confusion in his eyes disappeared and they registered their assurance on her own. In a matter of minutes he was asleep.

This was precisely when Olivia's attributes began to shine. She began by explaining his chart, what it said and what it meant. Then she systematically went about educating Renee on Rory's condition in language that she could understand.

"Did Dr. Becker explain the type of seizures that Rory experiences?"

"Yes, partial seizure. But when I looked it up the description didn't match his movements. Has it changed to something more serious?"

"Probably not. The actual diagnosis was partial seizure secondarily generalized, where the seizure activity begins in one part of the brain and spreads to involve the whole brain. The result is a generalized seizure that does match Rory's loss of consciousness and the shaking that involves his whole body."

"So I've been worried about that for no reason?"

"Probably, yes."

"And being worried about which drugs he's taking, it that also moot?"

"Now that's a legitimate concern. The wrong drug can make things worse. Rory's been on a pretty safe combination of drugs, though, and now that he's four the doctor can start him on Trileptal."

Obviously distressed, Renee asked, "How many drugs is he going to be taking?"

"Trileptal will be in place of the other drugs."

"What do you know about it?"

"It's been available here in the US since 2000, but it's been widely used in other countries since 1990. And besides the benefit of a single drug, if this drug works for him, Rory won't have to go through the regular blood tests to test his liver." She smiled, then added, "I did my homework for you before the doctor even prescribed it because I knew you would ask."

"Can you tell me what you think personally?"

"If Rory was mine, I'd put him on it without hesitation."

Renee nodded and looked over at Rory sleeping soundly. "He's just a little boy," she said, her eyes watering with tears. "I don't want him to keep going through this." She turned to Olivia. "I want to do the right thing for him."

Olivia slipped the chart back in place, Renee's near tears urging a desire to provide some peace. "You are," she said. "This is the right thing." She looked toward Rory and then back to Renee. "He's a lucky little boy in so many ways."

Renee looked down with a frown.

"He has you caring for him and loving him. I experience how important that is every day. There is no medicine like love, and it's clear to see that he has plenty of that."

Renee lifted her eyes directly to Olivia's. "I wish that was all it took."

"He's going to be fine. We're just going to give him a little help." Olivia pulled a pamphlet from her pocket and handed it to Renee.

"I have this information pamphlet for you to take with you, but I want to go over a few things with you first." She motioned for Renee to sit with her. "There's a list of possible side effects to watch for. But I don't want you to worry—if he does experience any of these, they'll probably be quite mild. Most patients don't experience any at all. And I put my phone number on the back, and my break time, just in case you're not sure about something and don't want to bother the doctor with it."

Renee read the list, then the rest of the pamphlet from beginning to end while Olivia waited patiently. Finally she asked, "When can he start on it?"

"The doctor wants to start tonight so that we can see how he does before he goes home. Sometimes it needs to be combined with another anti-seizure drug, but he wants to try it by itself first."

"So the twenty-four hours will be to see how the new medication does?"

"Yes," Olivia replied. "I'm afraid you're stuck with me for at least one more shift."

"I'm afraid you're the one who got stuck. Hopefully, I won't have as many questions tomorrow."

"Your questions and concerns are valid and important. You ask good questions, Renee. Part of my job is to take as much of the fear out of a hospital stay as I can. And that doesn't just go for my patients. Kids can sense their parents' fear. Relieving your stress relieves Rory's."

Renee nodded. "And you have."

"Then let's get your little guy started on the right track, shall we?"

Unless a person was drugged or comatose, it was hard to believe that anyone could actually sleep in a hospital. Renee lay awake, the semi-darkness of the room and the sounds from the hallway preventing every attempt to fall asleep. Squeaking shoes and muffled voices, nondescript clicks and bangs and shuffles, and an occasional child's cry—all just part of the night.

Rory slept soundly, his breathing deep and regular. Olivia breezed in and out, checking her patients like clockwork. And Renee, sometimes eyes closed, sometimes staring at the shadows on the ceiling, thought.

Her thoughts jumped and jangled, and morphed from one to another. They spanned years, revisited places she had once called home, and questioned what might have been. Then somehow they made their way all the way back to the moment that Olivia Dumont had become the most important part of today.

Olivia didn't know, she couldn't know, how important she had suddenly become. Olivia Dumont had come to work, done her job no doubt as capably as on any other day, and unknowingly became the anchor in someone's life—at least for today.

I wonder how many times she has been someone's anchor, holding them stable, grounding their drift, knowingly or not. Part of her job, to be there if they need her. Not part of her job to be their anchor, but I'll bet she is just that.

There had been many anchors in Renee's life—temporary stabilities—there for a while, then gone; holding her steady, then setting her adrift. Some had been there longer than others, her mother of course, and her stepfather. Their loss taught her life's most important lesson—anchors aren't meant to be permanent. But the lesson didn't stop her from looking for others, for needing others—it merely kept her from counting on them for very long.

The soft squish of Olivia's soles announced her before her silhouette appeared momentarily in the doorway. Renee lay still, feigning sleep, and watching Olivia quietly check her patients.

The interest wasn't in *what* she was doing—the routine was familiar enough now—but in *how* she did it. She seemed to glide, one motion seamlessly into the next, fluid and light. Pretty movements—like the fingers of a pianist or the fluidity of an athlete in slow motion. It was something innate, Renee was sure, something she was born with that made whatever she did a thing of beauty. Like the way she bent over the bed—a soft gray form in two dimension with one shoulder lower than the other, her head tilted gracefully in concentration. An image that should be preserved, and then framed and displayed in the lobby of the hospital.

It wouldn't be, of course, so Renee vowed to archive it in her memory where she could pull it up whenever it pleased her. She'd bring it up whenever she wanted that special feeling it gave her, the warmth that enveloped her and made her feel that all was well. The urge to hug her tightly and thank her for caring was overwhelming.

Instead, as Olivia passed quietly close to the end of the bed, Renee whispered, "Do you have a minute?"

"Of course," Olivia replied softly. "Did I wake you?"

"No," Renee replied, raising herself up on her elbow. "I've been lying awake thinking."

Olivia sat down on the edge of the chair-bed. "What's worrying you?"

"Less than usual, because of you. I want you to know how much I appreciate you being so patient and so caring."

"It's what I do, Renee."

She had spoken softly and, intended or not, so intimately that it caused a flutter of excitement in Renee's chest. "It makes a difference," Renee whispered. "*How* you do it makes a difference. I wanted to be able to tell you that."

She saw a soft shadowed smile just before Olivia replied, "Thank you, that was nice to hear." Olivia rose from the bed and leaned forward. "Now get some sleep."

Chapter 7

"J.J., will you be in charge of dessert?" Renee asked, placing a pan of chocolate-chip cookies on the table. "Only two each, and pour the milk. I have to make a phone call, so no interruptions."

She settled on Jenny's bed and unfolded the pamphlet she had carefully tucked into the pocket of her backpack. For a moment she stared at the number, hesitant, unsure if the call would be welcome. If it were only an update on Rory's health or a question regarding his medication, there'd be no hesitation. Olivia Dumont had been convincingly sincere about her offer. But this call wasn't about Rory's health, not exactly anyway. And it might be crossing some line of acceptability.

Renee audibly blew out the deep breath she had taken and dialed the number.

The sound of Olivia's voice stopped her next breath still. A momentary paralysis that surprised her. This was more than merely nerves.

She cleared her throat, testing her voice on Olivia's second "hello." "Olivia, this is Renee Parker. I hope you don't mind my calling during your break."

"Not at all, Renee. I was catching up on a bit of news and giving my legs a rest. How are you and Rory doing?"

"Rory has stayed seizure-free so far. He can't understand why

44

he can't go back to daycare yet. I'm an okay substitute, but he really misses the other kids and Stacy."

"The doctor wants him to wait until the beginning of the week, and that's probably best for him. But what about you?"

"Oh, no, I don't mind at all. Missing work is the toughest part, I can catch up on my classes; we'll get through it okay. Actually," Renee lifted her voice at the chance to bring the conversation on target, "that's more along the lines of why I called." She rose from the edge of the bed and struggled with the words in her head. Olivia seemed to wait patiently.

"I'm in a situation," she began, "where my guardianship is being strictly scrutinized." There, it was said. The words came easier now. "My capabilities were challenged when Rory was first diagnosed—too young, too much to handle on top of everything else—anyway, I have a very good attorney and the hearing went in my favor. But now, with Rory having to go into the hospital ..."

"It would look like it was due to inadequate care."

"Exactly."

"And we know that that isn't true," Olivia added. "So, is there something that I can do that will help?"

The relief of not having to ask was huge. "Thank you, yes. My attorney needs a statement, and I'm reading from her note here, 'from a health professional involved with Rory's care to attest to the cause and condition of his stay.' I could try Dr. Becker, but if you won't mind, I'd prefer to have her call you and explain exactly what she needs for this hearing."

"I'd be happy to talk with her, Renee. And I'll do whatever I can to help." Olivia's voice had taken on a distinctly more serious tone. "I understand now what I saw in your eyes at the hospital."

That Olivia had looked that closely, observed that acutely, was Renee's second surprise of the day. "I probably looked like a frightened little girl."

"You looked like a brave young woman unable to hide a deeper fear than I recognized."

"I like your description better. I'm really not that scared."

"Sure you are. I see frightened people every day. I've learned a lot from them. Probably the most important lesson they taught me was that once you identify your fear and you know the look of it, you can stand face to face with it and measure yourself against it. That's when you will realize that you're taller and stronger than you knew."

Wisdom, as Renee had already learned, wasn't exclusive to bald, middle-aged men with Texas accents. Olivia Dumont had joined her list of wise women.

"It's all right to be frightened, Renee."

"Not if you're me it isn't."

It was Olivia's turn at silence.

"But that doesn't mean I don't appreciate your wisdom, and your help. There's no way I can tell you how much I do."

"You don't need to try. Give your attorney this number and I'll expect her call. Oh," she said, much more upbeat, "tell Rory that Nurse Olivia said 'hi' and that I'm glad he's feeling so much better."

Chapter 8

Jenny passed her plate for Renee to dish a generous helping of mashed potatoes. "Can Rory stay home again tomorrow?" she asked.

"The doctor said he can go back to Stacy's Monday as long as he hasn't had any problems with the medication." She plopped a smaller portion of potatoes on Rachael's plate. "Why do you want him to stay home?"

"Because then you have to stay home again, and we don't have so many chores to do and you have time to fix mashed potatoes again."

"We've had them three nights in a row. Don't you get tired of them?"

"I could eat 'em every night for the rest of my life."

"Me, too," J.J. added.

"Let's see, seventy years times three-hundred-sixty-five," she worked the math with her finger on the table. "That's 25,550 nights in a row."

Their eyes widened as they looked at each other in surprise.

Renee just smiled and pulled the ringing phone from her waistband.

"Renee?" The voice she had heard in her sleep said, "This is Olivia—Dumont."

"Yes." The exclamation in her voice matched that of her heartbeat. "Hi!"

47

"I hope I'm not calling you at a bad time. I wondered if the hearing went well."

"No," she said quickly. "I mean, it's not a bad time. The hospital record and your statement was all the judge needed. She agreed with my attorney that Rory is getting good care."

"That's wonderful. And how is Rory? Is he experiencing any of the side effects that we talked about?"

"Nay, milk," Rory said, tapping his hand on the rim of his glass.

"Yes." She lowered her voice to Rory, "Just a minute, okay?"

"Yes?" asked Olivia.

"No, oh, I'm sorry. Rory wanted milk. No, no side effects so far. But I can't really tell about the sleepiness. He *seems* to be *less* tired."

"Good, good. Listen, I'm going to let you go, I've interrupted your dinner."

"Oh, no," Renee replied. "I mean, well yes, we're eating, but you don't have to go. I'll eat when the kids are through. I'm glad you called." She set the glass of milk down in front of Jenny instead of Rory.

Jenny rolled her eyes and pushed the glass over to Rory.

"It's so nice of you to check on him." She turned from the table and started toward the living room. "He's so excited about going back to daycare."

"And you can get back into a normal routine. I bet that will feel good."

"It will," Renee admitted, walking to the end of the room and starting back. "As hectic as it is, it is normal. Anything else just feels like I'm losing ground."

"What ground is it that you're gaining on in that normally hectic schedule of yours?"

"Higher ground," Renee replied, a more serious tone to her voice. "Solid ground. Solid enough that I can be sure that it won't drop away from under me."

There was no response from Olivia.

Renee dropped to the edge of the couch only to rise again seconds later and continue. "I hope that didn't sound as though I resent the time needed to take care of Rory. That's not it at all. I'll do whatever it takes to take care of these kids. It was my choice and I don't regret making it."

"No," Olivia said, "it didn't sound regretful in the least. You just had me at a loss there for a minute. More honestly, I'm still at a loss. Whether you have intended to or not, you've made me want to know more about you, about your situation. And now I'm afraid of sounding nosey."

Renee offered a soft laugh. "I guess I just assume everyone knows about me, about us. We were all over the newspapers and media four years ago. Really, don't worry. Nothing seems nosey after that."

"Then I missed all the excitement by two years."

"I don't know about excitement. My stepfather died and my mother is in prison for embezzling money to keep us afloat. I fought for custody. It's as simple as that."

"Nothing's that simple. And I was right, you are amazing."

"Now *I'm* at a loss."

Olivia laughed, a light soft tone over the phone. "Please believe that my sole intent in calling was to see if my statement helped and to check on Rory, because it was. And also, to see if there would be a time that I could bring something by for him."

"Only if you normally do this for your patients."

"I do."

Renee smiled. It didn't really matter—white lie or not, she wanted Olivia to come by. "During the week would be impossible?"

"Yes, and you and the kids probably don't get home until after I'm at work ... How does tomorrow look?"

"Yes," she exclaimed too enthusiastically. "You can come to Sunday dinner. One-thirty?"

"I would love to come to dinner."

"West End Apartments on Westview, apartment fifteen."

"I'll be there. Go eat."

Why did she even fantasize that a tiny apartment housing four kids could be made attractive enough to impress someone like Olivia? Keeping it clean enough from day to day to withstand a surprise visit from Mrs. Gordon was one thing, making it pretty was another thing all together.

"J.J.," Renee called from the kitchen. "Are those yesterday's practice clothes I still smell in the bathroom?"

"I told him twice," Jenny explained. "He's playing with the guinea pig."

"*Now*, J.J.! Nurse Olivia will be here in fifteen minutes. And spray deodorizer in there." She pulled the covered pan from the oven and placed it on top. "Jenny, can you help Rachael finish setting the table?"

"She's got the silverware backward."

"Do not," Rachael replied.

"The forks go on the left," Jenny said, following behind her and reversing the placing.

"Who says?"

"Renee says."

"Why do they go on the left?"

"I don't know, Rach," Renee replied, "they just do. Please just concentrate on getting the table ready. Okay?"

She turned and looked down the hall where there had still been no movement from J.J. This time she let go of a full shout. "Damn it, J.J., I'm not telling you again." She slammed shut the cupboard door and covered the distance from the kitchen to the bathroom in long, determined strides. With a quick lunge she scooped up the dirty clothes, then marched into the boy's room and threw them in J.J.'s face. "There," she said loudly, "maybe you couldn't smell them so far away. Now," she said only inches from his face, "get in there and spray the bathroom." She started to leave the room, but turned around sharply at the door. "And clean that guinea pig cage. It stinks in here."

Again she turned to leave, but standing just outside the doorway was Rachael. Her arms hung limply at her sides and tears stained a track over the full round cheeks.

Remnants of anger that had spewed from Renee's control now fizzled in regret. "Rach, I'm sorry. Come here." She knelt and passed her palms over the wet cheeks. "Don't cry now, every-

50

thing's okay." She placed a kiss on the salty cheek, then stood to face J.J.

He was stuffing his dirty clothes into a laundry bag, eyes down, face sullen.

Renee went to him, smoothed his hair back in place and pulled him into a hug. "I'm sorry, J.J., I shouldn't have acted like that. I was worried that you wouldn't get things cleaned up in time. I want everything to look nice and smell nice for Nurse Olivia."

"I'll get it done, I promise," he said, lifting sorry eyes to Renee's.

"And I promise I'll try harder not to lose my temper next time. Okay?"

He offered his forgiveness smile and a nod, and picked up his laundry bag.

Renee took Rachael's hand. "Everything's okay now. Come on, let's get dinner ready."

Predictably, Jenny was finishing the table.

"Is Nurse Olivia like Mrs. Gordon?"

Renee opened a new stick of butter and put it on a saucer. "What do you mean, Jenny?"

"If we don't do things right can she tell us that we can't live with you?"

The question took Renee by surprise. She set the dish down and sat on the closest chair. "Come here, Jen."

"Me, too?" asked Rachael.

"Yes, you too." She leaned forward and took their hands as they stood in front of her. "Olivia's job as a nurse is to help us take really good care of Rory."

Rachael sported her most serious frown. "So he doesn't have any more seizures?"

"Right. And she answers my questions when I don't understand why Rory doesn't feel good and then I'll know what to do to make him feel better. I invited her to dinner to thank her for being such a good nurse."

"Does she want us to live together?" Rachael asked.

"Yes, I think she does."

"Can she talk to Mrs. Gordon?" A good eight-year-old leap of logic.

51

"Well, you know what? Worrying about Mrs. Gordon is my job, and I don't want anyone else doing any of the worrying, and that includes you two. Okay?" Two heads nodded. "I made you a promise, remember?" One head nodded. "Rachael, do you remember that I promised that we will all stay together?"

"Always," Jenny added.

"Yes," Rachael replied, her frown finally dissolving.

"Okay, then. Sometimes when you get a little worried, you just have to say the promise to yourself. For now ..."

"For always," Rachael finished as if there had never been a worry.

"Oh," Jenny exclaimed with a quick turn of her head, "the door." Loyal to her self-appointed title of official greeter, she raced to open the door.

Peering through the crack of the still-chained door, she exclaimed, "It's Nurse Olivia." Quickly she shut the door, released the safety chain and welcomed Olivia in.

"I'm Jenny and this is Rachael," she introduced. "Rory is watching J.J. take care of the guinea pig. It's not ours; it's J.J.'s turn to bring it home from school for the weekend. He had to clean the cage today because his room smelled like guinea pig poop."

As adorable as the kids were, Renee was sure that Olivia's smile wasn't meant just for them, nor was it born of politeness. It was too spontaneous, too wide and bright and direct. And it made her return that awful smile that curled her top lip into a crease.

Renee reached for the packages that Olivia still held and put them on the coffee table, as Jenny continued, "Dinner will be ready in a few minutes. Renee has to mash the potatoes last so that they are nice and hot when we eat. Mashed potatoes are my very favorite."

"I think they're my favorite, too," Olivia replied, sending a wink in Renee's direction—a tea-colored gesture that sparked a little electrical charge in her chest.

Renee softened her smile and shook her head. "I hope we haven't scared you off already."

"Not at all. Jenny is the perfect hostess."

Jenny offered a self-satisfied smile.

"Your visitors know right away what the household status is, and that way they also know exactly where *they* stand. I like that."

"It also keeps the household always on alert to possible sources of TMI."

"And why would you worry about that?" Although nothing in Olivia's appearance said gay—no swagger or squareness; no fashion indicators, or lack of; nothing except very short hair, and *that* too coifed and feminine to count—there was something in her tone that hinted at something just shy of seriousness and dead-on for inquisitiveness.

"Right now? No reason." It was possible that they were speaking the same language—the one spoken in subtle expression and innuendo until one of them was sure—but for now, she'd just smile and let it go. It didn't really matter, after all. It was a fun challenge. You can never have enough lesbian friends.

"What's TMI?" Jenny asked, breaking her longer than usual silence.

"Too many interruptions," Renee answered quickly. "How about rounding up J.J. and Rory and getting them washed up for dinner? We've already lost Rachael to her other world. Round her up, too, while I whip the potatoes."

She left instantly and Renee returned her attention to a smiling Olivia.

"You're quite good, you know." She tilted her head to the side. "Too young to be that good."

"I've just had more practice than most my age, that's all. I'll only claim adapting well." She motioned for Olivia to follow her into the kitchen. "I'm a domesti-cat out of survival. The basics, I got them down in a hurry."

Dinner turned out to be warm bites punctuating a non-stop, energetic conversation like commas. There was school to discuss, and guinea pig habitat, and baseball, and a bazillion questions for their dinner guest. And all through it, Olivia listened and laughed and was quick to ask her own questions, which in record time gained her favorite-guest status, right up there with Jean Carson.

It wasn't until she returned from the refrigerator with milk for refills that Renee realized what, aside from having a special guest, was so different about this day. The attention, the energy didn't have to come from her. It wasn't coming from her. And because it wasn't she had time to watch and to think, right here at the table. She noticed things that she had never noticed before, like the very small bites that Jenny took, making it easier for her to stay in the conversation without talking with her mouth full. And that Rachael reacted to every topic with either a nod or a frown or a smile, joining in only when it seemed important enough to her. J.J., Renee realized for the first time, smashed his peas and mixed them with his potatoes just like his father had. And throughout dinner, she watched Rory watch Olivia. He was in love.

The time she'd been able to spend inside her own thoughts had brought on a sense of nostalgia, a feeling of familiarity and comfort tainted with sadness. Memories had a magical way of editing out the childhood squabbles and irritations, and forming a tireless loop of faces and voices and events that defined her world. A world, happy and secure, that she had never imagined would change. Back then, there had been not a thought that life would never again be that easy or that someone could be ripped from her life forever. It was the time before the toll of economic hardship, and depression, and death stripped her of her innocence. And she cherished today because of it.

Olivia caught her eye. "You've been so quiet," she said.

Renee leaned back in her chair with a nod. "It feels really good."

"I'm trying to imagine how tired you must get. Working a back-to-back double shift comes to mind."

"I once fell asleep at a tied championship Little League game—with screaming parents sitting on each side of me."

"That's beyond tired," she returned. "I don't know if I should admit this or not." Olivia stopped, clearly undecided, then stood. "Maybe this is a good time for dessert. I brought something special for the kids. Is that okay?"

"Of course," Renee replied. "If I can have some, too."

"I've got us both covered." Olivia continued into the living room with Renee right behind her. She opened the bakery box on the coffee table, revealing a dozen M&M topped cupcakes.

"If these are double chocolate, you know your kids."

Olivia smiled and handed Renee a cupcake. "With M&M's, triple chocolate."

"J.J.," Renee called, "come and take these to the table—and only one each." She waited for Olivia to take one, then sent J.J. on his way. "You can pour more milk for everyone, and when you're finished you and Jenny please clear the table."

"Aren't you coming, too, Olivia?" he asked.

"Let's give Olivia a little break, okay? We'll eat ours in here."

"Can we show her the guinea pig later?"

"I'm sure she won't want to leave without that experience. We'll come see it in a little while."

They settled on the couch with Renee leaning forward in obvious anticipation. "Okay," she said, nibbling an M&M off the top of her cupcake. "I did my part."

Olivia stopped before her first bite of cupcake and licked the icing from her top lip. "I missed something. What did I miss?"

"Here we are, no kids ... the 'maybe I shouldn't admit this' story?"

Olivia shook her head. "It's one of those image-destroying things."

"Not possible ... trust me," Renee said seriously. "It isn't possible."

"You say that now." Olivia rested the cupcake on her lap. "I want you to think I'm a good nurse, because I am, but I'd like us to be friends, so I guess the trust thing has to start somewhere."

Anticipation had just become apprehension. Don't let it show, Renee thought, and don't keep promising things you're not sure you can deliver.

"I was working in a hospital in Indiana before I moved back here. They were terribly understaffed. We'd all been working long hours, extra shifts. I was exhausted and shouldn't have been working. It was midday, bright sun streaming through the hospital window. I sat on a stool next to the bed and gave the patient a shot. The next thing I knew, he was asking me if I was all right.

55

Then we both realized that the syringe I had used on him was stuck in my own arm. I had passed out."

The realization of what that could mean was instantaneous and it must have shown on Renee's face.

"My expression must have been even worse than yours right now. I knew that he was gay, but there was no indication on his chart that he was HIV positive. He kept reassuring me over and over, 'It's okay, it's okay. Don't worry, you'll be all right, I don't have anything.' But when something like that happens you hear the words, but they don't do much to take away the panic. I was a wreck until my second set of tests came back negative."

"Then you were a wreck for months."

"Months of not knowing what was happening to my life. I thought about all of the things I had hoped to do, the things I had dreamed of, and how with just one act, just one mistake it would all be changed. It was the most horrible feeling I've ever had."

"Had you ever thought about your own mortality before that?"

Olivia shook her head. "No. There had been no events in my life, except grandparent deaths, that prepared me for that thought process. I hadn't even worked with terminal patients yet, so it caught me completely unprepared."

"It changes your priorities, doesn't it—realizing that life as you know it could be gone tomorrow?"

Olivia's eyes narrowed slightly as though she was focusing harder on something difficult to read. She said nothing.

There it was, the reaction Renee always looked for, always expected—the "she knows nothing of what she speaks" reaction. Most often she ignored it, kept further thoughts to herself and moved on. Convincing people otherwise took time and energy that she just didn't have. Today, though, the effort seemed important. Olivia seemed important.

"I know that you think I'm being pretentious, and I do know what the word means, but I understand more than you think."

"Oh, yes," Olivia's eyes twinkled as though she was smiling, "you do."

Renee was still staring into Olivia's eyes, no words readily in mind, when Rachael edged up beside her. She looked inquisitively

56

at her face and placed her small hands on Renee's cheeks. "Ooh," she said, a deep line pressed between her brows. "You have a fever."

"No, Rach," she said, drawing the hands away, "I don't have a fever."

"Are you sure? Your face is hot just like mine when I was sick."

"Go get Rory, please. Olivia has a 'getting well' present for him."

"Okay, but I think you're sick."

Renee chanced a glance at Olivia and found her finishing a bite of cupcake and smiling, this time with more than her eyes.

Renee was still searching for what to say when Olivia spoke. "You asked about priorities and you were absolutely right, they have changed dramatically. But, we're probably going to have to keep that discussion for another time. The priority for now is going to be an excited little boy and a Bob the Builder truck."

"Thank—"

"No thank you needed."

Chapter 9

The movie hadn't held Sylvia's attention as well as the two women sitting on her right. Twenty-some inmates occupied the folding chairs in the television room, some watching silently, some commenting and conversing. But it wasn't the light conversation of the two women that distracted her. They were holding hands in clear view of Sylvia's peripheral vision.

In her nearly four years here it wasn't as though two women holding hands would be a shock, or even anything of interest. It had taken less than a month for her to see far more than she ever would have seen in her outside life. All these women, nesters by nature, forced to live together, work together, eat together. There should be no surprise that personal space would be coveted and protected, working relationships strained, or alliances clearly drawn at meal time. And in this environment it was to be expected that emotional needs, more pronounced and pushed to their limits, hadn't a single quarter's chance in Vegas of being met.

So, noticing that these two women were holding hands was not the distraction. It was more than visual, it was knowing why. It was knowing what they needed from each other, imagining what they felt when they met the other's eyes, and understanding the measures and risks they took to have time alone.

Sylvia watched the guard, a male guard not inclined to overlook a rule violation here and there. He'd been watching the movie, but now began to move along the wall, looking casually over the group of women. When his next step was about to give him a clear view of the offending couple, Sylvia leaned forward, elbows on her knees, and rested her chin in her hands. She stayed there until he had made his turn and returned to his favorite position near the window.

Although she knew the women by name, nothing was said until the movie was over and the women were walking single file down the hallway. Just before Sylvia reached her cell the woman behind her said, "I saw what you did. Thanks, Professor."

Sylvia turned at the door and met the woman's eyes. She replied with only a smile and a nod.

"What was that about?"

Sylvia took a seat on her bed facing her cell-mate of a year and a half. "It was nothing—just a thank you."

Brandy Tanner gave her a sly look and raised her eyebrows. "For what, Sylvie?"

She frowned her denial. "I helped her and her girlfriend out and now I'm trying to figure out why."

Brandy pulled her feet up on her bed and leaned back against the wall. "They say the closets disappear in here."

"I'm serious, Brandy. Would I have done the same thing if it had been my Renee?"

"You've gotta come to grips with this queer thing, Sylvie."

The frown lines deepened considerably. "Why do you have to use that word? I don't like it."

"Queer, gay, lesbo. What difference does it make? It all means the same thing. You just get all pissy because it's your daughter."

Sylvia looked at her—too thin, too young, street-wise, and apparently free of the sexual hang-ups of an older generation. Many nights when sleep was impossible, Sylvia was aware of Brandy taking care of her own sexual needs. Something she'd never been able to bring herself to do, even in here. An obvious remnant of a Methodist upbringing long ago left behind. Funny, she thought, you'd think that that remnant never would have survived the rebellion of her teens. Having a baby out of wedlock at sixteen had certainly shaken her mother's medieval view of sex.

When you have sex only for the purpose of procreation, do you have an orgasm? Did Mother ever have an orgasm?

"I'm sorry, Professor," Brandy was saying. "My ol' man used to say 'You ain't got the polish spit gives a shine.' Maybe that's why he took out with the secretary at his shop. I knew you were pissy and I go and make things worse."

"You didn't make things worse. You got me thinking." Sylvia shook her head. "Wondering why I react the way I do about certain things ... Does your mother have, you know, certain hang-ups about sex?"

"Hang-ups?" She added a harsh laugh. "My mother's too drunk to know if she's having sex or ridin' the nickel pony at Wal-Mart."

Sylvia caught herself smiling despite knowing the situation didn't warrant it. She couldn't help it, Brandy was an anomaly. Unlike anyone she'd ever met, Brandy could make you laugh at even the saddest of circumstances. It was an ability she envied.

"What if *your* daughter grows up and wants to be with other women?"

Brandy shrugged. "It would make me wonder what I'd done right. If she wasn't pregnant, or drunk, or callin' me from jail I'd want a DNA test to make sure the kid was mine."

"I'm serious, Brandy."

"So am I. It's just that the things that worry you and make you afraid for your kid aren't the same things that make me weird out."

"You wouldn't try to change her mind, or at least hope that she would eventually find a good man?"

"Hey, you know what?" she asked, dropping her legs and leaning forward on her hands. "I'm not sure they exist anyway."

"They do, Brandy. You just had some bad luck."

"Yeah, let me count," she said, holding up one hand and counting off her fingers.

"*I* found one," Sylvia insisted.

"And look at the mess *he* left you in. You ain't no better off than I am."

"It was a hunting accident. He didn't mean to leave us like this."

"No, he meant to leave you the insurance money."

"I don't believe that. And if I could have afforded it I would have fought the insurance company."

"Shit, Professor," she said, plopping down on her bed. "You gotta get real. He couldn't pay the bills, he couldn't take care of his family—shit, had he even hunted before? He tried to make it look like an accident so you'd get the insurance money. You would've wasted your money fighting the insurance company."

Sylvia dropped her head to her hands. She needed to make her stop. She couldn't hear anymore. It wasn't true after all, John would never have left her, not on purpose. What does she know, what could she know? John was a good man, a good father. Nobody has the right—

"Hey," Brandy said, moving to sit next to Sylvia, "my ol' man was right." She put her arm around Sylvia's shoulders. "It's not like we can go anywhere to get outta each other's space; we're stuck at this fancy resort with each other. I know you can't leave outta that door like my ol' man did. I ain't the easiest person in the world to live with, but I'll try to be more sensitive. Okay?"

Sylvia dropped her hands and nodded. "And I need to be *less* sensitive." She turned to look at Brandy. "I miss him." Tears had formed. "I miss my family."

"Yeah," Brandy replied, putting both arms around Sylvia and hugging her. "I know."

Chapter 10

Shayna Bradley greeted familiar faces, and navigated the halls of the County Building as if they were home. And they might as well be. In the thirty-two years that her father worked here he'd had his own version of "take your daughter to work day." Any of his children who were so inclined could pick a day of the week and that was their day all summer long to spend time with him at work. A couple of them visited once or twice and that was all they wanted. Some made a summer ritual out of it for the year. But Shayna had made it an education from the beginning of her seventh grade year to the day she passed the bar.

Now, as a child advocacy attorney, she was here sometimes more than she wanted. She knocked her usual formality on her father's office door and went in.

He rose from his desk as he did every time, even if he was on the phone, and wrapped her in a bear hug. "Hey, baby," he said with a kiss to the side of her head. "How's your day been?"

"Productive. Good. But, why is it that I feel that's about to change?"

"Because you're my daughter, and you can read the tone of my voice like that comic book collection you know by heart."

"Well, that's scary."

He rumbled a short laugh before beginning an explanation for his phone call. "I overheard some talk at lunch and I wanted to give you a heads-up."

"Let me guess. Millie Gordon."

He leaned back in his chair with a groan. "Taking issue with Renee Parker's taking classes at the U."

"Why can't she leave that poor girl alone?"

"And I know you well enough to know you really expect an answer to that."

"Aren't they keeping her busy enough with cases that need her intervention, kids that are truly at risk?"

"She's up to her eyeballs with them, they all are. But sometimes a case becomes personal, and for some unknown reason this one stuck to her short hairs."

"Come on, Dad, you've known this woman for how many years? What do you think it is?"

He opened his big hands submissively, palms up. "What I *know* is that she's a straight-up woman, smart, dedicated to kids. She'll go the distance to get a kid out of danger, even face down the barrel of a 350 magnum. She may look like somebody's Great Aunt Betty, but she's a barracuda. This, I'm afraid in your case, is the last thing you want to hear."

"So much for what you know. What do you *think* is going on with her?"

"Aside from the obvious thinking that started it all, that the responsibility was too great for someone Renee's age, I think now it's more of a personal reaction to Renee. I could be way off here, but I just can't see any other reason."

"We're all human," Shayna replied. "I've got my likes and dislikes, too. But when your personal feelings start taking away your objectivity, it's time to step out and let someone else take the case."

"Can't argue with you there," he replied. "But just as she doesn't have anything tangible to substantiate her reaction, neither do we have proof that it's personal."

Shayna left her seat, circled behind it and stopped. "Am I being overly sensitive or does Millie Gordon suspect that Renee's a lesbian?"

"That would be my take on it."

She paced to the window and back. "Because she isn't shagging some guy, or because she's determined to better herself in a career so that she can get out of the system? What?" she asked with a scowl. "She doesn't look like a stereotypical lesbian; although it shouldn't matter if she shaved her head and wore Carhardts and construction boots. Who she chooses to sleep with or not sleep with has nothing to do with how well she cares for those kids."

He let her vent, watched her pace. He knew his daughter well. She'd be all right. She'd let the anger go, get rid of the negative energy, and then she'd get tough.

"This has all the trappings of a military gay-hunt," she continued. "Identify those that rise quickly to the top of the company, put in extra hours, excel in their field, and get rid of them—they must be gay. Typical government logic."

He waited still. She would sit back down soon, re-focus her energy and get down to business. Seconds later she did exactly that.

"Then she'll push for a hearing," Shayna concluded.

"Undoubtedly."

"We've got precedence going against us. Three years ago, maybe, a divorced mother lost custody of her child to her ex's parents because she was enrolled in college. They claimed she wasn't spending enough time and that a three-year-old child should have a stay-at-home parent. The court agreed and instantly set women's progress back decades."

"I remember thinking at the time that the court, by that decision, was virtually guaranteeing that this young woman and her child will remain on assistance and in the system. But then she surprised me by staying in school while she appealed."

"And lost," Shayna added. "And I can tell you right now that Renee Parker, if pushed to it, will not make the same decision."

"That will be a shame in so many ways."

"She's a proud young woman. I'm convinced that if it weren't the only way to keep those kids together, she would never take a penny of help. It goes against everything she knows and everything she's been taught. But what she doesn't fully understand yet is that it is that exact mind-set that caused her parents to do what they did, and what put her in this situation."

"It's ironic to think that the system she's resisting may actually be teaching her the temperance she needs."

"Even if she realized it, it wouldn't make it any easier for her. She made the decision to forego college once; I hope she doesn't have to make that decision again."

"I wish there was something I could do to help," he said. "But I'm afraid I don't carry much influence as far as Millie's concerned."

"That's no fault of yours. And I know I don't have to tell you that if I had my choice of a father who proudly loves me for who I am or one with influence with Millie Gordon, there would be no choice."

He responded with a hardy laugh. "Your momma would say that you're stuck with me."

"My momma's a lucky woman."

Chapter 11

"J.J.'s hogging the Skittles," Jenny yelled from the back seat of the mini van. Well, it was actually more of a shouting, loud enough for passing motorists to hear.

"I'm not hogging them," he replied, a decibel lower.

"Eeww," she screeched, "now he's sticking them in his nose and putting them back in the box."

Renee took her eyes off the road long enough to catch J.J.'s evil grin in the rear-view mirror, which changed abruptly to his never-quite-convincing innocent grin the second he saw her watching. "Knock it off, J.J.," she said, her eyes darting back to the road. "Rachael, hand the box of Ju Ju's back to Jenny."

"I don't want Ju Ju's, I want Skittles."

Renee responded firmly, "Then you'll have to take your chances on eating buggers."

She glanced quickly at Olivia in the passenger seat, seemingly unaffected by the continued taunt and whine from the back seat. "Just exactly what possessed you to spend your day off with this fine brood at Cedar Point?"

Olivia reached into the bag of snacks and pulled out another box of Skittles. She questioned permission with her eyes and received a cave-in go-ahead from Renee.

"I couldn't see turning down free VIP tickets," she replied, handing the box back to Rachael. "My brother's big on using his perks. There has to be something in it for repeating the same spiel probably 150 times a day."

"Hey," Jenny yelled, "Rachael's eating the Skittles."

"Rachael, pass them back to Jenny," Renee directed.

"But I want Skittles, too," Rachael replied.

"You picked out Gummy Worms," Renee said with a hard stare into the rear-view mirror. "Take a handful and give the box to Jenny." She made eye contact briefly with Olivia. "This is not the Parker family's finest hour. I promise the next hour will be better. They will lower their voices and share their snacks and play car games, or they will be tied up and gagged."

Her smile offered a quick reassurance. Then Olivia added, "I spend so much time with sick kids; it's really nice to be with kids that are healthy enough to be a pain in the patootie."

"*Okay*," Renee replied with enthusiasm. "I can guarantee you this crew will give you enough pain in the patootie to get you through the rest of the year. Of course, if you ever feel the need for a refresher, I'm sure they'd be more than willing."

"Why, thank you. I just may take you up on that."

"That must be one depressing job you have there," Renee said, half-jokingly.

"And rewarding as well. Please don't worry about me today. I'm going to have a really good time."

The Witches' Wheel, with enough centrifugal force to suspend spewed vomit in the air and deposit it on the face of some unsuspecting kid in a seat trailing the puker, should have been a pretty good test of Olivia's tolerance. Between Rachael, the puker, being taunted by Jenny, and a stranger's kid screaming uncontrollably, Olivia had her hands full.

Jenny, of course, reported the whole incident, minus her part in further agitating Rachael, when they met up with Renee and the boys at the old-fashioned cars. Tame by comparison, the cars were the perfect ride for J.J. and Rory to "talk cars." And, as it turned out, a lot less messy than the Wheel.

Rory was still exuberant over the Model T he got to drive and J.J. was naming each car as it moved past their bench, while

Jenny was recapping the spew hang time. Only Rachael, pale and still somewhat nauseated, was silent.

Renee watched Olivia stroke the damp blond hair as Rachael leaned up against her. It could have been worse; Olivia could have been cleaning vomit off herself and having to wear pukey clothes the rest of the day. Did she realize that? Or was she just thinking that the day wasn't over yet? Maybe she was making the best of what was proving to be a bad decision. Why on earth would any non-mother in her right mind choose to spend her day off like this?

Olivia leaned down and kissed Rachael's head. "Feeling a little better?" she asked.

Rachael lifted her face to look at Olivia. "I didn't mean to," she said with a deep frown.

"I know you didn't, honey. Is that what's making you feel bad?"

Rachael nodded, her eyes still on Olivia.

"Things like that happen so fast that you don't have time to stop it. You know, if *my* stomach needed to throw something up, I wouldn't be able to stop it either."

"Even if it was gonna splat someone in the face?"

"Even then. And then I'd do exactly what you did; I'd tell them that I was really sorry."

"Am I going to do it again if I go on more rides?"

Olivia glanced quickly at Renee. "Well," she began, "maybe we shouldn't have corndogs and candy apples," she looked to Renee with a sly grin, "all that protein and fruit, before the next ride."

"But I like corndogs and candy apples."

"But nobody enjoys them secondhand," Renee interjected, "like when they're all chewed up and spewed back out." She looked Rachael directly in the eye. "No more eating until after the rides."

"Can you tell," she directed at Olivia, "that we've never been here before? You could have warned me."

"I could have, but I'm careful not to cross the respect line."

"For me?" she asked as the children's patience reached its limit, and the women were bombarded with questions and demands.

"Why can't I eat? I didn't spew."

"We're riding the rollercoaster next."

"No, bumper cars."

Above the distractions, Olivia maintained eye contact long enough to nod and smile.

The feeling it gave Renee warmed her head to foot, as if the sun had burst into full blaze, bright and hot within her. Olivia Dumont, educated, professional Olivia respected Renee Parker— Renee knows-from-nothing Parker. Why didn't even matter, the feeling it gave stayed with her, paramount above all else as the day wore on. It took her higher than the steepest climb of the rollercoaster with all the anticipation of what would follow, and it spiked a thrill that rivaled that first drop off the edge of gravity. Nothing all day long could shake its hold on her. The kids laughed and screamed and whined and begged. They waited in long lines, dodged a short rain shower, hunted down bathrooms, and ate junk food until it threatened to solidify in their stomachs, but nothing altered that feeling.

She was respected. Not liked, or loved, or appreciated, all of which are needed and important, but respected, and by Olivia. After struggling and worrying about how to tell her how much I respect *her*, Olivia simply says it—to *me*. It doesn't even matter if I deserve it; it just feels so good that she thinks so.

Renee relaxed on the blanket alongside Rory, who had finally fallen asleep. Olivia had left them on the shaded lawn behind one of the gift shops while she took the other three kids to play games. Today had been not only fun for Rory, but a good test of his medication as well. He'd had an exciting, exhausting day without incident. That relief alone had made this day special. She draped her arm over Rory and closed her eyes. It had been a long time since she had felt this relaxed.

When she opened her eyes again she was surrounded by four smiling faces; Olivia and the kids were sitting quietly and waiting anxiously.

Jenny tried to contain her excitement in a loud whisper. "Look, Nay." She patted the head of a stuffed green dinosaur.

"I won it for Rory," blurted J.J.

Rory sprang to attention.

"Look, Rory, I won it for you."

Wide-eyed now, Rory reached for the dinosaur. He looked it over from head to tail, then clutched it tightly.

"How did you win it, J.J.?" Renee asked.

"Throwing baseballs," he replied proudly.

"*You* are awesome," Renee said with a high-five for J.J. "You're one fine baseball player."

"I tried, too," Jenny said, "and Olivia, too. And Rachael picked up ducks. We all promised we'd keep trying until we won something for Rory."

Renee sent Olivia a look of concern. "How many tries are we talking here?"

"I lost track," she said, then smiled at Renee's obvious frown. "Once the guy knew who we were playing for, the balls just kept appearing."

"And then J.J. won!" Rachael exclaimed, going from one to the next until she had high-fived everyone.

Renee turned to Olivia and said softly, "Thank you."

"It was fun," she replied. "We made a good team."

"You really are enjoying this, aren't you?"

"More than you know."

"Even if I could have afforded it, I never would have attempted a day like this by myself."

"No parent with full faculties would. Besides, like so much in life, it's so much better shared with a friend."

It wasn't until they were driving home, kids asleep from total exhaustion, that Renee found the courage to ask Olivia what she had been pondering for an hour.

"If I could arrange it," she began, "would you consider letting me thank you for today by taking you somewhere special—without the kids?"

Olivia turned from the window to Renee's profile. "No," she said.

Despite the bowling ball knocking the air from her midsection, Renee turned to now look at Olivia's profile. She'd gotten it all wrong. She needed to apologize, but the words wouldn't form. Her eyes returned to the road.

Finally, Olivia broke the silence. "I would, however, consider spending my next day off with you—alone—if you can arrange it."

Chapter 12

Out of courtesy, Renee waited ten minutes into Olivia's break before she called. She had begun envisioning Olivia during her breaks sitting at a staff table with something to drink in a favorite mug, maybe talking, maybe reading. A cherished time, clearly. No comparison, she was sure, to her own fifteen minutes away from the cash register or stocking shelves. But until she knew differently, she would take Olivia at her word that calls during breaks were welcome.

The sound of Olivia's voice was fast becoming an addiction, and luckily there was legitimate reason to get a fix today. "How is your day going?" Renee asked, shutting the bathroom door behind her to claim a few private minutes.

"A tough one today," Olivia replied.

"I'm sorry. I'll understand if you don't want to talk right now."

"Just the opposite, Renee. I'd really like to hear something happy or something silly right now—even something ridiculous would help."

Renee sat on the closed toilet lid and smiled to herself. "I can do that, probably all in one sentence."

Olivia's light airy laugh sent a twinge through Renee's midsection.

"Do tell," Olivia said.

"The Parker little people have set a new record—the happy part, by repeating your name five-hundred-and-thirty-seven times—

the silly part, and I'm holed up in the bathroom to get some peace—"

"The ridiculous part."

"Did that help?"

"I'm smiling," Olivia replied. "Yes, it helped."

"You know, any time you need a distraction, we'd be more than happy to help you out. There is never a shortage of material fit for distraction around here."

"I'm going to take you up on that, so I hope you're serious.",

"I am. And I'm also serious about thanking you for Cedar Point." She was standing now, pacing a tight circle in the tiny bathroom. "I never ever would have attempted anything like that on my own. It's all the kids talk about, it was the best time they've ever had. I don't know how I can thank you."

"It's not necessary, Renee, the thanking part. I've told you that before. I'm not the kind of person who does things because I think I should, I do them because something about it appeals to me. I see a lot of worry and pain in my job, and the day we spent at Cedar Point went a very long way to put back some balance. All that energy and laughter, all that joy lifted me up and made me happy. And for that, I should be thanking you."

"I believe that's a first. No one's ever thanked us for just being ourselves. It's a nice feeling, though, to make someone feel good. Who'd a thought it would be this easy?"

Another light laugh before Olivia replied, "Shouldn't it be?"

"Yes," Renee said. "*Something* should be easy ... Can I call you tomorrow and make you happy?"

"Please do."

Chapter 13

It had taken more than a little arranging, two weeks to be exact, to have a kid-free Saturday, but patience and perseverance had made it happen. J.J. had been easy. His best friend's father had come through with the perfect plan—watching the Detroit Tigers' play-off game with his teammates on a 50-inch HDTV screen. J.J. was thrilled.

Jenny's best friend, on the other hand, was at her grandmother's for the weekend. Another friend was committed to helping clean the garage for a yard sale the following weekend. Jenny was less than thrilled with the idea of helping until she found out that the reward was going to the movies afterward. Two down, two to go.

As anticipated, Rachael was the most difficult to accommodate. It had to be something special since she couldn't be included with her older siblings, and she couldn't feel "pawned off" with the "baby." So the clear choice was her classroom's most involved, most creative, favorite mother. A simple trade worked for everyone— Mrs. Brady would teach the girls beading this weekend and Renee would take them to the "Y" next weekend. Three down.

One more trade put Rory at Stacy's, and Renee and the kids doing her yard work on Sunday.

Getting everything arranged took so much time that Renee only had one day devoted to worrying about Saturday's details. Everything needed to be perfect. She wanted the van to be spotless, but relatively clean was all that was possible. Which would be best, late lunch or early dinner? Should they eat here or in Jackson? Would there be enough to talk about? Could she keep it interesting enough or would she bore Olivia into never wanting to see her again? And the Cascades, maybe it wouldn't be as special as she remembered.

The worries swarmed all night, annoying her, exciting her, keeping her from sleep. She was used to worries magnifying themselves at night. Sleepless, restless nights were nothing new. What made this night different was the strange mix with excitement. Each worry needed an answer, each answer needed to be the best possible solution. And each solution, if chosen just right, had the potential of making Saturday one of the best days of her life. She watched the clock toward morning, anxious for the day to begin; yet, in the next second wanting time for one more mental run-through. At five o'clock she was up and dressed.

After a morning full of questions and diplomatic explanations, each sibling safely in other people's care, and adrenaline threatening nausea, Renee finally settled herself in the restaurant of Olivia's choice.

"Do you mind eating at a buffet?" Olivia asked.

"No, not at all. And I love Chinese. Only I don't want you choosing a buffet because I'm paying and it's cheap."

"I worked my way through school, no grants and small loans," she replied. "I'm a buffet kind of girl."

That, along with a smile, was enough to relieve Renee's sense of impending nausea. She rose with Olivia and helped herself to a sampling of enticing entrees. By the time they returned to the table, Renee was actually feeling little pangs of hunger. What was left of her anxiety dissipated with laughter and a funnier-now-than-then recap of the Cedar Point escapade.

"I don't think you realize what a huge hit you were at Cedar Point," Renee said between bites. "The kids keep asking when you're coming over. And when they found out that we were going to do something together today, I really had a problem."

"I'm taking that as a very nice compliment, but I'm assuming you've had that problem before with other friends."

Renee looked up expecting the tea-colored eyes and the excitement they brought, but Olivia was concentrating on her dinner. Was there such a thing as being subtle and clear at the same time? Why do I think I need to be subtle?

"They've been jealous of my spending time away from them, but it hasn't happened often. Aside from parents of the kids they go to school with, there've been very few others, and no one my age interested in spending time with me *and* the kids. That has instantly made you special."

There they were, the beautiful eyes, working their sensual magic.

Olivia let them work for a few seconds longer, then smiled like she knew what they were doing. "So, do you think they know that I think they're special, too?"

"Oh. They know." She grinned, then mimicked, "'You didn't ask Olivia. If you had asked her, she would want us to come, too.'"

"They're precious."

"Uh, huh. They're precious, and I'm a heel. I only told them that we were going out to eat, I couldn't tell them where else we were going."

"Where *are* we going?"

"Jackson."

Chapter 14

The drive took just short of an hour, during which time Olivia cunningly tried to wear her down and Renee skillfully parried each attempt to find out where they were going. Whatever direction their conversation went—a movie, a play, a concert, shopping—Olivia tried to connect the dot. Each time Renee left the line hanging.

They were well off the highway now, across town, driving through an older southwest neighborhood. Vintage forties houses, five to a block, lined the tree-shaded streets. Renee slowed the car and stopped in the middle of the block.

"My mother grew up in that house," she said, "the stucco one with the cement block porch ... Mom and I came here and lived when my grandmother was sick."

"Are your grandparents still alive?"

"Just my grandfather, but he's in a nursing home. He's really sick with Parkinson's ... I wasn't going to come by here," she said, continuing down the street, "but we had a little time to kill before dark."

"After dark," Olivia mused. "Fireworks?"

Another block, then two, and Renee pulled the car across an intersection. "We're here," she announced. "Start watching through there."

Olivia focused on the area of silhouetted pines to the right of the street as they entered a dusk-shrouded park. "What am I looking for?"

"Just keep watching."

Suddenly, through an opening between the trees, she caught a quick glimpse of bright purple. The car slowed, and through the next break in the trees the color had softened to a lighter purple.

The car came to a stop at the mouth of a long, wide path lined with darkening pines on both sides stretching the full length of the park. At the path's end on the far end of the park was a waterfall now bathed in pink.

"Wow," Olivia whispered as the color changed gradually into a deep red.

Renee smiled to herself. It *was* as beautiful as she remembered. She watched with Olivia as the fall's colors morphed and mesmerized.

Without taking her eyes from the falls, Olivia asked, "Can we get closer?"

She studied the profile, so intent, so fine, and replied, "Yes, we can."

As the car started forward, the falls disappeared behind the trees. "The land for this park all belonged to William Sparks," Renee explained. "Over there," she pointed to the left side of the street, "is where his mansion stood for years." They followed the winding street along the edge of the park. "He had four hundred acres for his back yard. He made the falls, and a golf course and the park to bring visitors to this area. Building a lighted sixteen-tier concrete waterfall may not seem so special today, but in 1932 it must have been truly spectacular."

"It's still spectacular. And you just lived down the street a few blocks."

"I could hear the bands that played on certain nights from our porch. This park was our playground. There are ponds and miles of lagoons connecting them, and an island where my best friend and I use to pretend we were marooned."

Renee turned into the park and over a cement railed bridge. "After Mom met John, he used to bring me to the big pond, there, to ice skate in the winter. They had a warming shed with sawdust for a floor, and you'd walk right in with your skates on and sit around an iron stove and prop your skates up on a rail to warm up your feet ... Here's where we park."

"Come on," Renee said, exiting the car. "I promise to shut up and let you enjoy the beauty of this place without a running commentary."

"Don't you dare," Olivia said, running to catch up. "I want to hear your commentary." She followed through the gate in the wall that had hidden the falls from view. "Oh, wow," she exclaimed softly as she approached a wide shallow pool at the base of the falls. Tier after tier of flowing turquoise-colored water descended from the sixty-four-foot hill. The air was cool and moist, and the night filled with the sound of the water spilling from level to level. The color had begun a gradual change to a darker blue, starting at the top tier and following the course of the water until the new color filled the bottom pool. Olivia hadn't moved.

Finally, she turned her head to say, "It's beauti—" but stopped at Renee's expression. "What?"

"Nothing," she replied, slightly embarrassed at having been caught watching her. "I wonder if that's how I looked to my mother the first time she brought me here, that's all." Her focus went quickly to the falls now turning purple. "There are a gazillion lights under there, and control rooms under each level. A maintenance guy took me in and showed me how it worked one time when I was playing up here. My mother used to be able to play around the falls before they fenced it all in."

"The liability must be tremendous."

"And the maintenance. I guess they started having problems with vandals. I'm just glad they didn't shut it down."

"So am I. It's just beautiful, Renee. Thank you for sharing this with me."

"I haven't been here in so long, since we moved away from Jackson. I was worried that it wouldn't be how I remembered it."

"So, is it?"

Renee nodded, looking back at the falls now in deep red once again. "It's one of the few things that is ... Hey, there aren't many people here yet, do you want to play Rocky?"

"The steps?" Olivia asked, looking toward wide cement stairs hugging the curves on each side of the falls. "Is this why you said wear tennis shoes?"

"Are you game?"

"We're running the stairs all the way to the top?"

Renee pointed to the flag pole at the top of the falls, a large American flag blowing strongly to the left. "You take the left side and I'll take the right. Last one to the pole buys popcorn."

"You're on," Olivia said, taking off for the stairs.

"Oh," Renee shouted, on her way to the right. "I see how you are."

She raced up the steps, heart pounding with excitement and anticipation. Up the steps she flew, hugging the wall, faster than when she was a child, across the flat landing as it curved toward the second pool, and on to the next level. At the next pool she tried to find Olivia on the other side, but picked up her pace again when she didn't see her. As carefully as possible she worked her way around couples here and there, and started up the next level.

Then, just as she reached the landing, the six fountains spaced along the edges of the falls shot their pink spray into the dark sky. Renee smiled, jutted to the far right of the landing and raced to the next set of steps. Another level, more stairs, another spray, purple this time high into the air. Her legs were beginning to tire and she was breathing so hard that she could manage only a jagged laugh. A childish anticipation drove her tired legs upward. It wouldn't even matter if she had to buy popcorn.

One more level. She chanced a look across—no Olivia. Her legs were so heavy that her foot barely cleared the top step. She walked with shaky legs to the flag pole and leaned gratefully against it. God, did they shake this badly when she was younger? She remembered being so hot that they stood and waited for the spray to cool them off, but had she ever been this out of breath?

She rested for a few more seconds, then moved to the cement guard rail stretching across the top of the falls, rested on her forearms and watched for Olivia.

She had just begun to worry—had she fallen, was she all right, did she turn around and go back down?—when she caught sight of her walking slowly up the last few steps. The beginning of a laugh had already tightened the muscles of her abdomen and the instant Olivia was in clear view Renee lost control. She broke into laughter that bent her over the railing.

Olivia approached her, clothes soaking wet, water dripping from dark strands of hair across her eyes and down her nose. "You," she began, wiping a wet face with a wet sleeve, "are un-freaking-believable."

Renee gained enough control to lift her head and say, "You want to say it. Oh," she laughed, "I know you do. You want to say it in the worst way."

"But I'm not going to, because in some weird way it would just add to your amusement."

Renee, finally in control now, straightened. "Would it help if I apologized?"

"Not unless you can tell me, standing there bone dry, that you didn't know whoever went up the left side would get soaked."

Her eyebrows rose; her mouth opened, but nothing came out.

"Surprise, surprise. Then, at least, tell me ..." she looked straight up to see the flag flapping loudly in the wind to the left of the pole. "Never mind."

"Here," Renee started to remove the denim shirt she wore over her T-shirt.

Olivia held up her hand.

"Come on," Renee insisted, trying to hand her the shirt. "The wind is going to make you cold."

"Would it make you feel better?"

"Yes."

"Then, never mind." Olivia stepped to the railing and looked down over the falls. The colors were changing more quickly now, in time to music coming from unseen speakers. "You're lucky that this is a spectacular view."

"I'll take lucky," she replied with a smile. The view *was* spectacular, even better than she remembered. And if it provided her with a little forgiveness then all the better. For the next few minutes they watched the light show from their lofty position, but when Olivia folded her arms and hunched her shoulders, Renee suggested, "It's not as windy below; let's watch the show from there."

As if on cue, all six fountains shot high into the air. From where the women stood they could see the wind carry the sprays and heard them splashing against the concrete of the left stairs.

"Gee," Olivia said, "I hope no one got caught under that."

"Come on," Renee replied, unable to suppress a grin. "Try the dry side this time."

They descended in silence, watching the water as the colors danced and changed with the beat of the music. Olivia's thoughts were her own. Whether or not the prank had been taken as intended, Renee didn't know. She had used her own silent time to try to find the right words to explain it. She wasn't comfortable going much longer without trying. But, before she had put the words together and decided where and when, Olivia stopped in the circular jut-out overlooking one of the fountains.

She turned to face Renee. "Okay," she said, "I give in. Can I have your shirt? Point or no point, I'm cold."

Renee removed the shirt and draped it around Olivia's shoulders. "You did make your point," she admitted, standing close enough to smell the scent of shampoo in still-wet hair. "I've been thinking about it and you're right—you don't need an apology, you need an explanation. And I've been trying to—"

"No, Renee, it's okay." Olivia took hold of Renee's arm. "It *was* funny. I pour the teasing on too thick sometimes."

"But, I ..." she stopped, the words lost, unable to pull her eyes from Olivia's. Reflections of colored water danced in their dark centers. Renee finally exhaled. "I *want* to explain. I just have to sort it out a little better."

Olivia's voice was soft and low, her eyes unwavering. "For a moment there," she said, "I thought you were going to kiss me. But, since you didn't ..." She closed the short space between them, leaned forward and pressed her lips delicately against Renee's. They lingered and questioned, carefully, briefly—then leaving room, a tiny space filled with the warmth of her breath, for Renee to answer.

The eyes that had intrigued her from that first sight in the hospital opened, for a second, long enough to send their surge of excitement, for the second that it took for Renee to answer. She returned Olivia's kiss, a kiss she hadn't planned, hadn't even imagined yet. Gently, respectfully, she pressed against the soft warm lips as Olivia's arms encircled her waist. Yes, she would have imagined this, even wished it—holding Olivia, kissing her— but not planned it, not with Olivia.

Yet, here she was, Olivia's lips parting against hers, their kiss wetter and firmer, making the heat of its message undeniable. And just as her tongue began to explore the invitation, children's voices burst around the corner of the stair wall. The women broke contact immediately, turning from the sound of the voices to a crimson red fountain spray reaching its limit.

A moment later, Renee asked, "Still cold?"

"Actually," Olivia said to Renee's profile, "you managed to warm me up quite nicely." Profile or not, Renee's smile was apparent. "Do I need to thank you?"

"No," she replied, extending her smile to Olivia, "I don't think so." More approaching voices broke their intimacy once again. "Maybe we should go on down and watch the show."

"Maybe we should."

They settled on middle seats half-way up in the stadium seating along the wall that surrounded the front of the falls. Olivia wrapped herself in a blanket that Renee retrieved from the car.

"You must have been a good girl scout," she said, propping her feet up on the back of the empty seat in front of her.

"Never a scout," Renee replied. "I think it was the cookie thing. I love to eat 'em but I hate to sell 'em."

"I can relate."

"Kids have a way of preparing you better than anything else anyway. Even when you think you have the answer figured out and a foolproof plan in place, they can find a hole in it big enough to drive a real Bob the Builder truck through."

"Or an ambulance. Try answering their medical questions."

"Or why their father died and their mother isn't coming home." Renee scooched down in her seat and propped her feet up.

Olivia reached from under the blanket and took Renee's hand.

The silence between them followed like a natural lull in conversation, easy and warm, without expectation, without explanation. Everything felt right—music, old and familiar, colors as vibrant as the most spectacular sunset, and the company of a special friend. It was a place of comfort she missed desperately.

"I know why," she said suddenly, squeezing Olivia's hand.

"Why I kissed you? I thought that was apparent."

"Apparent that ..." Renee stopped before putting her assumption into words.

Olivia looked directly at her. "Apparent that I think you're someone special, someone I want to get to know better."

Special, a word used so often, for so many situations, and yet Olivia gave it a whole new sound. There was no other word that described it better. Special was exactly how this woman made Renee feel right now—very special, and very warm. "Even after I ran you, unsuspecting, through the Cascade gauntlet?"

"Were you testing me?"

"No," Renee replied quickly. "Not intentionally anyway. I was regressing. That's what I was going to explain. Being here, with you, without the kids, makes me feel free and silly. I always worry that I won't be respected and taken seriously because of my age, and here I am acting even younger than I am. And you still want to get to know me?"

"This place makes you feel good, and not just because it's beautiful. There's nothing wrong with that. Why do you think people love to hear the music that was popular when they were in high school and college? Why do they love the cars they first owned or had their first date in? For the same reasons this place makes you feel so good."

"You think?" she asked, acutely aware of their hands still holding tightly, warmly, and Olivia's eyes sparkling with reflected color.

"It takes you back to a happy time, when you felt safe and free."

"And I thought I had a revelation."

Olivia smiled. "My father owns a 1971 Chevy Malibu that he parks in the garage and covers with old quilts and drives in the Woodward Dream Cruise every year. My mother won't be caught dead in it, so I get to ride with him. It's great fun, but he definitely gets something different from the experience than I do. He becomes Bogey Boy—the nickname is a story in itself—right before my eyes. He gets animated and tells me stories of things he and his friends did when they were in high school. He loved that time in his life, you can see it in his eyes." She pulled Renee's hand up to hold it tightly against her. "I saw the same thing in your eyes."

Renee rested her head on the seat back, took in the blackness of the night sky, so clear and deep that the stars recessed into infinity. "I was really happy when it was just Mom and me. She had to work a lot, but other than that, I got to go every where with her—to see second-run movies at the dollar theater and shopping the sales at the Meijer store. When she met John I thought I wasn't going to like him. I wasn't going to give up my time with her. I wasn't going to share her. I don't know if it was John or my mother who figured it out, but what they did worked. My mother kept some of our special times just for us, and asked if we could include John at other times. The clincher, though, was when John started taking me places just with him.

"Like skating."

"Yes. My mother didn't skate. She didn't like the cold. And on Saturdays, I'd get up really early and go with him to have breakfast at this little diner and then visit his friend Ted who owned a used car lot. I'd get to sit in all the cars and Ted would give me ice-cold Cokes from his little frig. John loved car trading. Even after J.J. and Jenny were born, John and I still had our Saturdays. But when Rachael came, and John was laid off, things changed."

"That had to be tough on the whole family."

Tough? Renee could still see his face—the pride making a gallant, but losing, attempt to reassure them that everything was going to be all right. It wasn't tough, it was the first stage of devastation. "I wonder a lot," she began, "if Mom and I had known how tough, if we could have done something to help sooner."

"Was he out of work long?"

"It didn't seem like he was ever out of work for very long at a time, but they eliminated his position and after that he could never find anything full-time with benefits. He was a tool and die man. The big companies were downsizing and the small shops were either going under or offering only part-time positions. He started working two part-time jobs, but I found out later that he was making just over half of what he had been making full-time."

Olivia nodded her understanding. "Companies don't take care of their employees like they used to. My grandfather worked for the same company for fifty years. They took care of him when he had to have surgery. They even advanced him money for a down-payment on his first house. And, in return, he would have done anything for that company."

"We had a nice house," Renee said. "Nothing fancy, but nice, with a big back yard. John was so excited when he showed it to us for the first time. He took us from room to room as if the next one would disappear before we saw it. He was talking so fast, telling us what he envisioned for each room. When he finally stopped for a breath, my mother asked if we could afford it. He grabbed her and spun her around. 'You bet we can,' he said, all smiling and proud. 'I got a raise. They know a good man when they see one.' He could hardly hold still long enough for Mom to kiss him and tell him that she did, too. I guess I'll always remember that day."

Olivia nodded. "Of course you will."

"But how do you get rid of the ones you don't want to remember?"

"I don't know," Olivia admitted. "I'm not sure that it's possible to desensitize yourself enough so that they don't bother you. I've always had a particularly hard time seeing small animals that have been killed lying along the road. I couldn't help myself, I looked every time, and then the image wouldn't leave my mind. Even ones from years before still bothered me, so I disciplined myself not to look. Now it's the faces of children, sick and fright-ened, and I can't just not look. The only thing I've found that helps is to try to replace it with a good vision. Sometimes it's very difficult to do, to consciously fight to keep the good vision there, but it's worth the effort. I don't know that memories would be any different."

"And not try to answer the questions they pose then?"

Playfully, Olivia released Renee's hand and held her own up in submission. "Okay, now I've no doubt wandered over the line and contradicted advice from a much more qualified source. You should just tell me when I clearly don't know what I'm talking about. It's okay. Or, just smile and ignore what I just said."

"Never. I respect you too much to do that. And I do try to do what you suggested, but right now even some of the good images and memories are hard to keep."

"I won't even pretend to know what it's like to lose a parent." Her expression was serious, intent. "But I am familiar with the grieving process, the beginning of which often starts right where I work. I suspect someone has talked with you about it, but I'm not so sure you are letting it have its space."

"Would that be the space between getting four kids out the door in the morning and getting to work on time, or the one between work and school, or between eating and homework and bed?"

Olivia didn't respond, but maintained eye contact until Renee broke it and stood. She stared at the falls silently for a moment.

"Renee—"

"Hey," Renee said, turning and reaching out her hand, "I have something I want to show you."

"Does it involve needing a towel?"

"No," she said with a little laugh. "Come on."

Olivia took her hand and followed her to a small museum room on the opposite side of the enclosure. The walls were covered with old pictures and lined with glass showcases. Slowly the women made their way around the room, looking at original plans and sketches of the falls and pictures of the construction progress. It was an impressive dream come true, but not what Renee wanted to show her. She pointed to a picture in a series of photos of a group of uniformed men.

"That's my great-grandfather. Well, John's grandfather," she said. "He was a member of the Zouaves back in the twenties. William Sparks, the guy who made this park, was their commander."

Olivia looked closer at the men with their tasseled hats and their rifles. "Were they soldiers?"

"They were a famous drill team. They maintained a marching cadence of 300 steps per minute carrying regulation Enfield rifles. John showed me a film of one of the teams, they were unbelievable. They scaled walls using the rifles, like in that picture right there, to hoist each other up and over, and they never missed a beat. They traveled all over the world, and later teams were on television, too. See," she pointed to another picture. "There they are with Bob Hope."

Olivia did five quick steps in place, and then another five. "Three-hundred steps a minute would mean five steps a second. Doing it twice is tough enough, how could they keep up that pace for ..."

"Fifteen minutes in the film I saw."

"That *is* unbelievable."

Renee pointed him out in the other pictures. "He was famous," she said with a smile. "And since John claimed me, I get to claim his grandfather. Right?"

"Absolutely."

It was several minutes later, as they stood at the railing of the reflecting pool at the bottom of the falls, before either of them spoke again.

Olivia spoke first. "Did John adopt you?"

Renee's eyes with their catch lights of blue remained on the falls. "He asked me right here. I was ten ... He said that one of the things he wanted most in life was to have a daughter like me. Then he asked me if I would let him give me his last name so that everyone in the world would know that I was his daughter. It was as though we were giving each other a gift that no one else could give us. When I said yes, he grabbed me and twirled me around and around until we were laughing and dizzy. I couldn't wait to tell Mom ... He made me feel special—and safe."

"What a wonderful feeling that must have been."

Renee continued to stare silently at the falls as the last song of the night said its "good-night." "I wish it had never happened."

She had regretted saying it the moment it came out of her mouth—not because she didn't believe it, but because she was unprepared to pursue a conversation about it. Olivia, however, had not pursued it, and Renee was grateful for the lighter line of conversation during the ride home. She liked that about Olivia, her intuitiveness, her sense of comfortable boundaries. It made being with her easy, and very enjoyable.

"I'm not reneging on the popcorn," Olivia said as the car came to a stop in the parking lot of her apartment complex. "I just forgot."

"Which means, since they close the Cascades after this weekend to drain it for winter, we're going to have to go some place else for that popcorn."

"So, what's your pleasure, or should I say preference?"

"Say neither," Renee followed with a smile, "unless you want an honest answer."

Olivia looked at her, a reply smile stopping at barely detectable. She held the expression and Renee's attention for seconds before replying. "You know, you're really cute—and you're really naughty."

"Really? Cute?"

"Keep me up nights cute."

Renee leaned across the space between the seats. This time there would be no hesitation, no second-guessing herself or worrying. This time she knew that they both wanted this kiss. She touched her hand to Olivia's cheek, lowered her eyes to the lips she wanted, and covered them with her own.

How good it felt to be this close, this warm. Touching her like this. Letting the feeling fill her and excite her, and free her from all other thought. Olivia's lips pressed and parted, and things like social services no longer existed. Renee entered the warmth with her tongue, immersed herself in the wetness and heat and there was no thought of the past or concern for the future; there was only now and Olivia and a desire growing within.

She continued their kisses, pulling Olivia closer. Her hand found Olivia's waist, gained confidence over a denim-covered hip. The gentleness of their kisses began to give way to an increasing sense of urgency. Deeper they explored, their breaths coming quicker, their hearts pounding in tandem.

Olivia grasped Renee's hand, brought it to the inside of her thigh and moved it up the seam of her jeans to feel the warm wetness between her legs.

Her voice was low and breathy. "This is what you're doing to me."

Renee centered her finger on the thickness of the seam and traced it slowly.

Olivia responded with a throaty moan, grasped the back of Renee's neck and kissed her deep and hard.

A current of desire seared through Renee's body, its heat disconnecting thought and laying bare the purely physical. The kisses she returned came dangerously close to bruising; her fingers stroked the wet seam of Olivia's jeans with deliberation—every breath, every kiss, every stroke with a singular purpose—to bring this woman to orgasm.

Olivia had become *this woman*. The thought was disturbing. To have thought at all at this point was disturbing. Renee tried to block further thought by burying her lips below the collar of Olivia's shirt, the soft low sound of a moan filling her ears.

But the sound of voices approaching the back of the car halted everything. Both women jumped, separating to their seats without a word. Renee quickly wiped the steam from her window with her sleeve and looked straight ahead. As the voices continued past the car and faded down the parking lot, Renee dropped her head back against the headrest with a sigh.

Olivia let go of a gentle laugh. "Should we be grateful?" she asked.

"You don't think we would have come to our senses otherwise?"

"I'm afraid I was lost in a teenage world of back seats and Lover's Point. The adult thing to do," she said with a tilt of her head, "since we have no curfew, would be to go inside and enjoy the rest of the night."

But Renee didn't reach for the handle of the door, or make a move to pull the keys from the ignition.

"Are we moving too fast?" Olivia asked.

Is that what it is, moving too fast? Or is it something else entirely?

"It's okay, Renee." Olivia reached across and drew her fingers down Renee's cheek. "I shouldn't have rushed things."

"If that's what we were doing, you weren't doing it alone. I'm sorry if I ... not staying tonight, is that going to ..."

"Not staying tonight means that we're both going to get a little more sleep, that's all."

She leaned across the car and kissed Renee gently on the lips. "Sleep well."

Chapter 15

It was past one o'clock in the morning and from her pull-out bed in the living room Renee could hear the occasional hum of tires traveling the busy street in front of the apartment building. There were other sounds as well—the loud muffler of the neighbor's car two doors down as he backed into his parking spot, a short heated exchange between a couple in the parking lot. Yet, this was the quietest night she'd ever experienced. It was the first time in her life that she was completely alone. No parents or grandparents, no lover, no children. It was an aloneness, an emptiness, void of promises and reassurances, a clear and scary reliance totally on self. A self Olivia wanted to know; one Renee wasn't sure she herself could identify.

She lay on her back, arms folded over the top of the blanket. A wide-eyed uneasiness kept her too alert to sleep. Not being able to sleep after the evening she just had was expected. It should be excitement keeping her awake. The heat of sexual attraction barely cooled, the scent of Olivia still on her lips. And surely that was part of it. The rest was a mixed mess of unidentifiable pin pricks and adrenaline spikes. Emotional limbo.

The quiet, the aloneness exaggerated everything like the throb of a paper cut in the middle of the night. Emotions were suddenly bigger than life—fears flashing one moment, excitement spiking the next, until worry and fear encapsulated and chilled her excitement.

What if I can't pull this off? Four kids counting on me, and I make decisions based on what? What a father may or may not do if he were here? Or a mother whose lack of judgment, whose lack of honesty left them in this mess? Who's to say that I'm not screwing their lives up even more than our parents, concentrating so hard on Rory that I neglect the others? Not seeing their needs, not meeting them. What if Millie Gordon is right?

The consequences were scary, the thoughts frightening, and there was no one there this time to divert them, no one to shush away the fears or shrink their monster-sized shadows. There was, in fact, no measurement or perspective beyond her own thought. Tonight she'd have to stand and measure, just as Olivia had said.

She'd done it as a child. Certainly the risks were less consequential and the scale much smaller in comparison, but not to a ten-year-old child. The window by the refrigerator in the back room of her grandparents' house was tar black after dark. The perfect stage for a child to imagine the sudden appearance of a scary-eyed stranger. A sheer fear that paralyzed her in her tracks, hand on the refrigerator door, eyes staring at the window lock, unsure if locked was knob up or sideways and too terrified to test it. Then, one night, with her hands too full to flip on the light switch, she made her way through the darkened kitchen and there it was—the window, lighter than the room, with a clear view of the garage beyond it. The solution was simple. She knew the kitchen well enough in the dark to leave the light off and the window went from a fearful unknown to a security checkpoint. It was an easy transition from there to the confident sentry checking the windows of room after darkened room. Olivia was right, she was taller and stronger than she knew.

So, what fears are making me so uneasy? Find the dark window and light it up. Rory's health had loomed large such a short time ago, but the decision has been faced and made and it's a good one. Worrying about future health problems is pointless and its energy best used on other matters. Mrs. Gordon? Of course her constant scrutiny, her influence affecting us, is a continuous concern. Yet, against the worst of odds we won the custody battle—the biggest hurdle run at straight-on and cleared.

And keeping custody, taking good care of the family? Well, a better support system simply didn't exist. There is always someone, a caring and competent someone, only a phone call away. Be prepared, be vigilant, but don't fear what may never happen. Rationalism begets calm, calm begets peace.

Renee breathed in deeply, turned on her side and snugged the pillow under her arm. She closed her eyes and drew another deep breath. Yes, peace. A whole night without needing to worry, a night completely to myself, a night to rest.

Yet, it didn't seem to matter how tired she was or how much she knew she needed sleep; her mind wouldn't allow it. Thoughts wandered aimlessly, always coming back to Olivia. And why not? She was intelligent and fun and desirable, and she had added a whole new dimension to life. It was that dimension, the defining of it, Renee realized, that was nagging the edges of her thoughts.

At first the attraction to Olivia was masked with desire for her to respect her, to take her seriously. When it became apparent that the need to be with her had superseded the need for her help, Renee worried that needy and doubtful wouldn't translate into sexy and mature. And today, wanting to be with her began to border on discomfort, physical discomfort. It was no mystery what relieves that kind of discomfort. What was a mystery was why she came home alone.

What she *was* feeling and what she *should* be feeling were not lining up sure and clear. Quite the contrary; the more she thought, the less clear everything seemed. The decision not to spend the night with Olivia was not a decision Renee Parker in her right mind would have made. At least not the same mind that two months ago couldn't wait to drop off the last sibling, pick up some wine coolers, and get skin-to-skin with Shari Jacobs. Ready for a no-sleep night with every minute of it geared toward one purpose, no time to waste on chitchat or niceties. They both wanted one thing, went for one thing, and got it. They did whatever it took, did it over and over. Their hands searched frantically for those places that brought the most pleasure; their kisses sought to excite; and without any other explanation, they drove their bodies to orgasm. What single, or otherwise, right-minded lesbian wouldn't want the same thing with Olivia Dumont? A woman whose eyes alone, their gaze catching her own for even a second, flush every inch of skin.

It hadn't been only one time with Shari, and Shari hadn't been the only one. But with each of them there had been no promises, no expectations; their time together no more than a hyphen in time—needed by both, lamented over later by neither.

Renee turned to lie once again on her back. She arranged her pillow and laced her fingers together under her head. So why not Olivia?

Chapter 16

The answer, of course, was right there, like the proverbial elephant, and there wasn't enough camouflage in all the armed forces to hide it. But acknowledging its presence wasn't as much the problem as deciding what to do with it. And there was only one person who could tell her what she needed to know.

Renee sat in the little office adjacent to the girls' locker room and waited for Jean to return from her end-of-the-day duties. This year's crop of athletes, full of school chitchat, were busy changing clothes and getting ready for practice. It seemed a lifetime ago that she had been one of them. Full of excitement, full of pride, part of a greater whole destined for at least fleeting glory. Those days had held such promise, scholarships and college just a year away. She watched them through the large glass windows of the office. They seemed so fresh and young, so full of expectations for tomorrow. None of which, she was sure, were of unwanted pregnancy, or abuse, or divorce. And, as hopeful and naïve as these young women were, they surely didn't expect to have their dreams shattered. No one would. No one should. It's a special place they're in, and for some, it'll end way too soon.

"This place has more than one attribute," Jean said, choosing a small round table at the back of a coffee shop. "It's off the beaten school path and it serves a sinful hot chocolate."

"Both sound good to me," Renee replied.

Only minutes later they were warming the falling temperatures by sipping very hot hot chocolate and easing into more personal conversation.

"Oh, Renee, I am so glad to hear that Rory is doing so well. He's such a good little guy."

Renee nodded. "He is. As many times as he has been in and out of the hospital and doctor's offices, and prodded and tested, he just seems to take it all in stride."

"And I'm sure he's made a few fans along the way. I know I'm one. I'll take him any time you need a break."

"That's been a blessing you know I appreciate." Renee wrapped her hands around the warmth of her cup and dropped her focus from Jean's smile. "He has another fan after this last hospital stay." She looked up to add, "That's partly what I wanted to talk with you about."

"Rory's fan base?"

"No ... well, yes ... sort of."

"Okay," Jean said, adding a smile, "there's no need in explaining that any further. The color of your cheeks has done that part for you. Who is she?"

"Rory's nurse, Olivia." But it wasn't about feeding the smile on Jean's face, or needing to tell a trusted friend exciting new-love news. It wasn't that at all, and the smile would be short-lived. "I need serious advice," she said and watched Jean's smile fade. "Honest, intimate advice, with no reservation about hurting my feelings."

Jean's face was serious now, her eyes boring into Renee's. "I'll certainly be honest, Renee. But are you sure Shayna wouldn't be the better advisor?"

"Yes, I'm sure ... she didn't have to make the kind of decision that you did."

"About being together?"

A nod from Renee. "Only what you're comfortable with. If it feels too personal I'll understand."

"There's not much that I wouldn't talk to you about, especially if it's important."

"I don't know if the subject has ever come up in any of your conversations with Shayna, but my love life, committed or not, would probably be grounds for losing custody of the kids. But I've been very discreet." She stopped and offered a half grin. "That's a nice way of saying that I've kept my one-night stands out of the apartment."

"Good to know we're both going to be honest here."

"It's not always pretty, is it?"

"No. It doesn't have to be. Now, what ugliness do you need to hear from *me*?"

"Not ugly, I'm sure." She hadn't anticipated that Jean's answers might be more embarrassing to her than to Jean, but it was too late now. "Tell me how you knew it was the kind of love that you should risk everything for."

"I suspected that that's where this was going. And I'm not sure I can tell you anything that will help."

"Can you tell me how you felt about Shayna?"

"She was the one person, is the one person I would trust with my life—my *whole* life. I knew everything was safe with her—my feelings, my fears, my dreams. She was my best friend and then I realized that I wanted more than a friendship, needed more than a friendship. But I didn't realize the power of that want until I couldn't imagine my life without her."

"That's when you realized that your relationship with her would jeopardize your job?"

"I'd never had to worry much about my job. Even in physical education I was immune to the usual rumors because I was married. I was totally unprepared to deal with homophobia on a personal level. I'd intervened on students' behalf almost daily, but it didn't prepare me for the decision I had to make."

"To come out or give up your relationship?"

"To give up a love that made me happier than I had ever been. And I tried," Jean replied, dropping her eyes and running her finger around the rim of her cup. "I thought it was best. I thought I could." She lifted her eyes. "But I couldn't eat, couldn't sleep. I couldn't even get out of bed and get dressed. It taught me the meaning of despair."

"What if you had known the risk before," Renee asked, her brow knitted in thought, "would you have allowed it to go beyond friendship?"

"I've given a lot of advice and guidance over the years that I've taught, but I don't think I've ever answered a question this difficult. And I'm concerned that applying my answer to your situation could cause you to lose custody."

"You don't have to answer," Renee replied. "But I think you know me well enough to know that I will weigh whatever you do say, and make my own decision. I always have."

"And I've always worried anyway." Jean sipped the now cooled chocolate as Renee waited patiently. "You asked me if I would have *let* it go beyond friendship ... I wonder," she said with a stare that seemed to look past Renee, "if there's any conscious decision that can stop love at a certain point and let it go no further—if you can consciously say I'm feeling this much but no more ... and if it is possible, would I have done it? And just because *I* could or could not have done it, could you?" She finally smiled and once again centered her attention. "I think I'm off the hook here, aren't I? If you love this woman, no amount of advice, or thinking, or deciding is going to make one bit of difference. You're going to feel whatever you feel, and if she feels as much for you, then no matter what the circumstances you'll find a way to be together."

"And if this isn't the love I think it is?"

"You're the only one who's going to know that."

Chapter 17

The little grill on the north side of town was a favorite of hospital staff partly because of its location and partly because of the food. Unlike in the hospital cafeteria, the potatoes were real, the meat cooked to order and hot, and the salads contained more than iceberg lettuce and one cherry tomato. And as a plus on Wednesdays, it was the perfect place for Olivia and her sister to cap off a morning together before work.

They waited patiently just inside the narrow entrance until a couple left and the table was hurriedly cleared. They squeezed around tightly placed tables to a booth in the back and settled their bags beside them.

"Thanks for being so patient next door," Alisa said, referring to her favorite secondhand store. "You'd probably never set foot in there if it weren't for me."

"Oh, I wouldn't say never," Olivia replied. "I like to look through their books."

"It's the absolute best place for me to keep Keith in jeans and sweatshirts. I even find some with the price tags still on them." She rummaged through a bag and pulled out a new sweatshirt and showed it to Olivia. "Keith's gotten even worse after he and Todd started the business. He came home from a job site the other day covered in the usual layer of sawdust, and when he leaned over to pull his tool-belt out of the truck I saw a split in his pants that went from the waist band all the way to his zipper.

Olivia laughed, both at the vision in her head and at the disgusted look on her sister's face. "I love Keith. He's a treasure."

"Yeah, a real gem," she said, taking a quick look at the menu.

Olivia shrugged. "So he's not cover material for GQ, but he's in construction, what do you want?" She laughed lightly, then added, "He stays in shape, and he cleans up real nice when you take him out in public."

"I know. I do appreciate him." She acknowledged the waiter. "A number five with a Diet Coke."

Olivia followed suit. "Same thing with an iced tea."

"And at least we do get out in public," Alisa continued, "unlike my anti-social sister."

"I'm not ..." Olivia stopped and looked at Alisa with a frown. "Anti-social."

Alisa rested forward on her forearms. "Well, what would you call it?"

Another frown. "My social life?" Then a little smile and a lift of her brows. "Minimal. But, with my hours ..."

"Hey, I've got two kids and a man with his own business, and *I* get out." Alisa sat back from the table as their lunch was served. "That's what I like about this place, no frills, no thrills, just good hot food right away."

It made Olivia smile. Alisa was their mother's "good eater." But she put it to good use. Four inches taller and thirty pounds heavier, little sister had been an all-around athlete in high school. If anyone was judging on looks alone, Alisa would be their pick for the lesbian. It had always made things interesting. Girls would hit on Alisa and guys would hit on Olivia. And when they went places together, other lesbians would assume they were a couple. If she were even half as competitive as Alisa, it would have been much more interesting. It would, in fact, have produced battles of Alexis and Krystle proportion. But, she wasn't. So, she could smile and enjoy the contrast.

"For you," Olivia began, "it was more of a priority, the whole dating, hooking-up thing. It just never has been for me. I mean, it was all right now and then, but it wasn't as important as my career."

"And now?" Alisa asked between bites. "Let me see. I think the last woman I remember was Brenda—geez, how many years ago was that?"

"Not many people available for socializing at the time I am."

"Mmm ... probably not a lesbian one in the medical field with your hours. We only have, what, a dozen hospitals within driving distance?"

As if on some invisible cue, a woman with hair cut shorter than Olivia's and gelled into short spikes stopped at the table. A hospital badge hung from a cotton lanyard. "Olivia," she greeted cheerfully. "How are things on third floor?"

"It's been a pretty good month so far, Paula. It's always a good month when we don't lose any kids."

"I couldn't do what you do. I like that I can work my magic numbers with them and they're sleeping peacefully by the count of four—no time to get attached."

"Kids are especially tough," Olivia replied with a nod. "Paula, this is Alisa," she hesitated slightly before adding, "my sister. Paula's one of our anesthesiologists." The widening smile on Paula's face was exactly why she had been tempted to leave off the sister part of the introduction. Olivia let the greeting remain just that, offering no further conversation. Professional and polite—the best way, she had decided months ago, to handle the situation.

The pleasantries done, Paula moved on to her table and Olivia was left to deal with a typical Alisa reaction—the raised eyebrows and smug expression.

"Oh, don't go there," Olivia warned her. "I'm working. I'm focused. I'm happy. I have all I need. Just let it be."

Alisa lifted her hands, palms up. "I'm just saying."

"And I'm just saying you have a way of putting me back in high school faster than flipping through a yearbook. Every dyke is not necessarily dating material, just as every guy isn't, or wasn't, for you ... no, let me rephrase that. Just as all guys *shouldn't* have been for you."

"Come on," she said, "those were my frog-kissin' years. And there were some warty toads that didn't get kissed."

"I'm sure there were." She waited until Alisa took another bite. "I think you kinda miss those days. That's why you want me out there kissing and telling—you get vicarious enjoyment and you don't have to cheat on your prince."

Alisa couldn't swallow fast enough. "Mom's right," she managed quickly, "you're going to live alone unless you start taking finding a mate as seriously as you do your career."

A warning her mother had already worn out and, it had seemed, given up on. "You don't have that universal fear that all daughters have, do you?"

Alisa returned a questioning frown.

"That fear," Olivia continued, "that one day you will look in the mirror and see your mother staring back at you."

"Hey, when she's right, she's right."

"Like when she decided that your kids should go to church with her because you don't attend?"

Alisa took the white paper napkin from her lap, stuck the prongs of her fork through its corner and stood the handle in her water glass.

Olivia laughed lightly and refocused on her lunch. Now was not the time. Mentioning what may most likely end up being merely a friendship with Renee would serve no purpose and only encourage Alisa's wasted speculation. It wasn't necessary.

"I only want my big sis to be happy," Alisa said. "Okay, that's all I'm saying ... I am all over this baked chicken, and as usual I'll get the quarter."

With her ability to eat right through a conversation, Alisa did indeed finish her lunch first, earning the childhood reward promised by their grandmother.

"We're pretty lucky, aren't we?" Olivia offered between last bites.

"In what way?"

"Many ways. Still having grandparents in our lives. Having grown up in a family with both parents still together and reasonably happy. Aunts and uncles and cousins—fun, fascinating, quirky, annoying—we've got a little of everything, don't we?"

"Yeah. But I think you can add weird to that list. Don't forget Cousin Eddie."

Olivia slid her empty plate to the end of the table. "But what if we didn't have them?"

Alisa pushed her brows into a triangle above her nose. "Huh, we'd have no weird Eddie stories to share at holidays. Or ... be able to bet on how long Aunt Susan's latest marriage will last."

Olivia eased forward to rest her folded arms on the table. She locked her focus on Alisa. "We'd have no structure, no sense of belonging."

"You mean if we didn't have any of them?"

"What if we just had each other?"

Alisa's expression turned decidedly serious. "It's not anything I've ever thought about."

"What if when you were in junior high and I was in high school, we were left alone—no dad embarrassing us by talking to everyone about insurance, or boring us with details about the workings of a Deluxe '54 Ford. No mom with her weekly housework list, or Avon sales, or hokey family meetings. No grandparents. Nobody."

"Damn. What did I say to put you in such a morbid mood?"

"Seriously, Alisa. What if?"

Alisa stared, clearly contemplating, as the waiter placed a fresh Diet Coke on the table. "I'd be scared as hell," she said with a frown.

Olivia nodded, her eyes focused somewhere past the table and out the window. "Me, too."

"No," Alisa replied. "You couldn't be. I mean, I wouldn't want to *know* that you were. That would really freak me out." She waited for Olivia's eyes. "Really freak me out."

Olivia nodded again.

"I'd be expecting you to have the answers, you know, even if I didn't ask."

"Like Mom." Olivia offered a slight smile.

"And I'd believe you. I'd have to believe you. Wouldn't I?"

"Even if I didn't know the answers. Even if I made promises that I didn't know I could keep." Olivia's eyes made their way back out the window. Walk a mile in their shoes. The thought wouldn't leave her. This was as close to walking in Renee's shoes as she could get. How on earth could she ever know what it was really like? But there was this need to know, this unrelenting need to get inside Renee Parker's head and truly understand.

"Hey," Alisa broke the silence, "where are you?"

"Sorry," she said, returning her gaze. "I was trying to figure out where I'd turn for answers; who I'd trust."

"Geez, I'm thinking I'd end up in church. Now that's scary."

"And if you didn't feel welcomed there?"

"Okay," Alisa said making direct eye contact, "just what is it that's got you so unnerved?"

"I told someone recently," she replied, "a young woman with guardianship of four little kids, that it was all right to be frightened. I said that without knowing how complicated that could be."

"So, this scenario you created was to understand what she's going through?"

Olivia looked hard into her sister's eyes. "You and I will never be able to understand what she's going through."

Chapter 18

With a groan, Olivia dropped onto a chair in the staff room and stretched her legs out to rest them on the chair next to her. She flexed first one foot, then the other. First thing tomorrow. I've got to pick up a new pair of shoes, *tomorrow*. No more putting it off. I can't keep working on these pieces of cardboard.

She closed her eyes for a moment and tried to remember what else it was she was supposed to do tomorrow. Annoying. She couldn't even pull up her mental list. Her brain was as tired as her legs. With a sigh she gave up the effort and pulled her day planner from her bag. That's it, she promised, snatching the envelope containing her insurance payment—no more filling in for co-workers. Saying no is not a sin, it's self-preservation.

While she was at it, Olivia retrieved her phone, turned it on and checked for messages. Mom's reminder about what she needs for Dad's birthday dinner. Alisa giving her the girls' soccer schedule. Renee. Olivia sat up and listened intently.

"If you get this message before morning, ah, before eight a.m., please call. I could really use someone to talk to. Don't worry about what time you call."

Without hesitation she pushed the call button. Renee answered on the second ring. "Did I wake you?" Olivia asked.

"No, I'm up. I was hoping to be able to talk to you. Are you on your way home?"

"Just resting my legs. Haven't made it to the car yet. Is Rory all right?"

"Yes, he's fine. It's me. I just need to talk."

"If it's about ... well, you don't need to explain. I haven't brought it up because I knew you needed time, I understand that. And I haven't tried to see you because I've had this horrendous week filling in for a co-worker whose son is home on leave. I agreed to do this before—"

"No, Olivia, that's not it. If anybody understands a 'too-tired-to-think' schedule, it's me. Please don't worry about that. And, because I do understand how tired you probably are, I hate to ask you—"

"Ask, Renee."

"Could you stop by here on your way home?"

"I'll be there in fifteen minutes."

The door to Renee's apartment opened before she could knock. She would have knocked softly; not waking sleeping children was something she was used to. But then, so was Renee.

What Olivia *wasn't* used to was the effect that being face to face with Renee had on her after a week and a half. Phone conversations had definitely commanded her attention, causing a familiar twinge of excitement at the sound of Renee's voice. The warm rush that accompanied looking into the serious dark blue eyes was expected; she was, after all, admittedly attracted to this woman. She had not, however, anticipated the pure joy that she now felt standing so close to her again. The feeling burst open, glowed warm and bold as she stepped into the apartment. The sight of Renee, backlit with a soft yellow glow from the living-room lamp, quickened her heartbeat.

Renee greeted her in soft tones. "I really appreciate you coming over."

"Are you all right?"

"Mostly, yes," she replied, taking Olivia's arm and ushering her to the couch. "I didn't mean to worry you. I need some objective advice."

"About what?"

They settled, facing each other on the couch, and Renee began.

"I got a phone call from my attorney; CPS is challenging my guardianship while I'm taking classes."

"On what basis?"

"That 'too-tired-to-think' schedule that you and I are all too familiar with. I can't possibly dedicate the time required to do both successfully."

The delicate balance between anger and fear was evident in the tone of Renee's voice and the hard line between her brows. Olivia reached for Renee's hand. She wanted to quell the fear, soften the anger. "But you *are* doing both—successfully."

"For now." Renee dropped her eyes momentarily, then brought them up quickly. "What if they're right? What if I can't keep this up?"

"Would you be doubting yourself if they weren't challenging you?"

"I doubt myself a lot ... there just aren't many people that I dare admit it to."

"Is your mother one of them?"

"Tell her that her children may be split into foster homes, or not getting the proper emotional support, or that their physical health could be in jeopardy because I am making decisions that I'm not qualified to make? Make her helplessness and guilt even greater than it is? Oh, I've been tempted, believe me. You don't know how many times I've run down that list in my head, times when the frustrations or the anger get to me; I'd imagine letting her have it, point by point, every hardship *her* decisions have caused."

"And why haven't you?"

Renee let go of an audible sigh and relaxed against the back of the couch. "Honestly, I don't know."

Olivia watched her for a moment, waited for the troubled look in her eyes to rest on her own. She released Renee's hand and gently stroked the side of her face. "Maybe," she said softly, "it's simply because you love her."

Renee made no response except to close her eyes.

Olivia leaned forward and pulled Renee into an embrace. There were no words and no tears, and that was all right.

"I've tried to imagine," Olivia said, stroking the shoulder-length hair free of its usual ponytail, "how you must feel. It isn't possible; you know that, don't you?"

Renee nodded and sat back from their embrace.

"Not without experiencing what you have," Olivia continued. "But I want to understand everything I can. Will you let me?"

"Of course," she replied, looking directly into Olivia's eyes. "It's funny," her directness softened, "I know I have people around me who care, but no one's ever asked that before."

"Well, now someone has, and I truly do want to understand what being you is like."

"You may regret that wish before long."

"I'll take that chance."

Renee turned at a noise in the hallway. She rose from the couch and asked, "Will you wait?"

"Sure. Go."

For a moment she could hear the high soft tone of a child's voice, followed by Renee's hushed tone, then movement back down the hall. She envisioned Renee putting one of the little ones back to bed, patient and reassuring, leaning over them or lying next to them as she had in the hospital. Her priority was exactly as it should be, in there smoothing tousled hair and chasing away shadowy monsters. Just as she should. Just as any good parent would.

The vision was endearing. Appealing. As appealing as the glint of mischief she had seen in her eyes at the falls, and the adoration that she had seen at the hospital. Possibly even as appealing as the thought of kissing her again, long and deep and as sensual as any in her memory, or the anticipatory thought of what would follow. As she was discovering, there was a lot more making up this attraction to Renee Parker than she first thought. And each time she saw her it seemed to grow faster than she could put reason to it.

Renee swept quietly into the living room. "I'm sorry, Jenny had a bad dream. Can I get you something to drink, or a snack? Did you eat?"

"No," Olivia answered, reaching for Renee's arm. "Come and

sit back down and talk with me." Renee settled again next to her, wafting a faint scent of Tommy Girl and stirring excitement that Olivia immediately ignored. "What frightened her?"

"She saw her mother taken from the house in handcuffs. Sometimes she wakes up and thinks that they took me, too. She usually comes out here and crawls in bed with me and goes back to sleep."

"Little miss 'put-me-in-charge'?"

"Yeah, she's been very busy making a good disguise for that frightened little girl inside."

"And she's certainly convincing. She's lucky that you know what she's doing."

"She doesn't understand why, but there's no way she could hide that little girl from me."

The soft light from the lamp in the corner cast a warm golden tone over Renee's cheeks and lightened strands of hair falling loosely over her forehead. Reflected light sparkled in her eyes, and Olivia was aware of an intense need to take Renee's face in her hands and kiss her. Instead, she said, "You must work hard, too, don't you? Keeping *your* little girl hidden?"

"It's a must. I'm all they've got."

"But who do you have? Who does Renee turn to when she's frightened?"

Renee didn't say anything; she didn't have to. The answer was in her silence. Olivia touched her fingertips to the side of Renee's face, stroked them lightly over the glow of her skin, and all the while she held the fragile trust she saw in Renee's eyes as safely as she could with her own.

Olivia's voice was just above a whisper. "I don't have all the answers."

"I have a lot of choices for advice. I've learned to seek it out wherever I can. What I *don't* have," she said and stopped. She broke contact with Olivia's eyes and looked down for a moment.

Olivia waited patiently for the pretty, but clearly perplexed eyes to lift again to hers. Whatever Renee needed from her needed to be in her own words. It was like listening and letting a patient describe their symptoms; they need to find the right words, the right comparisons. Only they know what they're feeling. Only Renee knows what *she's* feeling.

Renee lifted her eyes and tried again. "I don't have an emotional net. Someone who can catch the important stuff and let the rest drop through the holes ... But I don't know if it's fair of me to ask that of you."

Once again the paths of rapid firing synapses making Olivia warm and increasing her heart rate had to be redirected. Again, her physical responses cooled to a simmer in favor of a higher priority. And that was all right.

"Most people aren't so forthright ... or analytical. Past their physical needs, I've found that few people put much thought at all into the beginning of a relationship."

"To be honest, it's not something I've ever done before. I've never discussed beginning a relationship with anyone. It just was, or became, whatever it was—the person was a friend, or a mentor, or a lover. Neither of us ever discussed what it was going to be."

"Do we know what this will be?"

"What I want it to be is even more unfair to ask."

The possibilities flashed quickly. Casual sex, when and if, would surely have happened the night of the falls. Friend, close and intimate, non-sexual. Isn't that where we are now? The next step, taking that chance, risking friendship for a possible future together? "What *do* you want?"

Renee leaned forward and touched her lips to Olivia's in a gentle kiss. Her voice was discreetly low. "I want us to be more than friends." She looked down and took Olivia's hands in her own. She spoke without eye contact. "But if we were and CPS found out, I could lose my family."

She lifted Renee's hands, touched them to her lips, then pressed her cheek to them. "This is one of those times when I do not have an answer for you." She raised her eyes to meet Renee's. "No one can make a decision involving that kind of risk except you. What you need from me is a promise to honor whatever that decision is, and you have that."

"People think that I've made really hard decisions, giving up

111

a chance to go on to college, giving up the freedoms that most people my age have, but they weren't hard. They weren't even decisions. Not like this. This is the hardest thing I've ever had to decide, and I don't want to be the one to do it."

"But you have to be ... and I want you to know that I'll be here. I'll be your friend regardless, for as long as you want me, or need me ... Don't be afraid to decide."

"I live from home visit to home visit, from hearing to hearing. You'd be locked in a closet with me, hiding from everyone. There wouldn't be anything normal or easy about trying to be together."

Olivia stood and pulled Renee up with her. "This isn't about me, Renee. Other than a chance to get to know you, to see if we could have something special together, I have nothing to lose here. And I don't want you to feel obligated in any way to decide before you're ready. So," she added, with a kiss to Renee's cheek, "I'm going to leave so that you can get at least a couple hours of sleep."

She crossed the room to the door with Renee following, and turned to say goodnight. She wanted to make it easy—give Renee room, and minimize her own emotional investment. But that hope vanished as Renee backed around the corner out of view of the hallway and pulled Olivia to her.

It was clear, in her eyes, in that instant before their lips met why this couldn't be easy. Renee needed her, in a way that went beyond the need for sex or friendship—she didn't want to be alone anymore. That realization made her embrace more poignant, the touch of her lips more honest.

Olivia slipped her arms around Renee's waist and leaned into the kiss. Warm and gentle, she loved the feel of it, the honesty. And the way she held her, with such tenderness, such sincerity. A strange mix of security and sensuality like she had never felt before.

As their lips parted, Renee whispered, "I don't want you to leave."

"I know," Olivia said softly against her ear. "I *do* know."

Olivia nestled into the embrace and felt Renee's arms tighten around her. "Your explanation to Jenny alone would be worth the risk of staying." She felt Renee's smile widen against the side of her head. "But I can't stay here and kiss you without that risk."

"Fair enough."

"When is the hearing?"

"Nine-thirty Friday. I have to take off work."

"Will you stop by when it's over?"

"Good news or bad?"

Olivia chanced one more kiss then turned quickly toward the door. "That's what a net is for."

Chapter 19

"I live from home visit to home visit, from hearing to hearing." Olivia couldn't get the words from her thoughts. They hadn't been spoken with sadness, although their meaning was terribly sad. That may be what had implanted them so stubbornly in her thoughts. Renee had spoken them as matter-of-factly as telling someone that she worked afternoons or that she traveled a lot. It was simply part of her life.

And it wasn't the constant scrutiny and evaluation, as annoying and frightening as it must be, that bothered Olivia most about the situation. It had to do with living with such uncertainty. She couldn't conceive of it in her own life, her structured, well-organized, predictable life. She stayed with an unpopular shift at the hospital because it meant she could keep it as long as she wanted it. Vacations always included quality time with an intact family. Her job paid her enough money to pay the bills without worry, drive a two-year-old car, and travel if she wanted. She liked certainty, like people she could count on, planning ahead, and Wednesdays with her sister.

The little north side restaurant was warm and humming with friendly conversations. The busy sizzle of the grill filled the air, as it did every Wednesday, with smells reminiscent of her father cooking on the patio, a familiarity of time and place that made it easy to understand the comfort Olivia felt here.

Alisa was on her second Diet Coke, and rummaging in the plastic bag next to her in the booth. She pulled the waistband of a pair of jeans into view. "Do you believe the gonga I got today? Three pair of Levis, five bucks apiece, and they still have the tags on them. They're new."

"It pays to look every week," Olivia answered absently. She sipped from the same glass of tea that had lasted through lunch and glanced around at the unassuming surrounds. Cramped and old, with standard restaurant-fare furnishings and chalkboard menus and advertising signs as décor. It wasn't the ambiance that kept regulars coming back. "What do you like about this place, aside from it being next door to your favorite jean source?"

Alisa stuffed her find back into the bag. "Are you kidding? A great lunch. I didn't have to cook it, and I don't have to clean up after it. What's not to like about that?"

Olivia offered only a nod.

"There you go again, wandering off into thought land. Was I ever this absent around you?"

The inference made Olivia frown. "I didn't see *you* for almost a year when you and Keith first started dating."

Alisa returned the frown. "Really?"

"I like this place because it's familiar and comfortable and reminds me of shopping with Mom on Saturdays and stopping for lunch. I like our Wednesday routine and spending time with you."

"Yeah. It's a feel-good place. I guess I just subconsciously enjoy feel-good things in my life without actually acknowledging them ... except when you get all analytical and force me to."

"I'm not trying to force you to see anything. I'm only being comfortable thinking out loud with you."

"That's okay, it's good for both of us. 'Hey, this tastes good. What's in it?' is as analytical as Keith gets. And I don't take much time to do any on my own. You know me, as long as I don't get a call from the school counselor or smell foreign perfume on Keith's sweatshirts, I'm not going to analyze anything."

"Everyone's guilty of that to some extent. Life keeps you busy just living it."

"So what's got you all sentimental today?"

"Renee, the friend I told you about last week ... and the kids." Olivia continued in an effort to fill in the blank look on her sister's face. "I take so much for granted, happy memories, things and places that make me feel good and safe. Lately, I've been wondering what kind of memories those kids will have when they grow up. I already see how conflicted Renee's memories are, and as hard as she is trying to make things better for the kids, there's only so much that she can do. It's like trying to plant a garden with your hands tied behind your back."

"So, who's more frustrated, Renee or the nurse who sees pain she can't heal?"

"The two can't be compared. She's living that frustration, I can walk away from it."

Alisa hesitated a moment, watching her sister divert her focus to her now empty glass. "Can you?"

Olivia's eyes snapped back to Alisa's.

"I grew up with you," Alisa continued. "I knew about your crush on Ms. Jenkins, and the reason you went to the library so much after school when you were a senior. Therefore," she said with that look that always accompanied a discovery, "I also know that you walk away from the pain you see at work with great difficulty, because you know you must; it's your job."

"So what makes you think that I can't walk away from this, too?"

"The tone of your voice every time you talk about them. It's different, I don't know if I can describe it. It reminds me of how you sounded when you got me through the James Adams crisis."

"God, you were a mess. He put you through hell."

"What I put you through wasn't too pleasant, either. I didn't stop crying for a week, but you stayed with me every minute. You forced me out of bed, made me shower, made me dress and made me eat. All the while, the thing that kept me going was the sound of your voice. All that week, day or night, whenever I needed to hear it, and for the whole next month, every night I'd hear your voice and I knew how much I mattered to you ... that's the sound I hear now, for Renee, and those kids."

"But, there's a difference," Olivia said. "I made promises to you that I knew I could keep. I was going to stay with you for as long as it took. I would have taken a leave of absence from work if I had run out of vacation days. I knew Mom couldn't know about the abortion, and she still doesn't know. Those were promises I knew I could keep. But I've made promises to Renee that I may not be able to keep."

"Can you tell me what they are?"

"You may be the *only* person I can tell."

Alisa waited with uncharacteristic patience.

"I promised that I would be there for her as long as she needed or wanted ... in whatever capacity she decided was appropriate."

It took a moment for Alisa to reply. "I take it that the 'being there for her' part is not the problem. But you'll have to translate the verbal hieroglyphics for me."

"I don't know if I can stay that close and just be good friends."

"Whoa. Couldn't you get your feet wet without jumping into a riptide?"

"I didn't see it coming. The last I knew, I was standing in ankle-deep water admiring the beautiful shells."

"They say that's how it's supposed to happen, but, damn, Liv, a riptide?"

"Maybe it won't come to that. Maybe she'll decide that whatever we might have together isn't worth risking custody of the kids. In her place, I don't know if I could make that decision."

Alisa was slowly shaking her head. "I'm putting my kids and Keith in the scenario, and I don't think I could, either ... are you sure there's that big of a risk to custody?"

"*She* is, and that's based on what she's experienced so far within the system, and counseling from her attorney. I have to assume it's accurate."

"No wonder you want to think that you could walk away."

Olivia leaned forward on her elbow and dropped her head tentatively to her hand. She took a breath, closed her eyes and let go of a long exhale. Thinking out loud had its points; coming to undeniable conclusions just happened to be one of them. When she finally lifted her eyes to Alisa, leaning toward her in concern, she admitted, "I'm as conflicted as Renee."

"And in love."

Accounting for an unprecedented amount of patience and restraint, and an emotional pull she had never expected to feel. Olivia nodded.

"This is the time in your life when I'm supposed to be able to tease you like only your little sister can. I couldn't wait for my way-too-serious sis to be so goofy in love over someone that even Mom would have to smile about it. I wanted to prod you for all the juicy details and watch you turn bright red and pretend like you don't want to answer me ... This," she said with a half grin, "isn't fair, Liv."

"No," Olivia replied, "it isn't."

Chapter 20

Renee stood alongside Shayna as Judge Mary Botsworth took her seat on the bench. "Here we go again," she said as they were told to be seated.

"And that's all right," Shayna replied, "as long as the alternative isn't an option."

"It's not."

"Then here we go."

The judge began. "The matter before the court today is whether or not Renee Parker can provide adequate care of her four siblings while attending college." Older and more formal than the judge who originally granted guardianship, Judge Botsworth directed her question to Shayna. "Ms. Bradley, I see that Ms. Parker is currently carrying seven credit hours at the university?"

"Yes, Your Honor."

"What is her GPA?"

"A 3.0 at this point."

Renee watched for a reaction, an expression from the judge indicating if that was acceptable, but there was nothing. No sign one way or the other, only a businesslike concentration on the reports before her.

"Mrs. Gordon, you've indicated in your report that you feel the children aren't getting the time and attention that they need from Ms. Parker."

"Yes, Your Honor, based on a number of visits with the children."

"Now, was there visual evidence of neglect?"

"No, they appeared clean and well-groomed. I believe they probably eat too many fast-food meals, but that unfortunately is common in many families. My concern is the effect that the lack of attention is having on their behavior."

"Specifically, what behavior has you concerned?"

"Well, specifically, the two older children seem to be on their own a lot during the evening hours when they really need quality time with an adult. They're expected to do their homework while Renee is studying, and they informed me that they were not supposed to go in the room where she's studying. The youngest child has very limited time during which he can play and interact with Renee or the other children so he interrupts their study time and I'm afraid that the older two may be starting to view him as an annoyance. The six-year-old, though, seems most affected. She shuts herself away from the others in a closet area she's made into a little hideaway. They just are not being given the time and attention necessary for normal family interaction."

Renee leaned close to Shayna and whispered, "She's making it sound awful. It's not like that."

"We'll get our chance," Shayna whispered back.

She missed the judge's next question, but not Millie Gordon's answer.

"Yes," she said, "I'm just as concerned about what this is doing to Renee. She is trying to do too much—working in the morning, going to school in the afternoon, taking care of four children and all that that entails—school, friends, doctor appointments, trying to take the place of two parents—and then trying to study every night. She cannot do it all, and trying to is already taking a toll. She's exhausted and falling asleep in her classes. We have to think about how the children would be affected if Renee were to get sick." Millie Gordon was showing how formidable thirty-one years of experience was and exactly why judges listened. "It's a task," she continued, "too great for many established couples, so I have a tremendous amount of respect for her even making the attempt."

Judge Botsworth nodded her agreement with a raise of her eyebrows. "As do I." Her focus rested momentarily on Renee, then moved to address Shayna. "Ms. Bradley, can you enlighten me as to why Ms. Parker wasn't privy to a voice of reason in this matter? Merely because the opportunity was made available to her does not mean that taking college classes is a wise thing in her situation."

Shayna stood, pressing fingertips against the top of the table, and began. "I'll do my best to explain what went before that decision. I want you to know that it was made after a great deal of thought and discussion. And at the core of that decision is Renee's unshakeable desire to get herself in a position to take her family out of the system." Shayna placed her hand on Renee's shoulder and squeezed it. "Renee is a proud young woman," she said and removed her hand.

"I'm sure everyone here is aware of the statistics," Shayna continued. "The number of people on welfare and in assistance programs is staggering, and now that the state has passed legislation to limit the number of years they can remain on the rolls it's even more important that she find a way to become self-sufficient and independent. That desire is second only to the welfare of her brothers and sisters. That's something that she has made clear from the beginning. And since no one can express that better than Renee, I think it best if the court hears directly from her."

"Yes," Judge Botsworth replied. "Ms. Parker, please come up."

With a deep breath, Renee left the table and moved to the front of the room. She was barely aware of being sworn in and taking the seat next to the judge's bench. Her thoughts were scrambling for organization, anticipating the first question, trying to ready an answer. She looked quickly at Shayna—so at ease, so confident—looking for the smile that said all will be fine, and got it.

But her moment of relief ended at the sound of Judge Botsworth's voice. "Ms. Parker," she said, leaning across the bench on folded arms, "we're all here with the same purpose in mind; we want what is best for you and your family. With that in mind, try to relax and answer my questions as completely as you can. The more you can tell me, the better I'll be able to understand how you and your family are doing."

Her hesitation seemed to require a reply. Renee nodded and obliged. "Yes, Your Honor." Although relaxing was out of the question, she would do whatever necessary to make this woman understand.

"Let's start, then, with you describing a typical day. I know that things occasionally happen that throw a normal schedule out of kilter, so just describe a day when all would go as planned."

Renee began, grateful for an easy question. She could recite her schedule in her sleep, and had done so, in fact, waking in the middle of the night, unable to get back to sleep until she had examined every minute of it. It didn't occur to her until after she had taken the judge through the schedule from wake-up calls to tuck-in time and through the last hours of reading before she herself went to bed, how exhausting it would seem to someone else. She only knew how it felt. But, even if she had realized it earlier, she wouldn't have lied. It is what it is, and lying about it wouldn't change it.

"Well," Judge Botsworth said, straightening her posture, "that took me back a few years—quite a few years—when my three children were small. And you know, every time I think back on it, I wonder how I did it all."

But she did it, obviously. Raised her kids, went to school to have a career. She knows it's possible. Hope held momentarily as Renee searched for an expression of reinforcement from the judge. But the judge's brows tightened into a double crease above her nose. Thoughts of regret? Of moments in her children's lives missed and irretrievable?

"I don't wonder, however," the judge added, "how impossible it would have been during those years without the help of my husband."

Hope dissolved into a sharp pain tightening across Renee's chest. Her eyes shot quickly to Shayna, who offered a clear but subtle signal. She raised her hands, palms up, only inches above the table, and took a deep breath before turning them palms down and exhaling.

Renee followed with her own deep breath, letting it out slowly. Don't panic. You knew this wasn't going to be easy. Get ready for the tough questions.

"I know first hand how exhausted you must get, Ms. Parker. I found myself falling asleep not only in classes, but also in church, and even behind the wheel. Are you finding that happening to you?"

Truth. "I've fallen asleep in class and on the bus coming home." Just as true, at Little League games and every night trying to read.

"If you are allowed to continue this daily schedule, what would you do to make it less exhausting?"

Thank you, Shayna for anticipating this one. "I've already been thinking about what things I can do and one that I'm sure will help is to use audio books. I've reserved the books from my Lit 1 reading list that are available from my library branch, and I'll keep my name on the list from the main library for the rest. That way I can listen to them on the bus and at lunch, even when I'm cleaning or doing laundry."

"Is that going to give you more time after dinner with the children, and get you to bed earlier?"

Take your time, word it right. "I think it will do both, depending on the day, depending on what I have to do for my other classes. On light homework days I will be able to spend more time with each of the kids and get more sleep myself."

"And the other days, when you have to make a choice? Which will it be?"

The right side of the blade or the left? Renee wanted desperately to look at Shayna, for some magical telepathy, an answer, perfect and acceptable, that would effectively sheath the sword. But no one needed to tell her how that would look. Daily decisions weren't coached by an attorney, and answers here in court shouldn't appear to be either. Just be honest. If there's to be an error, let it be from honesty. "I would spend it with the kids."

Judge Botsworth dropped her focus to the folder without a response. She read silently for an uncomfortable moment, then refocused on Renee. "I want to address the children's reactions, because like Mrs. Gordon, I'm quite concerned about that, and I'd like to get your input."

Finally. Thank you. This time she did steal a glance at Shayna, long enough to register a subtle nod of encouragement.

"Have you noticed the behavior that Mrs. Gordon described to the court?"

"Yes, Your Honor." Please just let me explain.

"If there is anything you can add that will help me understand things as you see them, now is your opportunity to do that."

"Thank you, Your Honor. I know that Mrs. Gordon is just doing the best job she can," Renee offered what she hoped appeared to be a gracious smile in Mrs. Gordon's direction, "but, you really have to know my brothers and sisters much better to understand what their behavior means. They are all dealing with losing both their parents. And each one deals with it differently. J.J., the oldest, expresses himself through anger, mostly directed at his mother. But he talks to me about it because I think instinctively he knows we are a lot alike. He is also very protective of the younger ones, maybe too much so sometimes, so Rory's little annoyances really don't bother him. Jenny is the next oldest and she is the most fearful of them all. So she has become a mother hen, rounding everyone up and knowing where everyone is at all times, for fear of losing someone else." Without realizing it, flushed and intent, Renee had leaned forward in her seat. "Rachael is next, the one who has created her own space in the closet. She is introspective and hard to read, but I truly believe of all of them she is the most well-adjusted. She asks questions like 'What do mothers do?' and 'What do dads do?' I told her that they make sure that their children have a warm place to live and food to eat and clean clothes, and they show them how to treat other people like you want them to treat you. But most importantly, that they love you so much that they would do everything they could to be sure they were safe and happy. So she thought about it for days and then she said, 'I've decided you must be a modad. That's what I'm going to tell my friends.'"

The judge's smile was the first sign Renee had that something

124

she said had pleased her. If only she could stop here and leave with the best thought. But the judge was waiting for her to finish. So Renee continued. "Rory is the youngest. All he knows is," she smiled and shrugged, "life with modad. Our mother, to him, is the nice lady we visit in the prison. He calls her 'Mom' but the concept isn't the same. His health is my biggest concern and my top priority. I'm never without my cell phone," she indicated her waistband, "set on vibrate, in case he needs me." She hesitated long enough to take an extra breath. "I don't know if it's possible to tell someone else what I know my brothers and sisters feel; I can only say that they depend on me and they trust that I will never leave them." Still tensed and flushed, Renee slid back to the back of her chair, relieved only to have the most stressful part over with.

"Thank you, Renee, you can step down now." Judge Botsworth's tone remained professional, not a hint of emotion in her words or her expression. After Renee was once again seated beside Shayna at the table, the judge said, "You're quite right; it's at best difficult to put the intangible into words. Poets are forever doing their best and still the words rarely do the intended." She closed the file folder in front of her and folded her hands on top of it. "But what you've told me has been helpful. The most difficult and the most important part of my job is to make sure I give all the facts and facets of a situation equal consideration so that I can weight the pros and cons of each, and then render a fair decision. In making my decision today I have taken into serious consideration the impact that it will have on all five members of the Parker family, not just now, but for their future as well."

Renee held her breath as she watched the judge's eyes. They seemed sincere, but still unreadable. They were now looking directly at her.

"Ms. Parker," the judge addressed, "do you have a computer?"

I don't like where this is going. "No, Your Honor."

"Ms. Bradley, you'll have to work with Mrs. Gordon to make a home computer available."

Shayna's response was less than enthusiastic but remained professional. "Yes, Your Honor."

"It is the decision of this court that Renee Parker be allowed to continue her progress toward a college degree by taking one online course per semester. She will retain full custody of her four siblings."

The thwack of the gavel set the decision and flattened the hopes that had so recently begun to soar.

Chapter 21

The moment Olivia opened her door she knew. Renee's valiant attempt at a smile, a flicker that lifted the corners of her mouth then dissolved into a serious line, fell far short of convincing.

"Come on," Olivia said, offering her hand. "I'm making lunch for us."

Renee took Olivia's hand and stepped into the apartment. A few steps into the living area, she stopped and gently pulled Olivia back to her. She leaned forward and kissed Olivia tenderly. "Thank you," she said.

"You haven't eaten it yet," she replied. Her body warmed with a desire to return the kiss, conflicting with her respect for Renee's emotional state.

"Thank you for having me over even with the chance that I wouldn't be very good company."

"Good company is relative. Don't you know that by now?" She locked her eyes onto Renee's and welcomed the shot of electricity they delivered to the middle of her chest. "I want to spend time with you *because* you're you. I feel quite lucky." She watched the way Renee's brows pinched quickly together and released when she was questioning. "Lucky, because I really don't like the whole dating thing. It's a ridiculous waste of time, trying to break through the façade someone works so hard to impress you with, and then finding out it's not much at all like the real person. You saved me from that."

"Even if I had time to create one, a façade wouldn't hold up long at my place. Five minutes is all Jenny needs to literally air the dirty laundry, and Rachael—"

"Is just a very observant six-year-old pointing out the obvious anyway."

Renee nodded. Her gaze lingered over Olivia's face, fine touches of a watercolor brush washing a pink blush everywhere it touched.

"Some things," Olivia said softly, "no façade can hide."

"Like what I'm feeling right now."

"And every time I'm around you." Olivia stepped close and circled her arms around Renee's waist. "Kids or no kids, three hours or three minutes, it makes no difference. I just want to be with you."

Renee's arms held her tightly, her face nuzzled against the side of her head. "Even if it's complicated? Living and loving between court hearings?"

Olivia pressed her lips into the smooth, warm valley just below Renee's ear and whispered, "Even if."

She lifted her mouth to meet Renee's, waiting and warm and not in the least hesitant. This time there would be no censure diverting her desire, nothing stopping what they both clearly wanted.

Their kisses said it better than words—tender seductive touches that probed and titillated until they moved with passion and parted with need. Olivia pressed her hips tighter into their embrace, welcoming the sear of heat, and drew her breath over Renee's ear. "I feel a little guilty," she whispered. "I haven't asked you about court."

"I hadn't noticed," she replied, taking Olivia's face in her hands. "And, right now, it doesn't matter."

"Come with me." Olivia led Renee through the apartment without a second thought that where they were headed was exactly where she should be. Something besides her work finally mattered, mattered enough to make a place, and make time, and make it a priority. Renee mattered.

Early afternoon light filtered through sheers to bathe the bedroom a milky white. Neat and Stewartly in fashion with its muted blues and plump pillows and comforter, it was a serene retreat from a hectic schedule and sometimes chaotic job. A contrast in living not lost on Renee.

Her gaze returned from its inspection. "I may never want to leave this room."

"I may not want you to." Olivia pulled the tail of Renee's blouse from her waistband and unbuttoned it from the bottom. "In here," she said, running her hands over the smooth warm skin to slide the material from Renee's shoulders, "there are no charts or worried parents." She touched her lips to the base of Renee's neck and placed a trail of kisses down the center of her chest. "No sickness, no pain." She felt Renee's hands caressing her back, in her hair. "No children, no worries," she whispered, and traced her lips over the thin cotton covering Renee's breast. "Just you," she continued, feeling the nipple stiffen under the sudden pressure of her lips, "and me."

"Then," Renee managed after a quick intake of breath, "I must be in heaven."

There were no words then, only fingers finding zippers, and quickened breath, and anticipation—sweet anxious anticipation. To touch what she had coveted for weeks, to whisper what now filled the emptiness. A greater need she had never felt.

Clothing slipped to the floor. Every kiss lingered longer, while hands caressed and dared and tested the limits of the fire until the limits themselves were consumed and the backdraft drew them down. Satin and puffed down caught them and cradled them as skin slid against skin.

Heaven, yes, Olivia agreed, surely this is heaven. Chosen, redeemed, right here, right now. A gift so rare. Olivia drew her lips slowly along the line of Renee's neck, acknowledged the responding quiver as she pressed the hollow above her collarbone. "I'm so glad you're here," she whispered.

Renee's hands caressed with such gentleness, over the planes of Olivia's back, warm gentleness smoothing the deep curve at the base of her spine and over the roundness of her buttocks. Her caresses so slow and unhurried, allowing time for shivers of sensation to warm at their touch. Such care, such exquisite care. They kissed, first with the tenderness matching Renee's touch, a melting softness that brought forth breathy sounds of desire, then more deeply. Slowly and deeply, again and again, as Olivia's hands offered their own gentleness.

She breathed her words against Renee's mouth, "Beautiful, so beautiful," as her hand covered the round firmness of Renee's breast. "I want this. I want this with you."

"Yes, yes." The beginning of urgency lifting to Olivia's touch. "I want this, too."

Perfect pink nipples hardened and pressed into her palms. Whispery murmurs, soft sounds of pleasure, breathed past her ear. The pleasure she was giving, with her hands, with her lips, had begun to shoot spikes of desire through her own body.

Pleasure from pleasure. She brought her mouth to the hardened nipples, tasting and stroking them with her tongue, unable to stop her own low moan of desire. The feel of her was exquisite. Renee moved beneath her, pressing and arching to every touch of Olivia's hands, every caress, every kiss. Desire was evident in every breath, quickening with each caress, light excited gasps matching the ardent rhythm of her hips.

Renee's body demanded more, pleaded for the gentleness of Olivia's touch to give in to the need to tighten, and press, to slide into the rhythm of Renee's hips. And Olivia gave. She slipped her arms beneath Renee, pulling her tight, feeling the length of her body close around her. It wasn't about decisions now—what will please, how long to linger—it was about letting her body go, letting desire have its way.

She matched the desperation of Renee's kisses, moved against her with the same intensity, hard and deep, let go of a throaty moan as Renee's hands clutched her buttocks and pulled her deep into the heat.

Renee's words came in short breathy gasps. "God ... Olivia ... I need you now."

"Yes," Olivia breathed, hot against her neck. "Oh, yes."

Desire burst forth in a gasp as Olivia's hand slipped into the wetness. Fingers slid in silky strokes, slowly, again and again.

Renee tightened trembling legs, held her breath within, as sensations electrified her body, then pressed full and open to bring the fingers in. Smooth and deep, as deep as the moan escaping Olivia's throat.

Renee's arms clung to Olivia's shoulders, her hips thrust once and again until orgasm, paralyzing in intensity, closed around the fingers and burst forth in a long, rapturous moan of release.

Olivia held her, and kissed gently the flushed skin at the base of Renee's throat. She waited, her fingers still held within until the quivers surrounding them yielded in lassitude.

Renee's arms loosened their embrace as she relaxed into the down of the comforter. She closed her eyes with a long sigh as Olivia's fingers left her. "I'm never leaving here," she whispered into the fine dark hair. "Never."

"Mmm," Olivia murmured against Renee's chest. "I like the sound of that." She brought her hand over Renee's side, a light brushing, and then she kissed the moist skin between her breasts. "I so wanted to please you, to take you somewhere safe and happy."

"And if I could stay there forever, I would. It's a beautiful place ... " She drew her fingers through the fine hairs and looked into Olivia's uplifted eyes. "Can I take you there?"

Olivia spoke softly without closing her eyes. "I want you to take me there. Only you," she said, and pulled Renee to lie beside her.

Desire would take little encouragement. She knew it the moment Renee touched tender lips to the sensitive skin below her ear. And wondered if she would be able to prolong the enjoyment of the lips barely touching, tracing their way over her shoulder, lightly around the contour of her breast, and make the quivers of anticipation last as they crossed her abdomen. Then Renee's hands, warm and soft, covered Olivia's breasts and caressed the nipples taut while the tip of her tongue drew a line of sensation from Olivia's navel, over the plane of her stomach and between her breasts.

Olivia trembled as a rush of heat centered and challenged control. She stretched up to meet Renee's mouth enveloping her breast—hot and wet—licking and sucking the tautness until Olivia could take no more. She found Renee's hand and thrust it between her legs.

"Yes, please," she called out. "I need you inside." She cupped the fingers and pushed them in, then closed around them with an urgency that moved her hips and quickened her breath. So close, so quickly. Ecstasy gathered itself in a sudden stillness, then released in a powerful shudder that shook Olivia's body. Heart pounding hard, she clutched Renee to her and pressed her lips against her head.

"Let me hold you," Renee said softly as Olivia's body began to relax.

Olivia settled into the comfort of Renee's arms, breathed deeply against the base of her neck and closed her eyes.

"One online class per semester," Renee offered from the bathroom. "In case you were afraid to ask."

Olivia loosely looped the ties of her robe. "I didn't want to ruin a happier state of mind. You looked pretty dejected when you first got here."

"It could only be avoided for so long. I have this need, which is probably good for me and not so good for you, to tell you everything. Even the bad. It's strange, I couldn't wait to get here today so that I could tell you the bad news."

"Not so strange," Olivia replied. "Bad news is a burden. It's easier to handle if someone shares the weight. And before you say it, it's not an imposition. It makes me feel good to know that sharing it with me gives you some relief."

"Spoken like the nurse that you are."

"Partly, I'm sure, it's my nature. But, mostly because of how much I care about you." She began selecting clothes from her dresser drawer. "More than I think you know."

Renee appeared in the bathroom doorway. "No, I do know. That's why I don't want to do anything to make you regret it."

"That," Olivia said, meeting Renee with a kiss that lingered only long enough to remind her of what she had no time for, "would be hard to do." She turned back toward the bedroom. "Talk to me. What happened in court?"

"Shayna knew before we went in that the best we could hope for was a compromise. There was a case right here only a few years ago where a college student lost custody of her daughter. And the kicker was that the father won full custody even though he worked full time and *his* mother would actually be caring for the child."

"What kind of message is that?" she asked, turning with a frown.

"Stay married, stay at home," Renee replied, "or don't have kids. It's archaic ... and it's arbitrary; it depends on who the judge is."

Olivia pulled underwear on under her robe and continued dressing as she spoke. "In other words, you've been lucky to have drawn sympathetic judges."

"I was hoping for a better compromise today, but yes."

There was something in the tone of Renee's voice, a match for the dejected figure at her door earlier, that made Olivia stop what she was doing. She sat on the end of the bed and watched Renee finish buttoning her blouse.

"Why don't you tell me what you couldn't say in court."

Renee stepped to the foot of the bed. She straddled Olivia's knee and teased her fingers through nearly dry hair. "I'm guessing you could tell *me* that."

"You think so?" she said, circling her arms around Renee's waist.

"Whatever I have neglected to tell you, you seem to know anyway."

A little straightforward knowledge, a little intuitive insight, and an insatiable desire to know all about her. "All I really know is that it's important for you to tell someone. Not just what happened, but how you feel about it."

"I'm not sure what I feel," she said, breaking from Olivia's arms. "I should be grateful—and I am. We're able to stay together as a family and that's what's most important."

Olivia waited patiently, watching Renee pace a short path right and back, watching her struggle with what she suspected was not only conflicting feelings but the decision to vocalize them. It comes down to trust, she thought, as most important things do. It is one thing to trust someone with your body—accepting it, pleasing it, caring for it—and still another to trust them with the essential you. Placing in their care those things, no matter how seemingly insignificant, that make you happy and make you vulnerable. Trusting that you would not be seen as less in their eyes for your fears, or for your inadequacies. Trusting that they would make every conscious effort to avoid causing you pain. Isn't that what love is?

Renee turned with a frown. "I'm selfish sometimes," a confessional tone that seemed to plead for relief. "And angry. And I spend so much energy trying to show everyone else that I'm not, that I believed it myself for a while." She held up a hand. "Before you say anything, I'm not looking for justification—I know there's plenty of that if I want it. I don't need to justify it, I need to own it ... and figure out a way to—"

"Express it, Renee. You can't own it, or defuse it, without giving it a voice. You can do that here, with me." She held out her hands and Renee moved forward to accept them. "You can tell me things that you can't tell anyone else."

Renee nodded. "I couldn't let the judge see me angry, or the kids ... or my mother."

"Here, in this apartment, you don't have to hide it. You're free to be you, to say what you're feeling."

Renee tipped her head back, closed her eyes, and released a long audible breath. "So many things ... how do I even begin?"

"Just get it out there. Don't explain it, just say it."

She dropped Olivia's hands, raised her arms at her sides and rolled her head away. "How far back do I go? My stepfather?" she began, shooting the words at the ceiling. "For leaving us, maybe on purpose? Or my father, for creating me and then not loving me enough to take care of me? And my mother ..."

Her eyes snapped back to Olivia, their fierceness more convincing than the strained tone of her voice. They convinced Olivia that she was right, Renee needed to say it, *had* to say it.

"My mother," Renee spat, "for everything. For putting pride before reason, and *now* before forever." Her arms now hung loosely at her sides. "There's too much, Olivia, too much. I can't make it go away. I make deals with J.J. to get him to hide *his* anger, for God's sake, because I don't know how to make it go away."

There was nothing like this kind of anger in Olivia's life, nothing that could help her to help Renee. Over the years there had been smatterings of misunderstandings and insignificant injustices, but nothing that wasn't soon forgiven. Sometimes the forgiveness wasn't even spoken—she couldn't remember making a conscious decision to forgive, there was just no more anger. And the other times, like forgiving an ex-lover for cheating, it had taken time and the effort to find its point of perspective. Where had it placed her in the big picture? What had it taught her about herself? Did it help her better understand the needs of others? It came down to recognizing the lessons, life's lessons, unplanned and unpredictable, and how they could make her stronger and better prepared for the next. But how do you help another?

"Maybe it would help to get inside their heads, Renee. Talk with your mother and find out everything you can about why they made the decisions they made. These are not evil people. I doubt that they set out to hurt you or to make your life more difficult."

"The result is the same. They left me with no answers and no solutions, and now the court has done the same thing. I can't finish school and get a job that pays enough by the time my cash welfare runs out." She finally calmed enough to come and sit next to Olivia on the end of the bed. "I have no choice but to accept hand-outs from the state." She tightened the muscles in her jaw. "It's as painful as lye on bare skin. I don't want charity, I need it. And being grateful for it does not diminish my loathing of it. I just won't do to my brothers and sisters what my parents did to me. That's the only thing that gives me control over my anger."

"What did your attorney say about the decision?"

"That we'll petition the court to reconsider after next semester."

"Will they allow you to finish your courses this semester?"

Renee shook her head. "A month to go. It seems like a terrible waste of the state's money, but that doesn't seem to be a concern ... their concern is the kids. I get that. It should be. I also get that Mrs. Gordon has me under a magnifying glass, and I can't afford to show anger or anything that she might think adversely affects the kids."

She didn't have to say any more. Complicated was only a nice generalization. What a relationship does, one like this that involves so much more than an occasional sexual liaison, is add a tremendous amount of risk to an already precarious situation. That Renee had chosen to pursue it said what words could not.

"There's something that I've learned never to say, or to believe, in the heat of passion," Olivia began, "but I want to say it now." She traced her fingertips lightly over Renee's cheek, then cupped it gently. "I'm in love with you."

Renee pressed her face into Olivia's hand and closed her eyes.

"I need to know," Olivia said, her words whispering over Renee's forehead, "if you feel the same way."

"When I wake in the morning, my first thought is of you." Renee lifted her eyes to Olivia's. "All throughout the day, I think about you, what you might like, what you might need. I wonder what it would be like to count on you being in my life every day ... and then the fear of you not being there makes my heart stand still." She shook her head slowly. "I don't know if I could stand that."

"It's all right," Olivia whispered. She touched Renee's lips with a tender kiss. "You don't have say the words."

Chapter 22

Relying on a pain reliever when you need surgery will only get you by for so long. Over the past weeks Olivia had been a wonderful pain reliever, sharing time, intimate and otherwise, covering and soothing the wounds. Renee's temptation was to enjoy the calm and not stir the waters by confronting her mother.

Thanksgiving had come and gone without fanfare. Even with Olivia working, her presence was felt, her phone call to the kids the high point of the day. Maybe it could have gone on like that for much longer, but the closer it got to Christmas and a new year, the more compelled Renee was to face the inevitable, to unload the unspoken and start afresh.

With Christmas just over two weeks away, the prison visiting area was more crowded than usual. Nearly every table was occupied, the room humming with anxious conversation and crackling with laughter. It was hardly the atmosphere for confrontational truth, but it was all she had. Renee met her mother at a table near the middle of the room.

"You didn't bring the children," Sylvia said. "What's wrong? First J.J. doesn't come at Thanksgiving, and now—"

"Everything's fine, Mom. Olivia is taking them to a free matinee so that I can come and talk with you. She's treating them with popcorn and Skittles and whatever."

"Why would she do that?"

"Because she's a good friend and she likes the kids." She met her mother's eyes reluctantly. Reluctantly because she knew what she'd see there—that look of knowing challenge, the same one that had stopped her mid-sentence in her first defense of unadmitted lesbianism. It hadn't changed over the years, nor had its effect. The only change, and *it* hadn't reached the desired maturation level, was Renee's forthrightness. "I had her put on your visitor's list. I want you to meet her."

Sylvia, evidently satisfied that she'd gotten the required mileage out of the look, finally continued. "Is she staying at the apartment?"

"No, Mother, she isn't."

"This is very dangerous, Renee. You're not thinking about your brothers and sisters."

Perfect. "And you *were* when you took money that wasn't yours, and kept taking it until restitution wasn't possible and the only future you could offer your children was a life without their mother? Was that how you thought about your children?"

The shocked expression on Sylvia's face wasn't any easier to accept responsibility for than the one of hurt that Renee had always worked so hard to avoid causing. Another vision that will surely haunt her nights. "You can think me insensitive or selfish, I can't help that, but I have to have some answers. I have to try to understand some things, I have to get rid of this anger, and you're the only way I can do that."

Shock no longer registered in Sylvia's now downcast eyes. "I didn't know," she said, barely audible. "Why didn't I know?"

"You didn't *want* to know." Renee, arms folded tightly across her chest, stared hard at her mother. With some effort, she swallowed the tirade of words bouncing off the back of her teeth. She forced air through her nostrils with a steady rhythm that finally brought about control. But the hard edge to her voice was still there. "And for some reason that I don't even know, *I* didn't want *you* to know. I guess I figured that you were dealing with enough. I thought I was avoiding my own guilt by not adding to yours. And maybe I was, but the anger's been there for as long as I can remember, and I can't make it go away."

Sylvia reached across the table, but Renee kept her hands tucked away. She forced herself to look at her mother's face and continued. "I felt selfish for a long time for how I felt—a very long time—before John came into our lives. I saw you working hard and not complaining, taking care of Grandma, and I realized that my father abandoned you, too. I had no right to be hurt or angry if you weren't."

"But I was. I didn't want you to be."

How could an answer be so simple? After all the years of confusion and misunderstanding, to bring realization in so few words. "It's a cycle, a damn vicious cycle, Mom, and it has to stop—it has to stop right now, right here."

Sylvia was looking around her, quickly wiping tears from her eyes before they made it to her cheeks. "I don't understand."

"Let it go, Mom. For once in your life, don't put on the brave face or give me tears of guilt. And don't stop these tears, the real ones, the ones that rip your gut wide open. Just let them go, damn it! Cry 'em, cry 'em for me, cry 'em for yourself."

Sylvia covered her face with her hands. Renee grabbed them and pulled them clear.

"I need to see them," she said. "I needed to see them all those years ago." The tears were streaming down Sylvia's cheeks, Renee's grasp firmly preventing her from wiping them away. "Help me stop doing the same thing. Help me help J.J."

They sat there like that for frozen, agonizing moments, tears purging their course until Sylvia spoke high and strained. "What can I do?"

"Start by telling me why my father left." She released her mother's hands, watched her gather her composure, and waited. The feeling was unexpected—strangely empowering. The usual mire of emotions battling each other for dominance was gone, and in its place was a mission-like quest. And as she looked into the watery blue eyes, she realized that there was something else different as well—an adult woman had replaced Sylvia's daughter.

"He was eighteen," Sylvia began, "a college boy. He had big plans. His parents had big plans, for his future. His dad was some kind of financial analyst, a lot of money," she said, wiping her nose once more and tucking the tissue into her pocket. "Getting married wasn't part of the plan, not that early. A baby was out of the question."

"Did he want you to get an abortion?"

"No. Well, he mentioned it, but it was more like he was laying out the options *I* had. Abortion, adoption, my parents were good people and would help me raise it. That's when I saw that it didn't matter to him, I wasn't going to be part of his future."

"Why didn't you make him help you financially?"

"His father never would have allowed that to happen; he knew my family didn't have the money to force it. And when I realized how selfish he was and what his family was like, I didn't want them to be part of your life."

"Why didn't you tell me? You lied when you said that he just couldn't take care of us."

"I thought that I could keep you from that hurt. I was so sure I could give you enough love to make up for it. And when John came into our lives and I saw how much he loved you, I knew everything would be all right."

"And for a while it was, wasn't it?" Even as a young child she had felt it, the sigh in her mother's life that was John Parker. They were the years of love and loving that brought laughter and security, and children. "When did it start to fall apart?"

Sylvia shook her head slowly. "I don't know exactly ... maybe if I had known earlier." She dropped her head to stare blankly at her hands folded on the table. "He hated that I had to work, but I knew if we wanted more children that I would have to. That was okay, I had always worked. But he wanted to make things better for me. He really thought he could."

"But if he kept things from you, he must have known that he couldn't do what he had hoped."

"He wanted to bear it alone. He re-mortgaged twice, and he wouldn't let the health or the life insurance go. One tool and die shop would close and he'd scramble to another, no matter what they paid him."

"I know he was mad when I dropped out of sports to help."

"Not at you; he was never angry with you. He was so hurt. It was the first time I ever saw him cry. He wanted you to play and maybe get a scholarship, and definitely go on to school no matter what. He wanted all of his children to go to college."

"Do you think that's why—"

"Please, Renee."

"But I need to understand. You certainly can't believe it was an accident; in your heart you must know. Could he have really thought that leaving us with insurance money would leave us better off than having *him*?"

Sylvia's eyes watered again, but she held them steady on Renee's for seconds before offering an obviously painful frown and nod.

Renee closed her eyes and rested her forehead in her hand. Hearing it, as much as she had needed to, was more painful than she had imagined. And the pain, realized in scorching embarrassment, was in her love for him. Had she ever let him know how much she loved him, how important his love for her was?

She felt her mother's hand stroking her head, sensed the loss they shared, and let it comfort her.

"I would have lived in a cardboard box with John Parker," Sylvia said, as unaffected now by the noise around them as Renee. "But I couldn't expect that of our children."

Nor could she allow her husband's death to be in vain. There was no need now for the question Renee had planned, even plotted, for years to ask. The answer was evident. Her mother had made her decision, a bad decision, out of emotion and blind devotion, and she nearly destroyed the very family she was trying to protect. The wrong decision, for the right reason.

"I'm sorry, Renee. I'm so sorry."

Words spoken so often, and now heard for the first time.

Chapter 23

Renee crossed the large crowded parking lot with Olivia, as the morning sun glistened over winter's first dusting of snow. The harsh commercial lines of the shopping mall vanished beneath airy puffs of white, and the main entrance welcomed them under a pine bough garland.

Tucking her hands into her jacket pockets, Renee drew a long, deep breath. The air sparkled with crisp anticipation, gleamed like a Christmas morning look of surprise. It brought forth memories, jumping for recognition, each waving a hand anxiously, all with promises of special billing. They were memories of surprises and surprised, wrappings and glitter, and love before the fog. And they hadn't been given their due remembrance in a long time. Today, they breathed free, and that made her smile. But today would also sparkle with the making of new memories.

"Are you a patient shopper?" Olivia asked as they entered the busy holiday clamor of the mall.

"I'm a non-shopper," Renee replied. "I haven't been in a mall since I was fourteen or fifteen. Unless you want to count shopping at Value Village or St. Vincent de Paul stores."

"The tiny little de Paul store on the north side? I've been there. I look through their books while my sister looks for jeans and sweatshirts for her husband."

"I never would have figured ... I always find books for my

mother there. It's awful what the prison calls a library. Anyway," she said, splitting around slower moving shoppers and rejoining Olivia a few strides later. "Anyway, that's where I shop. I get clothes for the kids there, too. But it's getting harder to find things for J.J. because he wants the popular stuff he sees the other kids at school wearing."

"Then I know exactly what he's getting for Christmas."

"Which brings me to something that I wanted to talk with you about."

Olivia slowed her pace and offered a concerned look.

"I have a rule," Renee said, "about gifts. Only one gift per child from each person. Mom can't even afford that, and I'm not much better off. Also, it keeps the years more consistent. With people coming and going in their lives, it makes it hard for them to understand lots of presents one year and very few the next."

"Of course I'll respect that," Olivia said, staring into the closest store front. She started forward, then turned back abruptly, stepping on Renee's foot and nearly knocking her over. "I'm sorry," she said, grabbing Renee's arms. "Not the store I was looking for. And, hey, what about Santa and their stockings?"

"We'll negotiate that. Just no surprises, okay?"

"I think you're in serious need of some good old-fashioned Christmas magic," she said, turning into a store without waiting for a response.

Magic indeed.

It was a perfect day. Stolen touches amid unaware shoppers pinked Renee's cheeks, and smiles and laughter and Mrs. Field's cookies lightened her heart. She was enjoying herself, enjoying Olivia, without guilt or worry. And with only one gift left to buy, there would also be time for intimacy before they had to share their day with the rest of the world.

"Who is his favorite Tigers player," Olivia asked, browsing through a rack of baseball jerseys.

"Justin Verlander, I'd say. J.J.'s sure he's going to get the Cy Young Award this next season."

"Perfect," she said, pulling one up to inspect.

"Damn, Olivia, look at the price. I don't want you to spend that much."

Her mind obviously made up, Olivia carried the jersey to the cashier. "You know he'll wear it until it's worn out. He'll get my money out of it," she said, handing over a credit card.

"Would you like this gift wrapped?" asked the cashier.

"Yes, thank you." Olivia signed the receipt as another woman behind the counter began to fold the jersey into a box.

"Oh," Renee interjected, as the woman began to remove the tags, "please leave the tags on it."

"You're not taking this back," Olivia said.

"No, that's not it at all. J.J. looks for tags. Some time ago he became aware of the fact that he was getting used clothes. It didn't matter that they looked like new, he started looking for the tags. So I started keeping tags from anything new that I bought and re-attaching them to things I got from the secondhand stores. I'm getting pretty good at it." The girl behind the counter smiled as she finished up the wrapping with ribbon and a bow. "But so is he. I have to go over his stuff so carefully. I look for any flaw, or loose thread, and I do a sniff test." Now they were all smiling. "He is going to be ecstatic when he opens that one."

Olivia accepted the box with a "thank you" and leaned close to Renee as they headed out the door. "Not as ecstatic as I'll be in about a half an hour."

The thought kicked her heartbeat into Zouave time, but she couldn't resist. "But I haven't bought *your* present yet."

"Not even you can convince me that that's an option."

Anticipation, fueled and fanned by vivid memories of their last lovemaking, quickened Renee's pace through the parking lot. Quickly to the car, then back to the store entrance to pick up Olivia and the packages, all the time her mind racing ahead to their perfect space of time. An unintended benefit that Judge Botsworth's one online class decision had afforded them. It would, as always, be too short, its parameters defined by work and responsibilities, but it was their space and time, and that made it perfect.

The excitement she felt, the pleasure she was about to feel, spurred Renee down streets she knew by heart and past buildings she hardly noticed. Olivia's fingers, however, she did notice. They slipped along her neck beneath her hair, and their touch sent shivers down Renee's arms and over her breasts. Without looking, she could feel the intent in Olivia's gaze, and she wanted desperately to look at her, to take her eyes from the road and let them answer. Yes, they would say, I want you, too. Now, she wanted to whisper, right now.

The apartment lot was barren, with most people either working or shopping at this time of day. Renee parked next to Olivia's Camry and quickly helped gather the packages from the back seat.

"I appreciate you keeping them all at your place. I've given up trying to hide anything in that apartment. I regularly impose on Stacy at daycare for the birthday presents."

"It'll get you back over here to wrap them, won't it?"

"Unless you want to do the wrapping today."

Olivia unlocked the apartment door. "I was thinking more along the lines of *un*wrapping," she said, grabbing Renee's jacket as she walked past and pulling it down off her shoulders.

Renee dropped the bags of gifts with a laugh and shrugged out of her jacket.

Olivia, with a bit of a head start, was on her way through the apartment to the bedroom by the time Renee kicked off her boots, nearly stumbled over Olivia's and started after her.

Moments like these were too few; the lightness and fun was cherished right along with their time for intimacy. They laughed easily today, with thoughts of work and kids and CPS banned from their minds, and teasingly unwrapped their gift to each other one piece of clothing at a time.

With only a pair of Hanes still in place, Olivia stood on the bed singing into her fist, "He knows if you've been bad or good, so be good—"

"Oh, I'll be good," Renee said, jumping on the bed and sweeping Olivia's feet from beneath her.

They fell in a tangled heap on the bed, laughing and kissing, and wrapping themselves around each other. Placing a kiss just below Olivia's ear, Renee said, "I think I'm going to love this Christmas present best."

"I'm going to make sure you do." Olivia followed her promise with a kiss that turned the lightness of their mood instantly passionate.

Renee snugged her thigh tighter between Olivia's legs. Olivia's kiss deepened in response. The rush of heat heightened Renee's senses—promising, promising ... until the sound of her cell phone intruded from the pile of clothes on the floor.

Olivia pulled from their kiss. "No," Renee whispered and buried her face between Olivia's neck and the comforter.

The sigh from Olivia was long and tainted with exasperation. With still no move from Renee to answer the ringing phone, she slapped her on the butt. "It could be important."

"It had better be," she replied, rolling from their embrace and dropping to the floor. She knelt beside the clothes and found the phone still attached to her pants. "Hello," exasperation barely disguised. "Yes, it is." Then the edge disappeared. "Is he all right?"

Olivia made quick eye contact. "Rory?" she asked.

Renee shook her head "no." "I'll be right there. Thank you." She grabbed her underwear and addressed a now upright and clearly worried Olivia. "Is there such a thing as rewrapping? J.J. was in a fight at school."

"Is he hurt?"

"Not yet."

A smile replaced the concern on Olivia's face and seemed to say, "Yeah, his timing really stinks." What she said, though, was, "Maybe it wasn't his fault. Don't judge him so quickly, he may have been defending himself."

"He threw the first punch. Three days before his vacation starts and he has to get suspended."

"Has he been in fights before?"

"Not that I've been made aware of." She pulled on her jeans and sat on the edge of the bed. "You know, when I talked to him that night after I visited Mom alone, I thought maybe it helped some. I tried explaining that it was all right to be angry at what she did, but not at her, and that I was trying to do that, too. It didn't seem like he was getting it, so I used a baseball analogy."

"Smart girl."

"Well, I thought so at the time. He seemed to understand that when Mom took the money she made an error, even though she was trying to help us, just like when he dropped the ball trying to make the third out for his team. He didn't want the team or the coach to be mad at *him* even though they didn't like that he made an error. But if he did understand it, it obviously hasn't done anything to curb his anger."

"Don't forget," Olivia said, "he's had four years for his anger to get a good foothold. You can't expect miracles in a week."

"I know. But I don't expect it to escalate, either."

"Sometimes things get worse before they get better. Something my dad used to say a lot when I was growing up. Of course, the advice didn't mean much at the time."

"I'm just feeling sorry for myself again," Renee admitted. "It would've been a perfect day," she said, her body finally relaxing its tension long enough to enjoy an embrace. The feel of Olivia's body, conforming against her back, eased away the rest. "God, you feel good. I just want to stay here and lose myself in the feel of you and the smell of you."

"That was the plan. But, short of drug-induced comas, there will be no guaranteed plans with children in our lives."

"Comas, huh?"

Olivia pushed her off the bed.

"If that's a new twist on foreplay, I know a young man who could easily spend the next hour in the counselor's office."

Before the idea had a chance for serious consideration, though, Renee's cell phone rang again. The look in her eyes was meant to reveal how tempted she was.

Olivia removed the phone from Renee's waistband and handed it to her. "This, unfortunately, does not have options."

With a look of resignation, Renee answered the call. "This is Renee ... is there another problem?" She continued to listen with her eyes closed and her face tilted toward the ceiling. "I see ... yes.

I'll be there in a few minutes," she said, dropping her focus once again to Olivia. "Principal Eller wants to talk with me before I pick J.J. up."

Olivia lovingly touched Renee's cheek, and kissed her. "I'm at the other end of the phone when you get home."

"I'll take whatever I can get."

Dr. Dorothy Eller was part mother lion and part eagle, a gryphon in a navy blue two-piece. She ran her school with a tenacity that got what was needed over what was wanted, and with an uncanny vision that could spot a wad of gum en route to a head of hair at a hundred yards. She was well known, well respected, and effective.

Renee, fighting a feeling of childhood discomfort of having been called to the principal's office, sat across the desk from her.

"Renee, J.J. isn't talking to the counselor—or to me. He has become increasingly withdrawn from adults here in the school setting. It began with his teacher," her focus was as direct as her message, "and now, well," she straightened her posture, "I hope he will talk to you. We have to find a way to turn things around with him."

"He does talk to me, about most things anyway, and I think he listens. I'm not sure he's able to act the way he wants to. Most of the time he's sweet and thoughtful. Yesterday he brought home a little wooden box that he found at the dumpster. He wrote Rachael and Rory's names on it and put it in the kitchen so that they can reach the sink." Dr Eller raised her eyebrows and smiled. "Other times," Renee continued, "he can be stubborn to the point of anger. Going to see his mother has become such a battle that I told him that the decision is his. He has to make arrangements to spend the day with a friend or a babysitter when he decides not to go. That seems to have helped some, but then today ..."

"You said that he talks to you about most things; what doesn't he talk to you about?"

"He doesn't say much about his father. Every once in a while he'll ask about him, like if he liked baseball, but that's it."

"I want to try something, Renee. When I was growing up we

wrote in our diaries, and it was strictly a female exercise. Now they're called journals and the world has figured out what we've known for years—that writing our private thoughts is darn good therapy." She picked up a little book next to her blotter and handed it to Renee. "The boys like the ones with cars or sports on the cover. I know how much J.J. likes baseball, so I'm sure he'll like this one."

"You've seen this help kids?"

"Many times. Sometimes it helps them start talking to someone after they've been writing for a while, sometimes it just seems to help them work things out on their own."

"Do you have one for me, too?"

"I sure do."

Renee's request for the two of them to think about things on the drive home was apparently a good one. J.J. sat in silence watching out the window until they got home. Eyes downcast, he continued into the apartment and waited obediently at the kitchen table for Renee.

Renee pulled her chair close to J.J. and leaned folded arms on the table. "So, who did you punch?"

"Ben Wilby," he replied, still not looking at her.

"Isn't he like six inches taller than you are?"

"Yeah."

"And you just hauled off and punched him? What were you thinking?"

No response.

"I mean, what made you mad enough to pick a fight with someone so much bigger?"

He sent her a sideways glance that disappeared so quickly that she wasn't sure she had seen it. His hesitation, though, didn't fool her. He was bouncing his heel against the leg of the chair, his personal timing system. He wanted to tell her. She waited patiently.

Two, three more bounces. "It was what he said." The sad little milk-dud eyes finally met Renee's. "He said, 'Nobody will ever trust your mother. They should keep her locked up forever.'"

The words straightened Renee upright, then forced her into

a conscious battle to keep from high-fiving her little brother. A milestone, she realized in the next moment, for both of them. Their anger had rumbled and roared, banged up against restriction and pushed holes of steam through walls of niceness. And now it had bumped itself around to press its back against Sylvia Parker. The anger was still there, just shooting its fire in a different direction.

"I understand why you punched him, J.J. I would have wanted to do the same thing." She noted a glimmer of hopeful redemption in his eyes. "But," she said, dashing it quickly, "I would've been more grown-up and handled it another way. I'm not saying that it would have been the easiest way, because the better way to handle things is a lot of times the hardest ... How do you think it would have been different if you had handled it with words, or even walked away from him?"

He mumbled his words, his chin pressed against his chest. "I wouldn't have been suspended."

"And maybe by choosing the right words you could have helped Ben to understand about Mom."

"He just wanted to be mean."

"Maybe. Does he play baseball?"

He nodded.

"Has he ever made an error or struck out?"

Another nod.

"Well, maybe if he tries to be mean again, you could ask him if making an error or striking out should mean that he should never get to play baseball again. Then explain what I told you about Mom making an error. Okay?"

He nodded again and pressed his chin back to his chest.

Renee smoothed his hair, mahogany brown like his dad's, and wondered if he would grow up to be as sensitive and compassionate as he was. Maybe not quite as sensitive, she hoped, but with better coping skills. He would be a good man, she was sure.

J.J. lifted his face, his eyes pleading. "Don't tell Olivia I got in trouble."

Renee tilted her head and raised her eyebrows slightly. "She already knows."

He folded his arms on the edge of the table and buried his face in the hollow.

Renee stroked the back of his head and his neck. Yes, she thought, he's going to be okay. "You know what, though?" she asked, adding a kiss to the back of his head. "She loves you anyway, like I do."

Chapter 24

Journal, First Entry

We named our journals. At first J.J. was going to name it J.V. for his favorite baseball player, but when I tried to name mine I realized that it couldn't be the name of anybody I know because I wouldn't feel free to say anything I wanted. I would think that I was talking to that person and maybe avoid saying some things that I wouldn't want to say to them. So, J.J. and I both decided to create an alter ego—someone we would be if we could, and that's who we would write to. J.J.'s journal is Bat Boy because if he could right now, he'd be the bat boy for the Detroit Tigers. He said he could tell Bat Boy anything. And I'll be talking to you, Co-Ed, because if I could, I'd be you.

Bat Boy

I write stuff in here for Bat Boy and no body else can see it. He isnt real so no body will get mad at me Renee said I can say anything I want but I dont think she means swear words sometimes I swear real low so no body else can hear one time Jenny heard me but I know her secret so she cant tell.

Co-Ed

I can't even say the words here. I thought writing them would be easier than saying them out loud. At least right now that's true. What I feel for Olivia remains whatever it is, without words. I think maybe my fear is bigger than my anger. At least this one is. I can't find all the edges of it. How do I know how big it is if I can't see the edges? How do I take hold of it?

Olivia. I like writing her name. Olivia. I like how it looks with its sweeping 'O' and strong internal lines. Writing it in my personal thoughts feels kind of reverent—I write it carefully, trying to make it perfect. It's nearly as beautiful as its owner.

Ownership. Odd, that word. Is that what it is, a prideful, adolescent kind of ownership that gives me the right to write her name in my private thoughts? She has given me that right, hasn't she?

An interesting realization, this is the one place I can be adolescent, or anything else I want.

Olivia
+
Renee

Bat Boy

How do bat boys get money in the winter? I had to go to see Stacy today so Renee could go to work and it snowed a lot last night I shoveled Stacys driveway and sidewalk before the parents came I had to get up real early I dont want Renee to be mad at me I don't want Olivia to think I'm bad because she wont come for xmas I hope it snows again.

Co-Ed

I hope I did the right thing. In my head it was right, in my heart it felt wrong. I told J.J. he couldn't accept money from Stacy for shoveling snow. He pleaded with me and told me that he needed the money for something very important. Which is more important, a nine-year-old's wish or the lesson that you shouldn't profit on punishment time? The "please" with tears in his eyes was almost enough to reverse my decision, but his anger when I didn't cave reinforced that it was the right thing to do. I wonder if he hadn't slammed his bedroom door, if I would have changed my mind before bed.

Bat Boy

I go to Stacys tomorrow and Friday to It snowed a lot Renee is still mad at me relly relly mad and I'm mad at me too because I say I'm not going to lose my temper and then I do Rory got scared and cried when I slammed the door I taught him the secret handshake that my team made up and I promised not to do it again so he stopped crying and I feel better.

Co-Ed

J.J. wouldn't tell me why he needed to make some money. I'm assuming he wants to buy more expensive Christmas presents than the $10.00 they each get to spend, or else buy more than for the person he drew. But, he has dropped the subject.

There are always consequences, either now or later. It's best he know that right now. Maybe this will help him understand Mom a little better. I sure hope so because I'm not looking forward to making him come with us to see her before Christmas.

Chapter 25

It was too easy. J.J. helped Rory with his boots and tried to tame his colic with water. He gathered the little gifts each of them had made and climbed into the car without incident. Renee had neither asked nor demanded that he go. He had just begun getting ready with the rest of them. Christmas magic? Maybe.

Her apprehension, however, remained front and center as they greeted their mother and settled around a table in the crowded visiting room. J.J. had allowed his mother to hug him, but his own arms had rested in placid non-commitment against her back. It was the first time since he was six that Sylvia had held her oldest boy in her arms. Was there a visible difference between joyful tears and those of sadness and grief? It seemed that there was as Renee watched her mother's face. Instead of staining drawn hollows, the shimmering stream this time curved over cheeks lifted high and round. No amount of Christmas glitter could outshine the beauty of it.

All around them families celebrated their joy with remarkable tenacity. Children, toddlers to teenagers, those lucky enough to have family guardians, succeeded in doing what a feeble attempt at holiday decorating had not. They brought normalcy, the sounds and scents of the world the women here missed so much. Their voices brought excited imagination and quiet wonder as they played, true testaments to their resiliency.

The room was a kaleidoscope of people, mixing and moving, their moods and lives changing predictably, unpredictably, living out their fates with what little control they'd been able to salvage. She'd watched the ever-changing picture for years, and in her own unengaged moments with her mother she had overheard hushed voices of hope and the silence of despair. And within those parameters she had witnessed women struggling for self-respect, searching for a semblance of power, and snatching up crumbs of hope from the most unexpected places. Some deserved so much more than they found. Some stole crumbs unmerited.

At first it was all too hard to watch. Peeking around the hands of embarrassment and intimidation that covered her face, she saw the women only in her head. She was afraid to look, afraid to see her mother there among them, afraid of knowing what her mother felt. She wasn't ready to see beyond, feel beyond, understand beyond. Not until Doreen.

Oh, yes, she remembers Doreen. Her mother doesn't know how vividly. Doreen was already sitting in the visiting area that day, her teenage son all bad and baggy and sprawled over a chair beside her. Mother hadn't come in yet, and suddenly Doreen was approaching. She stepped up close, looming dark and silent, sending a chill of trepidation through Renee.

"You the professor's daughter?" she had asked.

Fear clutched her throat closed and allowed Renee only a wide-eyed nod.

Doreen sat uninvited. She gestured sharply toward her sprawling son. "My boy." She waited, a silent demand for Renee to look. And after she did, "Sweet as they come 'til they killed his brother. Last few years he got no use for no one." She leaned forward in her chair, rested thick arms on her thighs, and clasped her hands.

Renee's sense of intimidation dropped right along with the dark eyes.

"Got no way to help him now." When she brought her eyes back to Renee's, they had lost the opaqueness that had made them unreadable. "'Til I got thinkin'. All your momma do is read. Everybody call her 'professor.' You think she'd help me to read?"

Right then the hands had left Renee's eyes.

"I was thinkin'," Doreen continued, "if my boy sees me learnin', tryin' to find a better way so when I get outta here I can do better by us, maybe he'll try, too."

It obviously hadn't occurred to Doreen, or perhaps it wasn't really relevant, that knowing how to read hadn't kept Sylvia out of prison. But what had occurred was a way to help herself; it was up to Sylvia to find her own way. Doreen had found some control, some minute grasp of power, a glimmer of hope, that could make her life better, and maybe someone else's as well.

It was after that encounter that Renee had begun to really look. And then the questions started. Each time she visited she learned a little more about the women here—what they had done and how long they would likely serve. But, more importantly, she became familiar with families much like her own that had been left behind when these women were incarcerated. At first, watching them, getting to know more about them, had fed her anger. So many women, so many children, such selfish, stupid choices that had separated them. She had automatically dismissed the choices made by childless women, they seemed less dangerous to anyone but themselves, and the added fuel would have been too much for her fire. It took years, as it was, for the flames to die down so that understanding could begin. And empathy didn't have a chance without understanding.

She'd begun to talk about these women to Shayna, and to her mother's attorney. They were the ones who finally set the perspective dots, the facts and statistics, that allowed her to draw the connecting lines. There were very few here, less than ten percent, convicted of violent crimes. The rest were serving time, a lot of time, for what Shayna described as crimes of the poor—drugs, prostitution, bad checks, larceny, insurance fraud. She saw it all around her—where she lived, where she worked, on the bus, on the corner—kids wanting what their parents couldn't give, parents wanting to give what they could not. Suddenly, poor choices translated into limited choices. And when she fractioned in the educational levels of the women, those limited choices looked much like bumpers in a pin-ball machine. The crimes were no less egregious, or the consequences any less harmful, merely the committing of them more understandable.

That understanding, however, hadn't expanded to her own mother until Renee was able to let go of some of her anger to make room for it. She wondered, as she watched the changing kaleidoscope, how long it would take others to forgive. Or maybe they already had.

"Renee." Jenny's voice demanded her attention along with the slap, slap of her small hand on the table next to her arm. "You didn't open your present yet. It's gonna be a frame. We all got frames. Mom made them."

"See, that's why I didn't waste all that energy opening it; I knew I could count on you to tell me what it is." Her quasi-serious expression was recognized by Jenny for exactly what it was. She placed her hands firmly on her hips and tilted her head in exasperation. "Then again," Renee added, "you could be wrong." She ripped open the present. "Or not." She held up the frame, decoupaged with pictures of pencils and rulers and books, and winked at her mother.

"They're all different," Jenny exclaimed. "It's special just for you because you're going to be a teacher." She stood her frame up on the table. "See, mine has little pictures of butterflies on it, they're my favorites. And J.J.'s is just like a baseball."

"I'm gonna put my team picture in it," J.J. offered in a tone usually denied his mother.

Sylvia's smile indicated that the change hadn't gone unnoticed. "And I'm going to wear your baseball picture right here," she said, clipping the large photo button to the pocket of her uniform.

Nor had it eluded Renee that her mother was making every effort to follow her children's interests. Their visits were accomplishing at least that much. The intangible was less obvious, and may not be clearly seen for years. But what she had seen today had given her hope, and for now, it made her smile.

"And I think the other ladies are going to be very jealous," Sylvia said, "of all the beautiful things you all made me." Jenny's blue-beaded bracelet adorned her wrist and Sylvia clutched the pictures drawn by Rachael and Rory to her chest. "But the best gift of all is being able to look at all your beautiful faces." She looked at each face, lingering, as if committing each to an unalterable memory. Then she smiled at each child, and each, beaming and bright, smiled back.

Her eyes reached Renee's, and there it was, absent for so many years, the declaration written in the absence of worry lines and tears, a smile written in the smooth, clear lines of youth. She'd forgotten how beautiful it was, and forgotten for years the picture that proved that it had once brightened her life every day. The picture wasn't a professional one, just a snap taken by a friend on the day Sylvia married John. And it wasn't posed, Sylvia hadn't even remembered it being taken. But it was perfect. In a moment almost too private to share, Sylvia had lifted the purest of smiles, pure joy and adoration, to John and her declaration had been captured and preserved.

Seeing that again touched something in Renee, something fresh and good, something that made everything seem ... possible, again. The picture wasn't lost, merely packed and neglected in a box of her mother's things. Now she had the perfect frame for it.

Chapter 26

"Gram," the voice skipped across the room in nearly-teen exuberance.

It wasn't the tone that made Millie Gordon cringe, it was the reference. She preferred to be called Grandma G and had made that quite clear. Disregarding her wish grated along the same nerve as children calling their parents by their first names. It suggested a lack of respect and a lack of proper parental authority. She did hesitate, however, to make that harsh a judgment of her own daughter on merely a lapse on the Gram issue. All in all, she was extremely proud of Sharon and Glenn for managing successful careers and raising two smart girls.

"I'm in the dining room, Sherry, with your mother," Millie answered.

She was on her way with her school project, a box of old family photos, and Millie's Christmas gift to her, a new Family Tree album. Christmas Eve with Grandma and Grandpa Gordon was a tradition and an excellent opportunity to get first-hand help with family history.

"I have to say, Mom," Sharon said, "this family tree project has *me* hooked. Remember when I first knew that I was pregnant and I began gathering family pictures? I even borrowed your old family Bible with the birth and death records in the back."

Millie nodded. "I remember."

"But of course," she continued as Sherry plunked the box of photos down on the table. "I had a few things take priority over that project. I never did get back to it."

"So, now you can help me," Sherry said, spreading out groups of pre-sorted pictures between her mother and grandmother. "These over here are Dad's side of the family. He's going to help me tomorrow night. These are the Gordon/Logan side. Mom helped with the chart, but," she opened the book to the partially filled page, "she doesn't know who Bernetta Logan is."

Millie studied the page. "Well, this one you know is my mother, your great-grandmother." She ran her finger across the line of three women's names and two men. "These are her brothers and sisters, and that makes them your great-uncles and -aunts."

"I know, but," Sherry pulled out a large black-and-white photo with a silver-and-black cardboard frame.

Sharon explained, "This picture shows only five children, like all the other family shots. I thought maybe Bernetta had died very young, but the record in the back of the Bible shows that all six lived into adulthood."

It stood to reason that the same propensity for record-keeping that kept her in good stead professionally would manifest itself in her personal life as well. But that talent for well-kept records that answered questions for her at work was now *posing* questions for her here. Past buying her granddaughter the album, Millie had been too busy lately to think about the questions that she should have anticipated. Most likely, if her daughter had years ago pursued the project further the questions would have already been addressed, but she hadn't. So, there it was, clearly unavoidable, the family anomaly waiting to be explained.

Millie sighed. "It was never really talked about, especially in my parents' day. My father never spoke about it, he didn't have to; my mother took care of that. It was clear that she felt it was her responsibility."

The eyes of her daughter and granddaughter waited on her explanation. They held the same wonder, the same questioning dread that her own eyes had undoubtedly held for *her* mother's explanation. She and her three siblings had been called together,

161

on the same weekend that her cousins were gathered in their homes. They were all old enough then to heed the warning; the oldest of the extended brood was eight, and the timing was imperative. Their Aunt Bernetta had left the sanitarium again.

"When I was twelve, your same age, Sherry," Millie noted, "my mother called us together to explain about Aunt Bernetta. You see, when she was a teenager her parents had to commit her to a sanitarium, a kind of hospital, because they couldn't control her behavior."

"Like nowadays," Sherry asked, "when kids get into a lot of trouble and they get sent to juvey?"

"Well, no. It wasn't the same kind of trouble that you're thinking of, like drugs or stealing, or fighting. It was the way she acted socially; she didn't act like a young girl was supposed to act. She acted more like a young boy."

"She was gay," Sharon concluded.

"I know about being gay," Sherry added. "Even before Mom explained it when one of the boys at church said he was."

"Kids are privy to so much information, and not all of it factual," Sharon explained. "I felt it was important that we talk about it as a family after the elders of the church decided that the boy would not be allowed to attend church any longer."

"I don't think that was right," Sherry said, arms folded across her chest. "He was really nice. I helped him put on puppet shows for the little kids. We made the puppets to look like people in the Bible, and acted out the stories so that the kids understood them better. The kids didn't understand why he had to leave; they were very sad."

"They may not understand now because they're so young," Millie said, "but some day they'll see that it was best."

"I don't know if that's true, Mom," Sharon replied.

"If it weren't for the contact with the children," Millie said, "I'd agree with you. How can the Church effect healing and change if those needing it most aren't allowed in the church?"

"That's not what I meant, Mom. I think it was good that my girls got to know this boy. They have a good value system in place and I'm learning to trust them to make good judgments." Sharon affectionately tucked a long errant strand of hair behind her daughter's ear. "This whole incident has actually opened my own mind. We're considering leaving the church if the elders don't reconsider their decision."

"Oh, I hope you don't do that, Sharon. The church elders have a responsibility to uphold doctrine, and also to protect the members—much like parents are responsible for teaching good values and for protecting their children."

"But when they make a decision that goes against our personal beliefs, Mom, I want the girls to see that it's important to stand up against it. And we should lead by example. Silence isn't acceptable. Those are things that you taught us."

"But you must look at the bigger picture. What about the parents with little boys? Don't they deserve protection? What if it wasn't a gay boy but a lesbian, how would you feel about their decision then?"

Sharon hesitated momentarily, then replied, "I'd like to think I'd feel the same way."

"I don't think you would. We're women, we're mothers; protecting our children is our strongest instinct. And unless you chemically alter it," she said with raised brows, "instinct will make those decisions for you."

"But how," Sharon began, then shifted a quick look at Sherry listening intently, "do you equate homosexuality with pedophilia?"

"It isn't only ... *inappropriate* behavior to worry about. There's the influence—"

"I know what inappropriate behavior means, Gram."

"Of course you do; you're a smart young lady."

"And, as I said, Mom, blessed with a good value system in place. This sounds like I'm getting very close to another *discussion* about born-versus-choice theory, and I really don't want to do that, not right now. I don't believe it's a choice and you're not going to change my mind about it."

Always a tug-of-war with this one, more headstrong than her two brothers ever thought of being. Discussion would not be the word Millie would use to describe her interchanges with Sharon; they would be more aptly described as arguments or, at their mildest, heated animated debates. And she was right, this was not the time or the place for it. But she knew her daughter well, and as much as she hated to admit it, Sharon seemed born with a tenacity that threw her headlong into whatever was before her, regardless of threat or warning. Right from the beginning, before she could even walk, Sharon wouldn't even be held like a normal child. Her brothers had nuzzled and clung to their mother like baby koalas, but not Sharon. With surprising strength she had pushed and twisted and insisted on being held facing out away from her mother's breast. And that had just been the beginning. Did that lend credibility to her sexual-orientation argument? No. It would take a lot more than a character trait to make that a clear and unchallengeable issue.

So there would be no debate today, but there was something she needed to tell Sharon, something Sharon needed to hear. "Yes," Millie agreed, "I'm sure Sherry will appreciate us getting back to her project, so I'll just tell you what I know about Bernetta Logan and we'll leave it at that. Okay?"

Sherry nodded her agreement while her mother offered the closed-lip one-corner-lift of her mouth that, over the years, had become her "I'll-concede-the-last-word-because-I-know-it's-coming-anyway" response.

Millie continued. "My mother explained that when Aunt Bernetta was in her early teen years she refused to wear dresses. She would steal her brother's shirts and trousers, and cut school and hang out in the pool hall with the older boys. They must have thought that she was a boy because no one made her leave. Her mother never would have gone in somewhere like that looking for her, so it was up to her brothers to find her. But they'd find her in one place and she'd just find somewhere else to go. She stole her father's cigarettes and smoked, and it seemed like she was rebelling against every socially acceptable behavior she could. She even took scissors into the school bathroom and cut her hair off real short. Her parents tried everything. They let her wear trousers to go riding if she would wear proper dresses at other times. When that didn't work, they tried not letting her go any-where except school and church; they even tried confining her to the house. They were probably exasperated at that point—seemingly nothing worked. But when they found out that she was acting like a boyfriend to one of her young female cousins, they must have felt there was nothing else they could do except commit her to the sanitarium."

"How long did she have to stay there?" Sherry asked.

"Off and on for the rest of her life. She evidently changed her behavior and did what was necessary in order to be released, but it wasn't long before they had to commit her again."

"And the purpose of that?" Sharon asked. "What did sending her there accomplish, except shutting her away from proper society?"

"Well, yes, it did do that. Sanitariums served a variety of purposes, one of them being an early version of a psychiatric hospital. Shock treatments and lobotomies are crude treatments by today's standards, but they were trying to find ways to change or control behavior. Frankly, there are days when I wonder if, with all our studies and drugs and our modern approaches, we're any more successful than they were."

"So none of that changed her, did it, Mom?"

"I thought you didn't want to go to that discussion."

"I didn't," Sharon replied. "But I didn't know your story was going to so beautifully rest the defense of my case."

"I'm not sure that it does. There are some successful programs out there now that are changing homosexual behavior. But like anything dealing with human behavior, you know, with the variables of influence and the human will, one method won't work with every person."

"And if you're wrong," Sharon said, "what are we as a society doing to these people? All they did for Bernetta Logan, with all their righteousness and experimentation, was to make her very short life a total hell. My God, she was only, what—"

"Twenty-eight," Sherry added.

Sharon shook her head. "And let me guess,' she said with a tone that could seat a nail with one blow, "she took her own life."

Millie ignored the tone—she had gotten quite good at it. Her expression said, "Yes, of course you're right," her words offered a stalwart defense. "When there aren't ready answers to help the individual, you have to consider what is best for the larger group." A philosophy she believed in its most literal sense. It was the mission that gnawed at her soul every day. "In Bernetta's case, she had to be prevented from doing things to young girls, like her cousin, that would affect them the rest of their lives."

Sharon rested her hand gently on her daughter's shoulder. "Sweetie, will you take a fresh plate of cookies to the other room for everyone?" She smiled and planted a kiss on Sherry's head. "Thanks."

"I'll bring some back for us, too," Sherry said, starting from the room. "Oh, Gram?" She stopped short of the doorway. "Thanks for telling us about your aunt Bernetta."

"You're welcome, honey."

"I wonder," Sharon said as soon as Sherry was out of earshot, "how close to the modern equivalent of a sanitarium commitment did *I* come growing up?"

"You've always tested the boundaries, even harder than the boys, that's true. But I always knew somehow that in finding who you were and finding your rightful place in the world that you would find a way to do it without self-destructing."

"You think Bernetta Logan self-destructed?"

"Of course she did."

"That's why, Mother, you will never stop wondering why we butt heads. You see no connection between Bernetta's struggle to be herself and mine."

"You're not a homosexual."

"And what if I had been?"

Millie rose from the table, coffee cup in hand, and without looking at her daughter, moved decisively toward the kitchen. "But you aren't," she said as she left the room.

Chapter 27

The tiny front room was in total disarray. Wrapping paper and bows lay unceremoniously where they had been thrown, and boxes emptied of their gifts lay like so many pieces of a shipwreck on a patch of blue carpet sea. Squeals of excitement had finally settled into a low babble of play, and Renee leaned over the back of the comfortable chair to whisper against Olivia's ear.

"I don't think I'll ever be happier than I am right now."

Olivia closed her eyes and pressed her ear only briefly against the warmth of Renee's lips. "It's pretty near to perfect, isn't it?"

"Pretty near," she replied, "moving around to sit on the arm of the chair. "Happy kids, and a full heart—I can't ask for more than that."

Olivia looked up. Renee's face, smoothed of its frown lines, was turned toward the children. If only it were possible, she thought, to freeze this moment in time, to capture forever the happiness there and replay it each day for the rest of her life. If only she could do that for her, she would in an instant. And to be included in that happiness was becoming a blessing Olivia hadn't anticipated. Love was a funny thing, not the fantastical notion of daydreams and movies where falling in love had promises of a happy life together, lovers wrapped tightly together in a fortress against worldly intrusion—forever. The reality of love was a far different thing, and Olivia had known that from the time she knew that that love would be with a woman.

She had held no fantasy of a life like her parents'—their love and commitment supported and revered by family and friends. And she had no delusion of a lesbian white knight sweeping into her life and making everything perfect. Yet, she had held hope for love, and dared to wish for happiness. She never expected both, however, to appear in the form of Renee Parker. How could she have imagined love within this unlikely context, or happiness amid the tension and drama of a family in crisis? But then, she had never met anyone like Renee.

Renee's voice broke her thoughts. "We may never get J.J. to go to bed tonight, it'll mean taking that jersey off."

J.J., proudly wearing his Tigers jersey, was busily placing his newest baseball cards in their protective sleeves while a captivated Rory looked on. "Maybe you should let him sleep in it," Olivia suggested. "It'll eventually make it to the laundry."

"Oh, no," Renee replied, "he won't sleep in it. All things baseball are treated with reverence. My bet is that it'll be draped over the back of his chair where he can see it."

"My brother-in-law went to high school with one of the Tiger trainers. I think we could get it signed in the spring."

"That, I want you to know, is going to lift you to hero heights, and not just in J.J.'s eyes."

"Well, if that's all it takes—" A small hand on her arm turned Olivia's attention to Rachael's round serious face. "What, sweetie?"

"Do you have any kids at home?"

"No, I don't. Only at work, where I take care of other people's sick children."

"Do you have a mother or father at home?"

"No. My parents live in another city."

"You don't have anyone there when you go home?"

"No, sweetie, there's just me."

The line between Rachael's brows deepened and her dark blue eyes bore deeply into Olivia's. The face of a cherub in serious thought. Then suddenly her eyes widened and her brows lifted away the crease. "I know," she said, "I'll make a bed roll like Jean taught me and I'll put it right beside the couch and sleep out here with Nay, and you can have *my* bed. Then you can stay here with us and you won't have to be alone."

There was no measure for it. The purity of her thought could not be measured by percentage or points like diamonds or gold. And how do you measure the sound of it, the tone of harp strings singing to the fingertips finding their heart? You don't measure it, you feel it. You let it find the heart of you. Let it sing its special song and make you cry at its sweetness.

Blinking back developing tears, and sensing that Renee was about to reply for her, Olivia lifted her fingers through the fine silky hairs at Rachael's temple. "I think that is the nicest invitation I've ever gotten. And if I could, this is exactly where I would want to be."

"But why can't you?"

"Well," Olivia began, "I really wouldn't get to see you much. See, I would be at home while you are at school, and then I'd be at work when you were home in the evening. And if I came in here after work I would wake you all up."

"You could be very quiet."

"But I wouldn't get to see you. I'll tell you what you could do," Olivia said, lifting her tone, "so that I won't feel so alone. You could draw me some pictures of you and your brothers and sisters. And I'll put them around my apartment, and when I feel lonely I'll look at them and think about the fun we've had together and about the next time I'll get to see you. Will you do that?"

Rachael's eyes were wide with possibility. "I'll draw you one right now," she said, turning abruptly. Then, turning back quickly, she added, "And you can take it right home with you tonight."

She hurried away with mission in her step to her new crayons and colored paper, and Renee waited for Olivia's eyes. "That," she said, meeting them with a smile, "was brilliant."

"That was also true, and not meant only for Rachael's benefit. Have you thought anymore about letting me stay with them during their vacation so that you don't have to take off work?"

"You sure you know what you're in for?"

"Unless there's something you're not telling me. Some family secret," she said, lowering her voice to a hushed whisper, "dark and scary, that will send me running in fear."

Renee responded with a gentle laugh. "Oh," she said, clipping her laugh short, "there is that little matter of their heads turning 360 degrees when they get mad, but—"

"But as long as I know a little something about exorcism, I should be fine?"

"Part of your nurse's training, right?" But before Olivia could continue their semi-private banter, a loud "Stop it, Rory" demanded their attention. "Just a minute," Renee said, and she was off across the room.

Rory, bored with picking up Christmas bows with the claw of his new crane, had begun trying to pick up Rachael's crayons and deposit them in his dump truck. A minute later, the dish of pine cones they had collected in the park for the table decoration had been emptied on the floor and Rachael's crayons were safe once again.

Renee picked up the beanbag chair, dropped it near Olivia's feet and sank into it. "You're sure," she said, more as a statement than a question.

"I am. I have two nieces and a few hundred pediatric patients in my experience cache, and you need to go to work. Also," Olivia added, leaning forward in her chair, "I don't believe your reservations have as much to do with my handling the kids alone as they do with your fear that they will somehow manage to frighten me off. You haven't had anyone willing to accept the whole package, have you?"

"It's not just that," Renee replied, before turning her posture away from the children. "I have more than one heart to worry about being broken, and keeping that foremost in my mind hasn't been easy lately. I've been so careful about letting someone into their lives who might be here long enough for the kids to begin loving them and depending on them, and then suddenly gone from their lives. They've already had two people they loved snatched from their lives. I watch them struggle with that every day and I know it's going to affect them for the rest of their lives. I have to do everything I can to keep that from happening to them again."

"*And* to you."

Renee shrugged. "I suppose. But at least I can see the danger coming—maybe even avoid it."

"Do you really think so?" Olivia asked. "Can you really see love coming? Don't we only see it once we're in it?"

Renee sank back into the beanbag. She watched the children playing happily, oblivious to their place in the adults' conversation.

"I practice professional detachment every day at work," Olivia continued, "but that ability didn't allow me to decide if I was going to love your family."

"You decided to get closer."

"And so did you."

"I could have avoided it," Renee replied, still watching the children.

"You knew it would be love you'd be avoiding?"

She finally turned her full attention to Olivia, eyes squarely centered. "I didn't know *what* it was."

"And now?"

"Now, my only choice is to deny it." She pulled her eyes from Olivia and refocused once again on the children. "They don't even have *that* choice. It's too late for them. Rachael has just made that very clear, hasn't she?"

"She has, and I hope I have as well." Olivia drew her fingers over Renee's hair pulled taut into a single braid. "I love them, Renee. Each of them has found their own way in and settled into a place in my heart perfectly suited for them." She smiled when she met Renee's eyes. "I fell in love with Rory before I fell in love with you."

"I think I did know that."

"What I want you to know now, deep in your heart know, is that I'm here for the long haul. I want you in my life—all of you. I can't imagine how empty and lonely my life would be now without you ... there *is* more than one heart to worry about breaking—there's mine, too."

Before Renee could respond, Rory was standing between them, planting his hands on Olivia's knees and demanding her attention. "J.J. didn't sing the song, 'Livia."

"What song, sweetie?"

"When he went to the bathroom and washed his hands. The birthday song."

J.J.'s voice preceded him across the room. "I did too." He marched toward Rory, his steps swift with threat, and stopped abruptly behind him. Hands clenched into fists and arms stiff at his sides, J.J. forced his words through tight lips. "You don't know anything."

"Yes, I—"

"Okay, that's enough," Renee said, taking hold of J.J.'s arm. "What difference does it make, Rory?"

"'Livia said."

"I taught them to sing Happy Birthday once through," explained Olivia, "to be sure that they're washing their hands long enough. You have to rub your hands together that long to actually kill bacteria."

"Is there any rule about singing it out loud?" Renee asked.

Olivia shook her head. "None that I know of."

"Good," Renee replied with a nod. "So, the song will work just as well if J.J. sings it silently in his head, don't you think, Rory?"

Rory answered with a vigorous nod.

"So it won't matter if you hear him sing it or not, right?"

"Right," he said with another nod.

"Then I say we give J.J. a high-five on it, okay?" Not a solution worthy of the Nobel Peace Prize, but very effective nonetheless. Rory got satisfaction without backing J.J. into a corner. They headed back to play without anger, or even a tattle-tale hangover.

"They can really use you in elementary education. *You* have methods."

"I just know what works here. I've helped to take care of them since J.J. was born; a lot of trial and error went before finding things that worked. And as far as any kind of education goes," she said, her eyes narrowing to warning level, "let's not go there."

"Even if discussing it won't ruin the day?"

"Can't imagine how," she replied, sliding deeper into the bean-bag until her head rested against it. "I just need to figure out my own solution."

"That's what I'm trying to get you to see." Olivia lowered her voice to just above a whisper. "Honey, I want to be a real part of your life. Let me help. You don't have to shoulder all the worries, and figure out all the solutions on your own. I can help you."

"What *you* don't see is how dangerous that feels to me. I want to believe that I can depend on you, that you won't drop out of my life—their lives—without warning. I want to believe that in the worst way. But the truth is, I did believe that my mother wouldn't let me down—that she would always be there for me, whatever it took, just like she had since I was old enough to know it. But then she *was* gone—no warning, no time to prepare for it, no acceptable reason why. And John, one Friday he is fixing fried chicken with me for dinner, and the very next day, he was gone. Dead. Out of my life forever." She turned her head to look at Olivia. "You don't know what that does to you, and I don't think I can tell you."

Olivia's voice was very soft. "I know you can't, honey." She leaned forward, as close to Renee's face as she dared, and whispered, "I want to hold you, right now, make you forget for as long as I can how much that hurt you." Her eyes lifted to see Jenny leave the kitchen table. "I don't have enough time with you. I want so much to take that hurt away."

"I know," Renee replied softly. She reached to discreetly touch Olivia's hand, one of so few touches they'd found possible throughout the day. "And you always do, every time we're together. I cherish every minute we have."

Olivia's eyes indicated Jenny's approach. She straightened her posture, and Renee lifted her hand in acknowledgment.

"Nay, can we play the Christmas CD again?"

"Don't break my new boom box, I'm pretty sure Olivia expects it to last past one day."

"I know how to do it."

"Will you and Rach dance to the Christmas Tree song for us again?" Olivia asked.

Jenny pulled her lips inward into a tight line that pressed deep dimples into her cheeks, exhibiting a barely controlled smile. She thrust herself against Olivia, threw her arms tightly around her shoulders, and said, "I love you, Olivia." Then she was off across the room on her music mission.

Olivia lifted her hands and offered Renee a look of mild surprise.

"Why do you wonder? She's just telling you that you're right."

The realization, the physical, audible reality of it, was sobering. The smile lines relaxed from around her eyes. Olivia knew the words in her heart before Renee said them. "She's telling you that it's too late, they love you. And so do I."

Chapter 28

Co-Ed

It's getting easier to write my thoughts down. I'm not skipping as many days now between entries. Maybe it's easier because happy thoughts are easier to write about. I wish writing them down would somehow preserve them and make them last.

I am happy. Rory is doing so well on the medication. J.J. is working real hard on his anger control. The girls are smart and happy and doing very good in school. And I'm in love. Life is good. Life is very good.

Bat Boy

This is the best xmas ever Im real happy because I got my favorite Tiger shirt Renee is real happy to becus Olivia was here all day.

Co-Ed

How is it possible to be this happy? How does loving Olivia make everything so different? I find myself feeling more confident and less frightened, even of Millie Gordon. I can't understand it, but I wouldn't change it now for anything, even going to school.

Some day, though, I will go to school. I have a plan for now and that is helping to make the wait more tolerable. Part of it was Olivia's idea. She told me about being able to test out of some classes, and I've already started preparing. I'm starting with the syllabus from the Lit course I had to drop. Dean is letting me bring home used books from the bookstore at night, and I'm taking detailed notes. I have a really good memory. I know I can do this.

Dean let me bring one of his video games home, too. I never thought I would waste time playing something like this. It's very violent, men coming at me with guns, and explosives and all kinds of hazards to avoid. At first I was getting annihilated pretty fast, but now I'm getting pretty good. Dean still laughs at my scores, but he says I'm improving faster than he thought I would. I've had to start setting my alarm, though, so that I don't play longer than forty minutes. It's addicting. One night I played until two in the morning. Even playing for forty minutes, I can't believe how much stress it relieves. I never would have believed it. I'm so anxious and stressed when I'm playing, but I'm blasting these guys off the screen and it feels great. This is one of those things, though, that no one else needs to know. Mrs. Gordon would have a lot to say about it, I'm sure.

Bat Boy

We read a book at school before I got kicked out about a boy named Billy His mother died He was real sad and so was his dad and then his dad got a girlfriend and Billy relly liked her and they wanted her to stay forever so Billy's dad married her and she adopted Billy Ive been thinking a lot about the story.

Bat Boy

Olivia is coming over every day this week and I promise not to get angry or lose my temper that way she will keep coming over I hope Olivia never goes away If she did I woud be even sadder than Billy Im going to ask her to adopt us like in the story and then she will stay.

Co-Ed

I feel like a complete ass. Stacy told me why J.J. was so upset about not being able to earn the money for shoveling snow. He wanted to buy his teacher some new perfume so that she didn't smell like Mom anymore. Stacy let him borrow the money and picked out the perfume for him. He thought I was so mad at him that he couldn't even tell me. I never want him to think that again. He's trying so hard. I told him how proud of him I am, and that I will always help him do the right thing. He already earned the money, I'll pay Stacy back.

Bat Boy

I asked Olivia but she cant adopt me like the lady in the story But I'm not going to be mad that our mother is still alive and that is one reason Olivia cant adopt us because I have another idea like in the story.

Co-Ed

I'll bet Olivia never imagined celebrating New Year's Eve with four children. Well, two and a half. Even though they all had long naps during the day to get ready, Rory fell asleep around nine and missed the whole thing, and Rachael only woke during the countdown to see the ball hit the bottom. She didn't seem too impressed, but it's hard to tell with Rach. She may come up with something a month from now that will indicate that she got the whole significance of a fresh start and new hope, the things Olivia and I were talking about. I've learned not to even try to second guess her. You just take Rach as she comes.

For J.J. and Jenny it was the best party ever. Olivia brought little bottles that looked like champagne and plastic martini glasses and hats, and we sang and toasted and made resolutions. And the kiss we wanted so badly we gave to the kids. Somehow that made it even more special. I don't know how it was possible for such a night to be so romantic. Romantic night with four children is an oxymoron. It shouldn't be possible—yet it was. And I keep trying to figure out how. Maybe romantic isn't the right word, or maybe my definition needs to be broader. I only know that what I felt last night was as memorable as a first kiss, and more touching than a candle-light dinner for two. The unselfishness of Olivia spending what should have been an adult celebration with all of us meant far more to me than even a night alone with her. And she knew that, without even asking. All evening I kept expecting some sense that she wished we could have spent the night differently, by some remark or just a look, but I saw nothing like that. I saw only joy. And if it was insincere in any way, then she should have gone home with a little golden statue.

I've been re-living the whole thing, from beginning to end, all day and most of the night now. I never saw those feelings coming; I never knew that they existed. I guess I just assumed that until there came a time in my life when I was truly free, probably when Mom was out of prison and able to take care of the kids, that there would not be an Olivia in my life. That someone like her wants me *and* wants my family is almost too good to be true. There are moments when I'm afraid to believe it. Will the novelty of it wear off for her? Will she grow tired of our limited time together? I wonder these things, and then she does something like plan the New Year's Eve party for the kids, or make love with me as if every week had a thousand Saturdays, and at least for a day I stop wondering.

Co-Ed

Okay, this is worse than thinking about Olivia having to discipline the kids, or at least it's going to make it harder for her to do. J.J.'s in love, and not with one of the little girls in his class. He's in love, however a nine-year-old envisions love, with Olivia. He took advantage of a few minutes alone with her, while she was looking at a Baseball Greats book with him, to let her know. He asked her if getting married was the same thing as being together 'For now, for always' like we've pledged each other. Olivia told him that she believed it was. So, then he said that he knew he was too young to

178

get married right now, but he wanted to know if she would wait for him to grow up and then marry him. I wish I could have seen her face. I could tell that it still touched her when she was telling me about it. Her eyes glistened and her smile would have looked sad if I hadn't known that she wasn't. Her response was perfect. She said that she would wait for him to ask her again when he is twenty-one, meantime, she pledged 'for now, for always' and that was all he needed to hear. She is amazing. I really love her. And J.J.? Well, I guess I won't have to worry about his taste in women.

Co-Ed

Part of me wonders if Olivia spending a whole week with the kids was a mistake. They miss her now that they are back in school and keep asking when she'll come and stay. That's not possible and before last week they didn't even mention it—except for Rachael. She's becoming more and more like me, I think.

Olivia is getting to know them so well. I can tell how much she loves them. She calls more often, checking on them, remembering something she forgot to tell them, or telling me that she picked up this or that for them for the weekend. And the weekend—my God, Olivia coming on the weekend—you'd think I'd just told them we were going to Disney World. They've been on their best behavior, especially J.J. Maybe it's good that Olivia isn't here every day, not that there isn't much I wouldn't give to make it possible. But, it's kind of a nice lever to have in case I need it.

Bat Boy

Im not so mad at mom anymore I dont think about it when Olivia is here and when shes not here I think about what were going to do when she comes over Olivia is going to help me with my science project Its going to be the best in the whole class.

Im not supposed to hate and Renee gets real mad when I say that word but I hate Brandon Getty He always tells me everything he does with his dad even stuff nobody cares about like cleaning out the garage Nobody cares if he cleans out the stupid garage and during baseball how his dad plays catch with him every day after he gets home from work He knows I don't have a dad but I told him how Renee plays catch with me and he said its not the same But Renee taught me lots of stuff like how on grounders you cant look up til you see the ball in your glove Brandon is scared of grounders becus he looked up and the ball hit him in the face I bet Renee can throw as hard as his dad can Im glad I dont have to sit next to him in class.

Co-Ed

I like this time of night; it's late and so quiet. I like the solitude of it. It's different than being alone or lonely. I don't feel alone, I feel content. For now, for this little space of time, I can think whatever thoughts feel good, make plans that I don't have to share with anyone. And I can listen to music and it doesn't matter if anyone else likes it. I love to listen to Billie Holiday and Sarah Vaughan and Diana Krall. Their voices haunt like a conscience, and make me think of lover's stolen moments, and soft lights, and intimate eyes. The words speak to me like no one else ever has, of lessons and discovery. They talk about love, powerful and painful. How to have it lights your life from within, and to lose it devastates more than death. I wonder if that's true.

Chapter 29

Millie Gordon was as far from everyone's thoughts as a snow storm in August. Blame it on the holidays—glitz, glitter, and a happy vacation—or blame it on love. It wouldn't matter, the result would have been the same. No one was expecting a Saturday morning home visit.

The day had been planned for over a week. Olivia was to take them all out to her sister's, where Keith and her nieces would teach them all to snowboard behind the ATV. The weather was perfect—thirty degrees, clear and bright—and the kids could barely contain their excitement. In all the scurrying to gather proper clothing and find missing gloves, Olivia was the only one to hear the knock. She called to Renee, "There's someone at the door. I'll get it."

She opened the door, greeting Millie Gordon's questioning look with a smile. "Good morning," she said cheerfully.

Millie's response was hesitant. "Yes ... let's hope it is. I'm the Parkers' case worker. Is Renee here?"

"Oh, yes. Come in. I'll get her."

Renee knew the moment Olivia entered the room that the day would not be going as planned. Her expression was one of concern. "What is it?" Renee asked.

"Mrs. Gordon's here."

The pained expression on Renee's face was all J.J. needed.

"No," he said, dropping hard onto his chair. "Now we can't go with Olivia."

"Maybe we still can," Olivia said. "How long does a home visit take?"

"It varies," Renee replied, picking the heaviest pair of socks from the dresser and handing them to Rory. "Here, buddy, put these on just in case."

"All right," Olivia said, "you do what you have to and I'll go down to the little café by the shopping center. Give me a call when she leaves."

"I'm sorry about this,"

"Things happen." She directed her attention toward the boys. "She'll be gone before you know it, and I'll see you in a little bit."

"J.J., get the girls, please," Renee said. "And meet me in the living room."

She'd lost count as to how many times her brothers and sisters had sat like stepping stones on the couch while Millie Gordon had prodded and pried their little minds. The number of times was irrelevant, the only thing that mattered was getting through this one.

They breezed through the initial niceties, also irrelevant since they rarely varied in tone or content. What the words were meant to convey was essentially lost in the delivery. But they were said and done and Millie was on to the more relevant holiday.

Yes, we all had a nice Christmas.

Yes, we visited our mother.

Yes, we gave and got some nice gifts.

And that's when things started to get shaky. There had been no time to prepare the kids for how to relate Olivia's presence in their lives. It's possible that there is no such thing as adequate preparation, for kids anyway. How can you expect them to avoid truth and not lie, or curb excitement over things that make them happy? No, there probably is no preparation.

But adults don't have the luxury of childhood exuberance. Renee needed preparation, at least a thoughtful run-through of possibilities, and she hadn't given herself that time. Now, she'd

182

have to rely on quick thought and careful answers, and it was making her more than usually uncomfortable.

"I would really love to see what you got for Christmas," Millie said. "Rory, why don't you and J.J. start by showing me?"

Or, more accurately, Renee thought, why don't I pretend to be interested in your gifts while I scope out your room and see if your clothes are clean and your room free of food and vermin, and you got more than an exciting trip to McDonald's for Christmas? It would pass the scrutiny, that didn't bother her. It was the fact that today's scrutiny represented only a base-level scrutiny. What bothered her was that *her* family faced a scrutiny that she suspected a lot of 'regular' families couldn't even pass. She wondered how many times they would have to pass these surprise tests before Millie Gordon believed what she saw.

"Do you think we'll be able to go with Olivia today?" Jenny asked as the girls awaited their turn with Millie.

"I think so, Jen. Olivia wants us all to meet her nieces. Even if we don't have a lot of time to learn to snowboard, we'll get to meet Olivia's family."

"But Olivia said she doesn't have any kids at home."

"She doesn't, Rach. Olivia has her own apartment. Her sister and brother-in-law and the girls live out in the country."

Rory, refreshingly unaffected by the drama surrounding him, came bouncing back into the room and jumped onto the couch. J.J. followed, now wearing his prized jersey. There was no doubt that the name Olivia was now in the mix.

"Jenny," Millie said from the hallway, "you and Rachael come show me your gifts now."

"Let's hurry," Jenny said, grasping Rachael's hand.

True to her mission, Jenny wasted no time helping Rachael show off her gifts, and then quickly displaying her own.

"Olivia got me this," she said, pulling a blue zippered case from under the bed. "It's for all my craft stuff. See?" Jenny unzipped the case and showed Millie all the compartments filled with multi-colored beads and wires and clasps. "I just finished this necklace. Do you like it?"

Millie fingered the strand of gold- and amber-colored beads. "It's beautiful, Jenny."

"You can have it. It will be like a Christmas present."

"That's very sweet. I'll wear it right now," she said, deftly fastening the clasp around her neck."

"And Renee gave me this," Jenny continued, holding up a journal with Harry Potter on the cover. "But nobody's allowed to read it, because I write my secrets in here just like Renee and J.J. do in theirs."

"I thinks that's silly," Rachael said with a frown.

"It's not silly," replied Jenny. "You're just saying that because Renee said you were too young for one."

"I am not. It's silly. It's a stupid book. I know all the secrets anyway."

Jenny quickly tucked the journal under her pillow, and stomped toward the door. "I'm telling Renee."

Millie, never one to let such a gift of opportunity slip by, sat down on the edge of Jenny's bed. "I know secrets, too." She leaned intimately closer to Rachael and put her finger to her lips. "My sister used to hide her lima beans in her socks because she couldn't leave the table until she ate them."

Rachael snapped her brows upward. It made Millie smile. "I never told our mother," she added. "You see, I couldn't tell because my sister knew that I had sneaked and read our mother's love letters from our father."

Rachael thought a moment, then said, "That's just like Jenny and J.J."

"Is it?"

"Uh, huh. J.J. made Jenny promise not to tell Renee about when he swears. If she tells, J.J.'s going to tell Jenny's friends that she's a big baby because she sleeps with Renee."

"Mm, yes," Millie replied, "she wouldn't want that. Does Renee sleep here with Jenny?" she asked, patting the bed.

"No," Rachael said with a shake of her head. "Jenny gets up at night and goes out to sleep with Renee on the couch. She thinks I'm sleeping. Renee said that I should let it be a secret, so I didn't tell J.J. He knew by himself."

"Mm, well," Millie said softly, "some secrets are hard to keep secret, aren't they?" Not waiting for a reply, she took Rachael's hand and stood. "Let's go back out with the others, shall we?"

Shit. Renee nearly said it out loud. The video game. Did I put it away? That's all Millie Gordon needs to see—and in the girls' room. Oh, please—I couldn't have been that careless.

Renee was struggling to tame the Mexican jumping beans that were flopping around in her chest when Millie and Rachael finally emerged from the hallway. Her stress level hadn't been this high since the first custody hearing. She had succeeded in gaining a moderate level of confidence in her ability to control the family destiny. Compromises could, and would, be made to keep them together. She would do whatever was needed for as long as it was necessary—that she had confidence in. But now she was doubting herself again, worrying about carelessness. And more critically, there was Olivia and compromises that could no longer be made. Merely the thought of what that could mean was too frightening to hold. The beans would not stop jumping over themselves.

"It certainly looks," Millie began, "as though you all had a very nice Christmas indeed. And, Olivia," she scanned the little faces, so attentive to the name, "seems to have been a big part of that."

Although they all nodded in affirmation, Renee realized that hers was the response Millie really wanted. "Olivia is Rory's nurse," she obliged. "She's a nice woman, very thoughtful."

"And very generous."

"She really likes the kids."

"And you, too," Jenny added. "She said—"

"She said she loved the nice things you made her," Renee interjected. "And so did Mom. I'm so proud of how creative you all are." She turned her attention back to Millie. "I see Jenny has given you one of the beautiful necklaces she made."

"It's so beautiful," Millie replied, "that I'm going to wear it to church tomorrow." She remained standing, making no move toward the comfortable chair left unoccupied for her. "Well," she said, turning to face Renee, "one of my concerns in coming today was J.J.'s suspension. He told me about the journal and I'm going to hope along with his principal that it will help him gain some control over his anger. I'll be keeping a close eye on the situation."

Oh, yeah, a close eye indeed. A whole lot closer than anyone had been watching the Columbine killers. "I am, too," Renee replied. "I'm working with him every day."

"Okay," Millie said, starting for the door much earlier than expected. "I'll leave you to your Saturday plans."

Renee began following her to the door, then turned to hold up a hand to shush the excitement stirring among the kids. They quieted momentarily and Renee concentrated on Millie's leaving.

Half-way through the open door, Millie turned. "Oh," she said, "was that Olivia I met when I arrived?"

It seemed that her eyes were more direct than ever before. Frighteningly direct, as if they were daring deception. It hadn't taken Renee long to realize that no question from Millie Gordon was merely pleasant conversation, but none had ever raised the hairs like this one. Her answer felt as if she was confessing to a major crime without benefit of counsel. "Yes. Nurse Olivia wanted to be sure Rory's dosage was adequate." Perjury. The word snapped into her mind. Millie's eyes wrote it in ink. No, no, just a white lie—a necessary, essential white lie—nothing more. It'll never come to perjury.

"How thoughtful."

Renee forced a smile. "Rory's got a lot of charm for a little guy. I think she has a soft spot in her heart for him."

"Yes, she must, to check on him like that on a weekend. Well, as I said, I'll leave you to your plans."

The final courtesies were barely uttered and the door not yet closed before the children were jumping with excitement.

"Okay, okay," Renee said in a futile attempt to calm them down. "I'll call Olivia. Just relax for a few more minutes."

She raced to the girls' room with a train of kids following her and saw to her relief that the game had been tucked safely away. Then she called.

Olivia answered quickly, surprise at the early call evident in her voice.

"Yes," Renee replied with a smile, "the coast is clear ... It *was* the shortest home visit we've had ... I'm not so sure it is a good sign. I had this horrible feeling as she was leaving that I was looking down the barrel of a gun I had just loaded ... It's hard not to worry, but I've got four kids here doing their best to take my mind off it. If you don't hurry I think they may self-destruct ... I know," she said, turning away from the surrounding chaos and lowering her voice, "and I hope you know, too, because I have four pair of ears that can't hear me say it out loud. We'll be in the car when you get here."

Chapter 30

The feeling, a foreboding unlike anything she had felt, haunted every thought Renee had, shackled every move she made for days. The moment she picked up the phone and heard the tone of Shayna's voice, she knew why.

Thankful for an understanding manager, Renee left work an hour early, raced across town, and hurried into Shayna's office. "I wish you would have told me what's going on when you called; I nearly creamed a truck trying to hurry out of the parking lot. Please tell me I'm scared for no good reason."

Shayna moved from behind her desk and pulled a chair next to Renee in the client chair. "Thank God you didn't have an accident. I thought it would have made you more worried to hear the short version. I'm sorry." She sat and leaned forward. "We do have a serious issue to deal with, and I wanted to be able to explain it thoroughly to you."

Renee breathed deeply in an attempt to calm the nervousness that was making her nauseous. She concentrated on the light brown eyes. If only there was a way to absorb their calm, to claim their confidence. She needed to believe in them, in Shayna.

"I've been notified of a complaint filed in Probate by Millie Gordon."

"About what?"

"She's claiming sleeping arrangements resulting in inappropriate touching and inappropriate sexual influence."

"What is she talking about?" Anger instantly replaced her nervousness. "*Who* is she talking about?"

"You," Shayna replied, "and Jenny."

There was at first confusion, her thoughts unable to pinpoint where or how the accusation originated. She searched frantically, frozen in a stare that Shayna honored. Then, suddenly, it was clear. "Rachael," she said, the anger draining from her face. "She told the secret."

Shayna didn't have to utter a word. The look on her face demanded an explanation.

"It's not actually a secret," Renee explained. "I didn't want the other kids to tease Jenny, so I told them that we should keep her secret. She has nightmares and thinks that the police are coming to take me away, so she comes out and sleeps on the couch with me. My God, Shayna, how can she say something like that? She didn't even ask me about it, just took what Rachael said and ran with it."

Shayna was nodding. "That's why I wanted to explain some things to you. I told you at the beginning that Probate Court is a whole different animal. It's not like any other court. There's no presumption of innocence, no burden of proof, only offering the best defense you can against sometimes outrageous accusations from over-zealous case workers, and hoping for the best. The only sure defense is to avoid accusations in the first place. That's why I tried early on to get them to give you another case worker. This is personal with Millie; but convincing them to switch any case, especially one already in the hands of one of their most dedicated workers, is improbable, and in your case impossible. Even so," she said with a lift in tone, "we've done pretty well."

"So what happens now? Another hearing?"

"No, this is different. A formal complaint calls for an investigation that will decide merit. In this case, whether or not the accusation has merit is going to be decided by a psychologist questioning the kids. We have to bring them in tomorrow. They don't want the kids being coached. Dad's information bought us the extra time."

"Tomorrow?"

Shayna nodded. "I'll have to get the kids right after school.

You won't be allowed to be with them during the questioning."

Renee's tone pleaded. "They're just little kids. They'll be so scared. And what if ... I've heard stories about them getting kids to say things that they don't even understand. People have been convicted of things that never happened because kids have been manipulated into saying things that aren't true."

"That's why I'm going to be with them."

"What if they say that there *is* merit? What happens then?"

"We go to court. But let's not get too far ahead. We're lucky that we can have an actual psychologist doing the questioning, and not a social worker. It's the best possible scenario, so try to be optimistic and trust me to do my job. Okay?"

"Should I talk to them first? What should I tell them?"

"You can come with me to pick them up and I'll explain it to them so that they won't be scared."

Renee hadn't seen the need last year when Doreen had added her name to the visitors' list, and certainly hadn't anticipated needing to see her alone, without visiting her mother. But here she was, without Shayna knowing, without even her mother knowing, making the contact she needed.

Doreen had only mentioned it once, quietly and discreetly, a year or so ago, an option Renee had dismissed but not forgotten. Now it was more than a viable option, it very well could be her only option.

The underground system, according to Doreen, was an old system, practiced and perfected by people passionately committed to giving the abused and threatened and oppressed a chance at a new life. It existed deep in the shadows of everyday life, protected by strict secrecy and an ingenious organization.

Doreen cleared her throat before beginning, shifted her large frame on the folding chair hidden beneath her. "When families are stressin' I truly do believe they should get away on vacation together," she said. "You know?"

Renee didn't, not yet, but she was about to. "We've never been able to afford a vacation."

"Oh, yeah, you got to get the best deals, talk to the right people," Doreen continued. "Like my sister knows. She can hook you up with a good travel agent. If you ever have need, I'll hook you up."

"I don't know if I could ..." In that moment, the whole thing suddenly became real. Real, possible, and now more frightening than she ever imagined. She had asked advice from no one, chancing no interference, and now carried the full weight of the decision on her own shoulders. Doreen was waiting.

With Renee's trepidation apparent, Doreen leaned forward over the table, her head low, her voice barely audible. She spoke without looking at Renee. "She'll explain it, answer all your questions. You need to talk to her, you know, just in case. Give me your number, she'll call."

The call came the very next morning. Renee ducked into the back room at work and listened to the woman who introduced herself only as Doreen's travel agent.

"Time is usually of the essence with our travelers," she said. "This trip is an important decision, one that often has to be made quickly. We understand that, so I'm going to give you as much information as I can, and a phone number, and the rest is up to you. I don't need to know why you need us, the fact that you do is enough. Here's the number."

Renee wrote it, as the woman had requested, without repeating it back.

"This system is successful," the woman continued, "because it runs on a need-to-know basis. Once the direction of your journey is decided, each person along the way knows only a phone number of the next—no name, no address, no chance for information to be intercepted or for anyone to interfere. You don't have to worry about anyone finding out your destination because no one knows it, not even you. Your best chance at a new life is to follow instructions to the letter and tell no one. You and your family will be cared for along the way and assisted in getting settled once you reach your destination. They will help you find a place to live and a job and get the kids enrolled in school. Travel as lightly as possible, bring only what is necessary, and make sure you have prepared the children for the trip."

The flood of information seemed other-worldly, the words floating past her, detached and unattainable. She felt obliged to listen without knowing why.

The woman asked for questions, but none came to mind.

"I know change can be frightening, sometimes more frightening than the situation you're trying to leave. It's a normal reaction to uncertainty. You would be leaving what you know, what you're familiar with, however bad it is, and facing all new challenges. It's never an easy decision. Just remember that should you decide to go, you won't be alone. There will good people at every step dedicated to making a chance at a new life possible for you. You would be starting over in a place where you and your family will be safe."

The only thought that finally formed was how Olivia would fit into the equation. "You said that I shouldn't tell anyone. What about someone that I love and trust?"

"That's a huge temptation. But my experience has been that involving others, no matter how much they care about you, only adds emotion and confusion. The decision must be yours. It is best to contact them after you have relocated."

The thought that she could not tell Olivia lost every ounce of possibility the moment she met her eyes. Renee greeted her with the expected look of concern and followed that with far more than what to expect from the children's interviews.

Olivia hadn't moved a muscle or relented her stare since she turned from the stove at the word "underground." Finally, "You're serious, aren't you?"

"Very serious."

Without responding, Olivia turned back to the stove, removed a pan from the burner and placed it on a hot pad. She continued working silently, her back to Renee.

"Please," Renee said, "can we talk about it?"

In the impending silence, Renee crossed the kitchen and slipped her arms around Olivia's waist. She pressed tightly against her back and laid her head on her shoulder. "I'm scared, Liv."

Olivia's arms slid atop Renee's. "Of course you are." She turned her head to press her cheek to Renee's head. "I'm sorry I reacted like that."

"I need to talk about it."

Olivia nodded, and added softly, "Come on, sit down."

They settled at the table, each of them waiting for the other to begin, both knowing it couldn't be avoided.

Finally, Olivia spoke. "So, what are you expecting of me? What exactly does this mean for us?"

"I don't know, Liv ..." Anguish showed in her face. "I don't know. I don't know what I have the right to ask."

"You don't have the right to ask me to break the law."

"No," Renee replied quickly, "I would never ask that ... I don't know what I'm asking. I only know that I can't take any more of this. I can't put those kids through any more."

The lines, rigid with hurt and anger on Olivia's face, began to fade. "And that's what I should be thinking about, too. I just don't see this as a solution, Renee, and I'm trying not to judge out of selfishness. Ultimately, what's this going to mean to the kids?"

"They'd be free of the system. We could start over."

"And you'd be working two jobs at minimum wage to keep a roof over your heads and food on the table. Who's going to be with the kids?"

Renee searched tea-colored eyes, looking for a hint that Olivia understood what she didn't dare ask. It must have been obvious.

"Don't you think if they wanted to find you, they'd just follow me? Even if we took that chance, Renee, it would be a long time before we dared try it. Meantime ..."

"The organization is set up to give us a real chance to start over. They have volunteers in place to help us make it. They're people who needed help in their own lives and now they are able to give back. They are used to making arrangements for mothers with kids. I have to trust that we'll be able to make it."

"But if you don't make it and they find you, all you've done is break the law and not the cycle that your parents started."

But the risk, she thought, isn't that justified? If you're wrongly backed into a corner, isn't any means of escape justified?

"You'd have to have a new name," Olivia continued, "a new birth certificate and driver's license so that they can't track you through your job. And the kids will have to have new documentation for school and health care. Do you know if the state you'll end up in has a health care program for needy children? And what about Rory? You won't be able to transfer his medical history."

Everything was so convoluted—no path out but a spaghetti bowl of improbability. Renee leaned over the table and rested her head in her hands. She had no answers, only odds, and none that looked worth the gamble. Yet, there were no other choices.

"What happens if Rory—"

Renee sharply clipped the words, "I know."

After a moment, Olivia's voice slowed its cadence and began offering its usual compassion. "I wish I could lay out a solution for you, honey. If I could do it, I would convince Mrs. Gordon that no one could love and care for those kids more than you. I'd find a way for you to go to school and really make progress toward your degree, and I'd get us a place so that we could all live together as a family. These are the dreams I have for you—for us—and I'd make them come true if I could. But all I can do is be here every day for you, to love you and support you in your decisions ... and help make the best family we can for the kids."

Renee dropped her hands to the table. "God, how I want that to be enough."

"It's not, honey. We both know it isn't. But we have a wonderful attorney and the truth on our side. We have to trust in that, and trust in the kids to do what we can't." She watched Renee leave her chair and move behind her.

The decision had been made. Renee wrapped her arms around Olivia and muffled her words into the soft cotton of Olivia's turtleneck. "I love you ... more than you'll ever know."

Chapter 31

Renee paced the length of the empty meeting room. There was nothing for her to do except wait. It was out of her hands, out of her control. It was up to Shayna now, and the kids. Even with the many days of foreboding, things moved too quickly. Justice, it seems, is swiftest when its justness is in question, like the other major events in her life. There had been only teases of time during which she dared to think, or hope, that her life had normalized. Today just proved that that wasn't possible.

She stood at the window. The rest of the world was moving along, living their lives, unaware of her turmoil. No one was aware of it except Olivia, and maybe Shayna. She must have read the distress on a lot of women's faces in her career. This one shouldn't have been hard to read, especially after the last and hardest question was asked. The answer to "Could I do jail time if things go badly?" almost sent Renee to her knees.

The reality of that possibility was just beginning to set in. She'd been pacing to get her legs to stop quivering, stopping at the window to place herself solidly in concrete and steel. How could this be? How could she make it through another nightmare? This wasn't a bad dream, or even the hope of one. It was real, and more frightening than she could stand. She took a shallow, shaky breath and reached for her phone. She paged Olivia with a grateful thought that she checked her phone on every break.

Fifteen anxious minutes later, Renee was spilling her fright in words and tears, and Olivia was doing her best from a distance to calm her.

"They're only kids, Liv. *Kids*. They can't understand how dangerous just one word can be. It scares me, Olivia. I don't know if I've ever been this scared."

Olivia sounded calm and controlled. "I'm going to call a couple of people and see if I can get someone to cover the rest of my shift. I'll be there as soon as I can. Meanwhile, you need to hold up your trust in Shayna. And remember how much those kids love you. They're going to say a lot of very good things. Hold that up in front of the fear. Okay?"

"I'll try, Liv. I love them more than I can tell anyone."

"I know you do. And I love you. I'll be there as soon as I can."

Rory's questioning was, at least on the surface, a formality. The "getting familiar" questions were clearly that, and the generic feelers apparently didn't raise any red flags. And it was hard to find fault with bathing answers like, "Renee says I'm a big boy. J.J. and me get the bathroom all by our self. J.J. lets me wear his goggles and I can find the penny on the bottom. He said it's good because I know how to hold my breath."

So Rory was in and out in short order, and J.J. was close behind. No questionable situations or answers indicating inappropriate sexual content. Nothing seemed to pique Dr. Aaron's concern.

The emphasis was clearly on the girls.

Shayna noticed the difference the first time the same question was rephrased and asked again. "Why did you keep the secret about Jenny sleeping on the couch with Renee?" became "Did you keep the secret because Renee asked you to, or because you didn't want Jenny to feel bad?"

Rachael's natural frown, which may have added insistence to persistence, deepened. "Renee asked me to so that Jenny wouldn't feel bad."

Patience was a trait and a job requirement that Shayna had witnessed before in the psychologists who questioned the children. Dr. Aaron was no exception.

With no hesitation and no change in tone, she continued. "Why would Jenny feel bad?"

196

"Well," Rachael began, her frown still intact, "wouldn't you feel bad if you were the big sister and I called you a big baby because you needed to sleep with *your* big sister?"

"Hm," Dr. Aaron's cheeks creased softly, "I see what you mean. I think I *would* feel bad. And, why do you think Jenny needs to sleep with Renee?"

"Oh, that's because she's afraid of being alone."

"But she has you. If she's scared she could get in bed with you, couldn't she?"

Rachael shook her head. "I'm not big enough to take care of her, like Renee. Renee's always going to take care of us. She promised us."

"Do you ever go sleep with Renee?"

"No."

"Does Renee ever come in and sleep with you in your bed?"

"No. Renee never gets scared."

Then came the bathing questions, which led seamlessly to the touching questions, which garnered Dr. Aaron many versions of the same answer, "Everybody has a private place on their body, and nobody else is allowed to touch it, and you should not touch anyone else's." She was concise and consistent and almost comical in her effort to make the slow-to-understand doctor finally get it. But it was her response as she was leaving that forced a smile from the doctor.

"You've been very helpful," Dr Aaron said. "Thank you, Rachael."

"You're welcome," she replied, her carriage way too mature for her age. "If you need more help, just call Renee and she'll bring me back."

It was Jenny, however, who held the key to the entire investigation, and no one was more aware of it than Shayna. She watched her every expression closely, just as she knew the doctor was doing. She had done this enough to know that it wasn't always *what* was said, but *how*. Merit in this case rested on the shoulders of a worried, frightened little girl.

It was up to Dr. Aaron, however, to work her way beneath the surprisingly well-crafted exterior that Jenny presented to the world. Legally and professionally, Shayna was there merely to protect Jenny's rights, and stepping past those bounds would do more harm than good. She watched patiently and listened carefully.

There wasn't so much as a hairline fissure to be seen in Jenny's composure or confidence throughout the preliminary questioning. She was her usual, convincing self, answering and conversing as if she were sitting through another Millie Gordon home visit. She was unflappable—until it came to the secret.

"Jenny, J.J. told me a little about his journal. He likes that he can write things in there that no one else can read. That's pretty special. Do you have a special journal, too?"

"Yes," she replied, "and Renee, too, because we're the oldest. Rachael and Rory are too young to have one yet."

"I imagine that you write things in your journal that you don't tell your brothers and sisters, right?" She noted Jenny's nod. "What if they knew what you wrote?"

"It's a rule," she answered quickly. "Nobody's supposed to read it unless I give permission."

"What if they knew without reading it?"

Jenny dropped her eyes and remained silent.

"I think everyone probably has at least one secret, don't you think? But I wonder why people keep secrets."

Jenny remained silent.

"I kept a secret once because my best friend asked me to. She was afraid that people wouldn't like her if they knew her secret."

Jenny lifted her eyes.

"Are you keeping a secret because Renee wants you to?"

"No," Jenny answered softly.

"Are you keeping it because you're afraid people won't like you if they knew?"

Her expression clouded into near tears. "We mustn't tell lies," she said, pulling her eyes down again. "So I make it a secret."

"I don't understand, Jenny. Can you help me understand?"

Tears were now making a stream down the pale pink cheeks,

and Shayna began to stand from her chair nearby. Dr. Aaron sent her a look of reassurance that convinced her not to step in.

Dr. Aaron leaned closer and spoke softly, "What is it, honey?" She gathered a couple of Kleenexes from the next table. "What's making you cry?"

"If I say, they'll be scared like me."

"Rachael and your brothers?"

Jenny nodded and wiped her eyes.

"What would they be scared of?"

"You mustn't tell," Jenny said with a touch of her usual protectiveness in her voice.

Shayna met the doctor's eyes with a silent warning. A lie will be challenged.

The doctor refocused. "I don't want them to be scared either, Jenny. I won't tell Rachael and your brothers. Okay?"

Jenny leaned toward the doctor and mimicked her soft tone. "We have a promise with Renee, it's 'for now, for always.' It means she won't ever leave us ..." She sat back in her chair. "But I have dreams at night."

"Dreams?"

Shayna felt a slight relief. Jenny was talking now. She just needed to *keep* talking. We can't afford any more gray assumptions.

And she did keep talking. "Renee says that scary dreams aren't real, but I think they are because they won't go away. And if they're real, that means Renee will go away like our mother."

"So, what do you do when the dreams scare you?"

"I keep them secret and I go sleep on the couch with Renee so maybe I can keep them from taking her away."

Dr Aaron smiled. "I think you're very brave, Jenny. And, you know what else I think? I think bad dreams are just when your mind won't go to sleep even when your body is tired, and it keeps worrying about things. Just because we worry about scary things doesn't mean that they're going to happen, though."

"Well," Jenny said thoughtfully, "I wish my mind would stop worrying then."

"Yes, I do too. Now, I have two more questions that I need to ask you. First, I need to know if there is anything else that you worry about and keep secret."

"I worry about Rory getting sick again, but I don't keep it secret. If I worry, I tell Renee."

"That's good. Okay, just one more question, Jenny." The doctor folded her arms on the table. "Rachael told me all about how nobody is supposed to touch the private place on your body. I just have to check to see if anyone has touched you in your private place."

"No. But if they did I would tell my teacher and Renee, and I taught my best friend, Cathy, the rule because she didn't know it."

"Good. That's a very important rule. And you've done a very good job of answering my questions today." She stood and held out her hand to Jenny. "Ms. Bradley will take you to join your brothers and sisters. Thank you for being so helpful."

"I appreciate your professionalism," Shayna said as she shook Dr. Aaron's hand.

"You have some charming clients there, Ms. Bradley," she said. "Tell Renee Parker that she has nothing to worry about."

"Thank you, Doctor, she will appreciate knowing that tonight."

Excitement exploded in shouts and squeals from the children the moment Olivia entered the apartment. They surrounded her, hugging and squeezing her and talking over each other. Olivia waded forward, trying to listen to each story and kiss each head.

"Okay, okay," Renee said, "let her get in the door. One at a time; she can't hear what you're saying if you all talk at once."

They lowered their voices to argue over who would get to go first. Olivia decided for them. "I'll hear all your stories," she promised, "but we're going to go oldest first. That means Renee is first." She looked up at Renee, standing a few feet away. "And I think she needs a hug, too."

The kids gave her room and Olivia moved forward into Renee's arms. "I'm sorry," she said. "I should have been there with you. This is the earliest I could get someone to relieve me." Then very softly she whispered, "I love you."

Renee held her tightly, eyes closed as she fought unexpected tears. There was so much she knew Olivia wanted to hear, so much more than the complaint being dismissed and we could all come home. But the words wouldn't come; they dissolved instead, void of form and substance, and ran together in tracks down her cheeks.

Abruptly, she turned from Olivia's embrace and retreated to the bathroom. Closing the door behind her, Renee sat on the lid of the toilet and cried. Whatever release the tears afforded *her* would only worry the kids, so this was where she would shed them.

Minutes later, she dried her tears and answered the soft knock. Olivia stepped inside and closed the door. "Are you okay?" she asked, as Renee welcomed the comfort of her arms once again.

"What did you tell the kids?"

"That your tears were because you are so happy to be home."

Renee nodded against her head. "I love you," she whispered.

"I know," she replied, and kissed the still-salty cheek. She held her for a moment longer, then pulled away enough to take Renee's face in her hands. "It's okay now. You're home, you're all together. It's all over."

For now. Renee looked into the eyes offering their reassurance. If only reassurance came with a guarantee.

Chapter 32

Sweet cherry-scented smoke wafted from the pipe Ron Gordon had smoked for the past twenty-three years. Millie spread her paperwork neatly on the coffee table and settled on the end of the couch closest to Ron in his favorite recliner.

"Still working?" he asked, diverting his attention momentarily from his evening news vigil.

Millie pulled a form from a folder and replied without looking up. "Mm, yes, amending a complaint." She shot him a quick "long day" look while she had his attention. "I warmed up the tuna bake you fixed. You're a dear heart. I missed lunch all together today."

"Is this still the Parker case?"

"The psychologist found no merit to my original complaint." Millie straightened and directed a quizzical look at her husband. "I was sure that Jenny would tell her something. And just because she didn't doesn't convince me that the couch incidents are merely the comforting of a little girl after a bad dream. But evidently I've underestimated the influence Renee has over those kids."

Ron seemed content to draw puffs from his pipe and let his wife talk.

"You wouldn't keep a secret of something you think is perfectly normal," she continued. "I *am* right about her being a lesbian, and I've met a woman that I'm sure Renee is involved with. Those kids are growing up with an influence that makes women touching each other seem like a normal thing, so it stands to reason that their answers wouldn't indicate anything being wrong."

"It may also stand to reason," Ron added, placing his pipe in its ceramic cradle, "that there truly is nothing wrong."

Millie offered her attention to the beginning of what she expected from her husband—a thoughtful, logical challenge of her conclusions. It was one of the things, although frustrating and aggravating at times, that had drawn her to him all those years ago. He had been that soft-spoken, thought-provoking member of their college discussion group who relentlessly challenged every assertion. He could just as easily represent the cons of an issue as he could the pros, and somehow managed to maintain a less-than-obnoxious persona. In fact, he had managed it so well, with his disarming smile and captivating eyes, that Millie had fallen in love with him.

He'd grayed over the years, found new reason to challenge, but his effectiveness was never more apparent. He'd honed it like a craft, balanced it with subtlety, and Millie had grown to depend on its consistency. It provided her with a sounding board that absorbed the extraneous while amplifying the germane.

"Wrong is more relevant than it is absolute," he said. "Make it adult consensual sex, put it behind closed doors, and what do you have?"

"I still have a lesbian raising and influencing four young children."

"And if you take lesbian out of the equation?"

Millie hesitated to respond.

"For the sake of argument," he added, "she's heterosexual and seeing a young man."

"I doubt that I'd have cause for complaint."

"You'd have no cause for concern about whether he would be an appropriate influence on the kids?"

"As long as there were no red flags, no indication, for instance, that he shared a bed with any of the kids."

"These are good kids, yes?" He acknowledged Millie's nod. "Polite, smart, pretty well adjusted?"

"Surprisingly so."

"So, aside from sexuality, you have no issue with this young woman."

"Well, there was the time issue when she was taking classes, but otherwise ..."

"Otherwise," he said, tapping the tobacco from his pipe, "she's remarkable. Wouldn't you say?"

"She certainly has managed, with the help of her attorney, to get the help she needs from every government program available to her."

"I'd say that's commendable," he replied. "But a young person, male or female, who sacrifices what should be their years of freedom and exploration to raise four children is remarkable ... would either of us have made that same sacrifice?"

"Of course we would have."

"No college, with all its excitement and challenge, no room for experimentation, for mistakes, no career ... would we have?"

She wanted to respond, to say, "Yes, of course we would have sacrificed. We would have done whatever was necessary." She wanted to believe that they would have, that *she* would have. But the truth was, he had exposed her doubt. There was no denying how much she cherished her college years. They were full of wonder and growth. They were like no other time in her life, the opportunity to find out who she was, and find her place in the world. If it had been a choice, would she have given it up? Difficult even now to answer. How hard would it have been then?

The answer may have been the most hard-fought of her life, but thankfully she never had to make it. That Renee Parker did make it may be admirable, but Millie questioned its bearing on the decision at hand. When pared to the core, it came down to whether this lesbian, remarkable or not, should be raising children.

Chapter 33

Relief had been measured in days. Five days for normalcy to find its level. Enough time for fear to retract its talons from Renee's innards and just enough time for the children's questions to revolve around something other than Millie Gordon.

Renee dropped the second laundry basket full of clean folded clothes on the couch. Doing the weekly laundry at Olivia's not only saved money, it gave them precious extra time together. Little by little they were finding and taking advantage of every available moment. The scheduling was tight but well worth the effort. Planned out right, she was able to get the clothes done today, enjoy alone time with Olivia, and get back home thirty minutes before she had to pick up Rory. Tomorrow would be towel and bedding day.

She moved with renewed lightness, switched on a CD and hummed along with Diana Krall. She was going to sleep very well indeed tonight.

Removing her own underwear off the top of the pile, Renee lifted the basket of the girls' clothes and started for their room when she heard an unexpected knock at the door. She slid the basket down the hallway floor and hurried back to the living room.

The instant she opened the door, her five-day relief stood face to face with a solemn Shayna Bradley. A familiar stab of fear sliced through Renee's midsection. "No," she said, barely able to utter the sound.

Shayna, her expression denying frustration, moved past Renee before replying, "We have work to do."

Renee followed her to the kitchen table. "What more can she do to me?"

Shayna flipped open the flap of her briefcase. "She can accuse you of being a lesbian." She pulled out a piece of paper and pushed it across the table to Renee. "Millie Gordon revised her complaint. This one," she said with direct eye contact, "will go to court."

Renee folded like a deflating air balloon into the chair. She dropped her forehead to her hands without a word.

"Hey," Shayna said, drawing her chair close. She placed a hand on Renee's shoulder and squeezed. Her tone was gentle. "Look at me."

Obediently Renee raised her head, defeat already pulling at her features.

"I know this is tough, Renee. And you know that I'm not going to pretend it isn't just to make you feel better. What I will tell you is that it's winnable. I wouldn't still be doing this if I didn't believe that."

"Winnable doesn't tell me my chances—realistically."

"That's why I'm here. I'm going to explain your options, tell you what I think you should do, and then you have to do the hard work and make a tough decision. Okay?"

"I wish I were paying you, then—"

"It wouldn't matter if you were," Shayna replied. "The tough decision still has to be yours."

"I guess you'd better explain my options then."

"That's the easy part. You only have two. You can deny that you're a lesbian and dare them to provide convincing proof, or you can admit it and force the moral decision."

"No," Renee replied quickly. "I don't need to be a hero. It's too risky."

"Hear me out before you make your decision."

"I've made my decision."

"Even if it means you'll always be looking over your shoulder?" Shayna asked. And without waiting for an answer, she added, "Millie Gordon, or someone like her, can continue to be a threat. You realize that even when your mother is released, there's no guarantee she'll be able to regain custody."

Renee merely stared as the realization settled in.

"Do you want to try to put a stop to this? We could strike a major blow to Millie's pursuit by winning this. Honestly defending your sexuality eliminates having to admit later that you lied, and it will go a long way toward discouraging future accusations that your sexuality has anything to do with how you're raising those kids. As well-respected as Millie Gordon is, if we can get another ruling against her it will look like she's crying wolf ... I'm only asking you to consider it."

"Consider losing the kids for a moral decision?"

"I don't know that your chances of winning on a lie are any better. Remember, this is probate, *convincing* is the key word, not proof. She doesn't have to prove that you're a lesbian and an inappropriate influence, she only has to convince the court that you are. That's much harder to defend ... you'd be taking the same chance of losing either way, but by admitting your sexuality and winning, you gain so much more."

"And if we lose?"

"The consequences are the same either way."

"How long do I have to decide?"

"I think we can expect Mrs. Gordon to be granted the first opening on the docket. There are always postponements and settlements that create openings. I'll know more tomorrow, Renee," she said, and softened her tone. "I've been doing this for fourteen years. I know the look in your eyes; I know it too well. It's why I do this. I want you to know that I will do everything in my power to take away that fear, regardless of how you decide to proceed."

"I know, Shayna. I wish I could pay you, even a portion of what you're worth to me. I appreciate you more than I could ever show you. You know that, don't you?"

"I do. And the best thank you in the world for me is to see the relief and happiness in your face when you know that you're all going home together. At the end of the day, if you're able to separate the chaff from the grain, you understand that that's more important than anything."

As expected, Millie Gordon, with ties older than Renee, was able to get a hearing scheduled for Monday. Five days to decide, to prepare. Maybe the last five days that the Parker family had together.

The call from Olivia during her break was expected and dreaded at the same time. Part of the worry caused by the upheaval in Renee's life now had everything to do with the effect it may be having on Olivia. It was one thing to deal with the normal ups and downs of family life, and the added burden of it being someone else's family, but when upheaval reached crisis level and occurred this frequently, no one could expect Olivia to stay the course. It just didn't seem fair.

Although Renee contemplated the idea, downplaying the seriousness of the situation wasn't possible. Olivia had become too well-tuned to the subtle tones of Renee's words for her to hide anything from her.

"What have you decided?" she asked after Renee's recounting of the situation.

"Not to lie, but I don't know that it matters," Renee replied.

"I thought you had more faith in Shayna than that. You sound as if you've already lost."

"It's not my faith in Shayna that's lacking. They don't come any better. But I feel like I'm grafted to a system that's rejecting me, and I don't think it's going to matter how she defends me."

"Us," Olivia corrected. "She's defending us. And our right to raise children. You won't be alone, Renee. We'll be fighting this together."

"I didn't want to drag you through this."

"You're not dragging me anywhere. I'm here because I love you, and I love those kids like I never thought possible. This is not a choice for you to make anymore. I'm here because I want to be here. It isn't a choice to be discussed any longer."

"I'm concerned about your job, Olivia."

"There's a shortage of nurses, Renee; they need me. Maybe not as much as you and the kids do, but they're not going to let me go because of who I sleep with. And you would have no claim to guilt over it if they did fire me, because *I* made this decision, not you. So let's start putting our thoughts and energies where they'll actually do some good. Okay?"

If only it were that simple. Not to worry, not to take on guilt, not to have branded in all conscious thought that loving me could ruin Olivia's life, or at the very least make her life less than she deserved.

"Okay?" Olivia repeated.

"I'll have to use the time we usually have together to review the questions Shayna gave me and go over my responses with her. I may not get to see you before court."

"That's all right. You and Shayna take the time you need to get prepared. Do you want me to take some time off work and stay with the kids so that you have more time?"

"No. Stacy or Jean will take them."

"Call me before you go to bed."

"If it gets late I won't wake you."

"Then go to sleep remembering how much I love you."

Chapter 34

The day had seemed longer than normal as Olivia slipped the key into the lock and entered her apartment. But the hours had been no different from the first of the week, or the week before for that matter. It was not seeing Renee that had made it seem so long, and so empty. And the apartment, as if missing some undefined essence that always lingered after Renee had been there, seemed a lonely place tonight.

Olivia collapsed into the pillows piled at the end of the couch. She laid her head back and closed her eyes. Her unwinding routine at the end of the day now included a call from Renee, but she doubted there would be one tonight. She knew Renee well enough now to know that the higher the stress level, the tighter Renee pulled the confines in around her. She needed to feel some kind of control, to feel confident, and the tighter she made her world the easier it was. She had always made the decisions and carried her weight. She'd seek, and listen to, advice from those she trusted, but there was no doubt whose decision it was in the end. She was thinking and worrying and going over her responses tonight, and that was all right. Olivia wouldn't be getting any more sleep tonight than Renee, but she would respect her process and not disturb her.

As the tension in her legs began to ease, Olivia consciously began warding off the "what-ifs." There were only two scenarios, she reminded herself. They could win and actually start a life together, or they could lose and spend as long as it took doing whatever it took to regain custody. Either way, no amount of worry would have any bearing on the outcome. She needed to stay positive, send the best possible energy into the universe, and be ready to do the same tomorrow. Impossible. But, she'd give it her best effort. Getting out of these clothes would be a good start.

Tired and preoccupied, she made her way through the apartment at a pace more appropriate to her patients and was half undressed by the time she reached the bedroom. She flipped on the light and started to drop her uniform top onto the bed when she saw the envelope lying there. It was addressed to her in Renee's handwriting. Expecting an "I missed you today," she opened the envelope and sat on the bed to read.

Dear Olivia,

Before you read any further, I want you to know that I love you more than I ever thought possible, in a way that before I met you I didn't know existed. What my mother had with John ended senselessly. I saw it only as something to avoid. What Shayna and Jean have I saw as something to hope for later when there might be room for it in my life and my heart. I didn't know that you can't plan it or choose it. It didn't know that my heart could ache like this for anyone except my family. But now that I do know, it makes this the hardest thing that I've ever done.

The kids and I are gone. I can't put you or them through this anymore. Being without you is going to be very hard for all of us, but I can't be responsible for them being put into foster care. I don't think I could live with that.

I want you to have the kind of life you deserve and I know now that with me you won't be able to have that. Just remember that I loved you enough not to keep that from you.

Renee

Olivia stared at the words. Her heart pounded hard against her chest, and her next breath, held in check only for a moment, exploded in a gasp of realization. They couldn't be gone—gone from here, gone from her life. They just couldn't be. She stood quickly, but her knees gave way beneath her and she slumped to the floor beside the bed.

She sat there for a long time, her brain unable to gain focus, unable to jolt her body into motion. Nothing had ever crippled her like this. She'd seen severe blood loss, and shock, and children blue from the lack of oxygen. She'd handled those emergencies, and children screaming in pain, without a second's hesitation, without one blocked thought, one delayed action. Her training served her well, partnered perfectly with what she'd been told was a natural disposition for calm under stress. If so, it was gone now. Her thoughts now twitched weakly, her body remained unresponsive.

It isn't real. Can't be. I would have seen it coming. I would've talked her out of it. Just like I did before.

She picked up the letter that had dropped to the floor and read the words again. She read them, clinging to denial and fighting tears.

She tried her legs again, more determined, insisting that they prove her denial. Still shaky, Olivia re-dressed, grabbed her keys and her phone, and ran to the car.

All the way to Renee's she tried calling her, leaving messages, redialing every time the familiar greeting began. The van was gone from its parking place, but it didn't stop her from racing to the door and using her key.

The switch turned on the lamp in the corner, illuminating the once noisy, busy room. Stillness hung heavy in the air, threatening to smother her last breath of denial. Olivia rushed from room to room. Dishes and pans and silverware still in the kitchen. Medicine cabinet in the bathroom empty. Beds still made, dresser drawers and closets empty.

She dropped to the edge of Jenny's bed, envisioning the faces, hearing the voices so clearly, wanting them to be real. Children should come running around the corner any second. But they didn't, they wouldn't—they were gone. All of them. Renee and the family Olivia had claimed, and loved and planned her future around. With this one realization, her life had slipped beyond her control. She curled onto the bed, buried her face in the pillow and let the tears come until she sobbed.

Not until they subsided, early into the morning, and she lay staring into the silence, did her thoughts move far enough from her loss to include Shayna. Did she know? Before last night, whether or not she knew never would have been in question. The Renee Olivia thought she knew so well would not have left Shayna, after all that she had done for her, to face the court unprepared. But now, with the faint beginning of anger making its case, she realized that she didn't know her at all.

So there was no hesitation to call Shayna, regardless of the hour, and no surprise that she didn't know Renee was gone. The only hesitation was in Olivia's voice, the only surprise was being able to control the welling tears.

"What do I do?"

"Stay there," Shayna replied. "I'll be over in a few minutes."

"This isn't good, is it?" Olivia asked the second Shayna entered the apartment. "I mean for Renee?"

"It puts a shaky situation firmly on the rough side of the fence," she said, assessing the questionable state of abandonment. "Help me look for anything that'll tell us where she went—phone number, address—check the waste baskets and all the drawers."

They searched the apartment thoroughly, checking every piece of paper left behind, but Renee had been careful. They found nothing of help.

Shayna's voice was controlled, unemotional. "How did she know about the underground?"

Unlike Olivia's. "A woman at the prison."

"How long has she been contemplating this?"

"Since before the interviews of the children. I'm sorry now that I didn't tell you about it. I thought that we had talked it out, that she had given it up. I'm so sorry, Shayna."

"You did what you could. We all did." She hesitated, then let

Olivia know that the bloodshot eyes and puffy face hadn't gone unnoticed. "Are you all right?"

The answer was simple. "No."

There was an audible breath, and Shayna replied, "That makes two of us ... for different reasons."

"You worked so hard for her. Was it all for naught?"

"No. This isn't the outcome I was working for, but even if I had known that this is the way things would be, I wouldn't have done any less. I have more than a professional investment in what I do, and that gives me the jaws of a mongoose. The good of it, as my dad likes to point out, is that I won't let go, no matter how hard the ride. And the bad of it, that I won't deny, is that I tend to expect the same of others. What I've learned over the years is that everyone has a different threshold for pain, whether it's physical or emotional, and their own level of tolerance. I understand where my own is; the difficult thing for me is recognizing where that threshold is for my clients."

"I understand thresholds very well," Olivia replied. "I just never applied it to Renee. Is that what it was, reaching her threshold?"

"She took all she could take."

"But it makes Millie Gordon look like she was right—that it was too much for her."

"It only looks that way because Millie Gordon *made* it too much for her. That's the irony of it."

"What will happen in court if we don't find her?"

Another audible breath from Shayna, weariness or maybe exasperation. "If I ask for a postponement it will only delay the inevitable."

"Which is?"

"Representing her *in absentia*. It's the one thing she still has going for her. Thanks to Jean she didn't end up in Probate without an attorney."

"What can I do? I have to do something. I'm too involved to just let it alone. I need to help somehow."

"Would Renee have confided something like this to her mother?" Shayna asked.

"Their relationship has improved lately. But enough to trust her with that kind of information? I don't know."

"Are you willing to try to find out?"

"Of course. Anything ..."

"Renee took the computer with her, but I might have some luck with her phone records ... Are you sure you're up to a prison visit?"

"I'm going to make myself as presentable as possible and go to work, and I'll visit Sylvia Parker tomorrow. I have to have something to focus on. It's the only way I know how to keep from falling apart."

Chapter 35

The problem with staying focused is that it can't be maintained twenty-four/seven. The span of time between the end of Olivia's shift and her drive to the prison the next morning was so filled with unmanageable emotion that sleep wasn't possible.

So, bundled against the cold, Olivia walked the ten blocks into the center of town. Her focus became her lack of focus. Each house along her route differed from the next, some with windows of late-night light, some darkened in sleep. And when the houses changed to storefronts, she peered absently into their windows, looking without purpose. Moving kept her thoughts random and tears at bay, and left only two hours for restless sleep still bundled and sitting in the living-room chair. Morning and her chance to meet Renee's mother couldn't come early enough.

Yes, she could see it in the eyes, lighter in color but the same deep set, the same expressiveness. Sylvia Parker seemed genuinely surprised to be meeting Olivia without Renee.

The expression accompanied one simple question, "Why didn't Renee come?" and dashed Olivia's hope for information before she had a chance to ask.

"I wish I could say that I came here only to meet you. I did want to do that, and I had imagined that it would have been with Renee. But I can't." Olivia concentrated on Sylvia's face—her eyes, the lines at their corners and between her brows. "I came to ask if you know where Renee and the kids are."

The signs were clear. Sylvia's eyes widened, the lines nearly disappeared. She didn't know.

Sylvia's voice edged on panic. "What do you mean? What has happened?"

"There's going to be another hearing, this one involving Renee's sexuality—"

"Because of you."

"I don't deserve that—not coming from you. We both know why Renee's choices are under such tight scrutiny. I won't take that blame." Her voice softened only slightly. "I don't doubt that you love Renee, and that you're sorry for what has happened. But I love her, too, and right now she and those children should be our first concern. Our relationship, yours and mine, isn't important right now."

Olivia had seen the look before, when blame, being pushed from place to place, was finally seen for what it was and the focus directed where it needed to be. Sylvia dropped her eyes in resolve and nodded.

When she lifted them again, she asked, "Tell me what has happened."

"Renee got information from someone here ... I'm fairly sure that she took the kids underground."

"I didn't know," she said. "I never know. I've made it so that she doesn't confide anything in me."

"If she didn't use the underground, is there anywhere else you think she may have gone?"

"There's no one."

"I was afraid of that," Olivia said. "I don't know how we're going to find her."

"Who did she talk to here? Maybe I—"

Olivia shook her head. "I don't know. Renee didn't mention a name ... And I don't think it would be a good idea for you to ask around."

"No, I suppose not ... when is the hearing?"

"Monday morning."

217

"What will happen if she's not there?"

"I've spent two days trying not to think about that. Shayna Bradley will do whatever she can, but there's a good chance that Renee will lose custody. Then we'll have no choice but to hope she's successful staying underground."

"Then we have more in common than our love for Renee. We're both helpless to bring her back."

Chapter 36

"So, what do you think my chances are?" Shayna asked, absently watching the morning traffic from the office window, her back to her father. "We can't find her. The phone records provided nothing, her mother knows nothing."

"You've had better," he answered. "Somewhere between near and almost impossible."

"That good, huh?" She turned and half sat, half leaned against the wide windowsill.

The old leather of his desk chair creaked as his weight pushed it back to its limit. "So, your no-show had an unavoidable family situation, a respected social worker will make a strong case for removing the kids from a morally corrupt environment, and, oh yes, you have Judge By-the-letter Botsworth on the bench."

Shayna leaned heavily on her palms against the sill and continued to stare at the floor.

"I think I liked your chances better with an admitted lesbian personally pleading her case."

Shayna nodded but didn't look up.

"It's all about character. You know that. You have testimony or affidavits from other parents and the principal?"

She met the eyes, always direct, always honest, that she had counted on since her youth. "And the nurse who took care of Rory, but I can't use her—not unless I want to defend her sexuality, and Renee's."

"If I'm Judge Botsworth, I want to see *Renee* defend her sexuality."

"Exactly. But then I lose an expert's opinion on how well Renee has cared for a little boy with special medical needs."

"It's a tough call."

Shayna looked at her watch. "And an hour in which to make it."

Cold cloths and make-up had minimized the puffiness caused by crying, and Visine had reduced the redness of Olivia's eyes. But the effects of a full day without anything else to focus on were still apparent as she met Shayna in a small conference room down the hall from the courtroom.

"You know," Shayna began in an understanding tone, "depending on what we decide here, you may not have to be here today."

"No, I need to be somewhere right now, anywhere but home."

"Everyone has to find their own way of coping with things like this, and I won't pretend to be able to advise you. I'll just say this once and then I won't bring it up again. If you need someone to listen, I'd be happy to do that for you. Just be warned that if you ask for an opinion you'll get a 'cut to it', no frills 'this is what I think,' which would have nothing to do with how much I care and understand what you're going through."

The honesty brought a weak smile to Olivia's otherwise drawn face. "Which is why you are so good at what you do. Thank you."

"That said, we need to make a decision, and quickly. If I introduce you to the court to testify to Renee's care of Rory, it will allow Mrs. Gordon, via the prosecutor, to ask you if you have had a sexual relationship with Renee. It puts me in a position of defending her sexuality without the court having the benefit of hearing from her personally. And that is never good when you have an otherwise sympathetic client. If I don't use you, I lose the personal, human accounting of what caring for Rory entails. I'll have to rely on facts like hospital and doctor visits."

"Do you think you can actually avoid the sexuality issue if you don't use me?"

"I can't address what I have no first-hand knowledge of, so yes, I can. My argument would be based on sexuality being irrelevant."

"But if you're not addressing what the complaint alleges ..."

"The judge could get very aggravated with me, and with Renee, and we could lose."

Olivia shook her head. "How do you make these decisions?"

"With as much input as I can get. What I need to know from you is how you would answer if you are asked about a sexual relationship."

"The same decision that Renee was faced with."

"Essentially."

Olivia stared silently past Shayna for a long moment. "If I had known," she said very quietly, "I would have asked her to move with me, out of the system, out of the state. We could have managed to take care of them together."

Respectfully, Shayna waited.

"All I have now," Olivia continued, "is the hope that she'll contact me. I don't care how long it takes, if I could just hear her voice and then I'd know somehow everything would be okay." But when she brought her focus back, Shayna dropped her eyes. She didn't have to tell Olivia what she was probably thinking. Olivia said it. "But, it wouldn't be okay, would it?"

"Not if we lose. If you went to her you would both be in jeopardy."

Not a revelation—Olivia had used the argument herself to talk Renee out of leaving the first time—but it was so much harder to hear it now.

"You were prepared for Renee to tell the truth."

"Yes."

"Then I'll answer truthfully, too."

"You're sure this is what you want to do?"

"The tiny bit of hope that I have left of seeing Renee again is only possible if we fight this honestly." She pushed away from the table and stood. "So let's give it our best."

It was not only the right thing, Olivia thought as they started down the hall toward the courtroom, it was the only decision that held hope. And hope would have to get her through.

Chapter 37

Olivia was starting through the courtroom door when the sound of her name rang through the hallway and turned her around. The sound, pitched high with excitement, repeated and bounded toward her as all four children raced down the hall.

Tears streamed down her cheeks as Olivia tried to hug each child before being engulfed tightly by four pairs of arms. Excited greetings mingled with a fragmented tale of packing and driving and a motel with a swimming pool, and there was no quieting them until Renee interceded.

"Okay, okay," she said with a hand on two of the four heads. "Give her a chance to breathe. You can tell her all about it in a little while. We have to be quiet now—remember what I told you about the courtroom."

She looked from Shayna to Olivia. "I'm sorry. I can't explain it now. Just know that I'm sorry for putting you through this."

Olivia straightened, locked onto the eyes she had doubted ever seeing again, and said nothing. Too much, too fast, and still too much at stake. She was grateful for Shayna's intervention.

"Are we proceeding as originally planned?"

"Yes," Renee answered.

Olivia quickly asked, "Do you want me to take the kids somewhere?"

"No," Renee said firmly. "Whatever decision is made in there is going to be made looking into those faces."

Shayna nodded. "It may be helpful. Especially, Olivia, if you sit in the middle of them." She turned to Renee. "Are you ready?"

Renee knelt in front of the children. "Don't forget what we talked about. Mrs. Gordon and the judge don't know how much we love each other, so we're going to try to tell them. And if they don't understand this time, then we'll come back another time and try to make them see how much we want to live together."

"And we might have to stay some place for a while," J.J. directed at his three siblings, "like when we stayed at the motel."

"But I'll make sure that we all get to see each other," Renee added.

"Olivia, too?" asked Rachael.

"You bet," Olivia answered. "I'd miss you terribly if I couldn't see you all."

Shayna touched her hand to Renee's shoulder. "It's time to go in. We don't want to be late for this judge."

Millie Gordon was noticeably unsettled, her attention drifting periodically to the children surrounding Olivia as the judge read the complaint.

Olivia watched her, smiled politely, and wondered if a woman so cloaked in self-importance ever looked into a child's eyes and really saw them. Did she ever see what they saw, or feel what they felt? Was there a chance she would see the difference between what the children need and what she thinks they should need? Olivia listened and doubted.

"Yes, throughout the years," the prosecutor was saying, "Mrs. Gordon has always exhausted every means to keep families together. She's worked with parents to get them into anger management, to stay off drugs, to take parenting classes, whatever is necessary to give the children the best possible family environment. But there are cases, and this is one of them, when we are unable to change the environment in the home. Children, especially this young, we believe should not be raised with a lesbian lifestyle as the norm."

Judge Botsworth had listened, too, without expression, making discreet assessments of the family awaiting her judgment. "And you're proposing foster care?"

"Yes, Mrs. Gordon has arranged for a family with a strong father figure to take the boys, and another good family for the girls."

The words surrounded her, squeezing in on Olivia, sucking the air from her lungs. She tightened her arms around Rachael and Rory sitting on either side of her. This could happen, this could really happen. She was trying to take a normal breath when J.J. whispered, a little too loudly, "It's going to be okay, Olivia. Don't cry."

She forced a deeper breath and attempted a reassuring smile. "Okay, sweetie," she whispered, touching her hand lovingly to his head. "We'll be okay."

Rachael put her finger to her lips with a shush. "Renee's going to tell them now," she whispered.

Olivia leaned down and kissed her head, then closed her eyes and made a plea of faith she hadn't made since her HIV scare. Please, God, please. She opened her eyes, and made herself watch as Renee answered the question that could change everything.

Without hesitation Renee replied, "Yes, I'm a lesbian and I've been involved in a relationship with another woman."

Judge Botsworth reexamined Olivia and the children. If she was surprised at all at Renee's honesty, she didn't show it. "And is this other woman in the home with the children on a regular basis?"

"She spends time with us as a family on the weekends and on vacation days and holidays. During the week she visits with the children by phone. She has her own apartment so she never spends the night with us, and any alone time I have with her is spent at her place when the children are in school."

"Is she in the courtroom today?" Then almost as an afterthought she added, "With the children?"

"Yes, Your Honor."

All eyes—except Shayna's, still intently studying the judge—were on Olivia. It was a silent, uncomfortable scrutiny. Not knowing was what made her uneasy, not knowing what was behind the silence, in their thoughts, in their judgment. Not knowing why, or from where their judgments came—even worse, suspecting that she knew.

It lasted only seconds, but it was long enough for Olivia to feel a fraction of what living with it every day must be like. Leaving was understandable—coming back wasn't.

"Do you understand," the judge asked Renee, "the concerns addressed in the complaint?"

"I understand what the concerns are, but they're unfounded."

"I would expect you to think so, Ms. Parker. What can you tell me that would convince me that they are unfounded?"

"I wish it was possible for me to tell you how much I love my brothers and sisters. That would convince you, I'm sure. But all I can do is to tell you how I live my life so that you can see that I would never do anything that would bring any kind of harm to them."

"Let me stop you here," the judge said. "I've read your file more than once. I'm familiar with the history of your family and the decisions you've made to keep the children together. That kind of sacrifice, although commendable, does not tell me whether your sexuality will have an adverse effect on your siblings."

Olivia watched Renee look to Shayna, and felt the painful thudding in her chest that Renee, too, must be feeling. There was no help Shayna could give, short of the preparation she had given days ago, no help anyone could give. It was a painful fixation, not being able to pull your eyes from something that you don't want to see. Don't be scared, please don't be scared. You can do this. You can.

After a visibly deeper than normal breath, Renee began again. "What is adverse to those children is having seen their mother taken from the house in handcuffs. It's visiting her in prison and not really knowing her. It's never having a chance to get to know what a wonderful, loving man their father was. And it's worrying from home visit to home visit whether someone is going to take them from the only security, the only family, they know." Her focus had changed from the judge to the children and then to Olivia. "They see no evidence of sexuality, not even what a prudent heterosexual couple would allow. What they do see, and what they understand even without words, from me and from the only woman I've allowed close to them, is unconditional love. It's the only thing we can give each other that doesn't cost any money, that isn't affected by where we live or what clothes we wear. It's the most important thing I can give them and I'm very lucky to have found someone who feels the same way." She turned her focus once again to Judge Botsworth. "If I were allowed to teach those children only one thing, it would be that to love someone unconditionally is the best thing you could ever give them."

"I don't doubt for one minute, Ms. Parker, that your altruism is real, or that you have succeeded in planting the seed for such unselfish love in each of your brothers and sisters. But what you have succeeded in doing here is to articulately avoid the heart of the complaint. Maybe it'll be easier if I have Mrs. Gordon ask some specific questions."

Millie Gordon stood at the judge's nod. "Well, one of my big concerns, Renee, is the absence of a strong father figure for the boys. As they mature into their teen years it is vital that they have a man in their lives who they can trust with questions, someone who will act as a positive role model and can help them grow into the best men they can be. How are you going to be able to provide that for them?"

Olivia felt a twinge of panic. We never really talked about that. Why didn't it ever come up?

"I am trying to answer your concerns," Renee said, addressing first the judge and then Millie Gordon. "But I'm not sure that not having a father figure in our home is any more relevant than in the home of a single heterosexual woman."

Olivia nervously suppressed a smile. Shayna had prepared her well. She wanted to believe that she had prepared her well enough to win this, but her fear that honesty would touch a righteous nerve and anger the judge was quite real. She studied the eyes of the woman who would not only decide the future of Renee's family, but her own as well. Was it wisdom she saw folded in the creases of her lids? Could it be compassion that deepened the furrows of her brow? Or was there something else there, invisible to the clarity of her sight, distorting what she saw? Just tell her, Renee. Tell her what she wants to hear.

"I'm very careful who I bring into our lives, male or female. I watched the way J.J.'s baseball coach worked with his team. I watched him coach when they lost and when they won. I talked to his wife, and parents of the other players, all before I would let J.J. play for him. He's turned out to be a very good influence in J.J.'s life; he's fair, even-tempered, and he stresses values like sportsmanship and honesty and hard work. J.J. thinks the world of him. And now, he and Rory have Keith, Olivia's brother-in-law, in their lives as well. He's young and fun, and as a father he's raising his children with the same values I believe are important. I think the boys would have no problem asking either of these men questions."

The judge deferred. "Mrs. Gordon?"

"I don't believe anyone can take the place of a father in the home. And having a man there on a daily basis who J.J. can count on may be the answer to dealing with his anger, which at one point escalated to the point of school suspension."

Before Renee could respond, the Millie Gordon concerns continued. "I also question," she said, concentrating on the judge, "whether a lesbian can adequately prepare young girls for healthy relationships with men."

The comment stunned Olivia. People didn't still believe such nonsense. *Women* couldn't still believe it. Am I so isolated in my own little world that I didn't know people like this? Maybe it's the woman's age, or her religion. Surely my mother wouldn't feel that way. And the judge?

"Possibly without even being conscious of it," Millie continued, addressing Renee, "you may in many ways be influencing the girls to think like you and act like you. As a parent figure you are showing them every day how to navigate the world—the normal course of things as you see it—from simple things like what and when to eat to the complexity of relationships and how to relate to both men and women. And the children living with you, especially the girls looking for their role models in life, will model what they see and hear. Have you consciously thought about that?"

Renee, possibly as stunned as Olivia, hesitated for a moment before replying. "For much of my childhood I was an only child. I was very close to my mother. I trusted her and counted on her, and I loved her very much. She is a heterosexual woman. She is also in prison for embezzlement. I did not model myself after her. I did, however, learn about unconditional love from her. And in the absence of my mother, and my father, that's what my brothers and sisters will learn from me. I don't know who they will love in their lives, but I do know that they will know how to love those people. That's the best I can do."

Millie's expression held firm. She directed her comment to Judge Botsworth. "In my professional opinion, that's not good enough. The best chance for the normal social development of the children is to be part of a traditional family unit, and we can provide that. We must consider the kind of life that we're expecting these children to live."

Then with a look of professional piety, Millie took her seat. Judge Botsworth thanked her with an equally professional tone, and directed Renee to step down.

"Ms. Bradley," she said, "I'm sure you would appreciate an opportunity to contribute here. And since it's unusual that I have two highly respected advocates for the welfare of children on opposite sides of my court, your input will give me a rare opportunity for a well-balanced overview."

Shayna stood with a nod. "Thank you, Your Honor. I appreciate your careful consideration, as I'm sure Mrs. Gordon does. It *is* about the children," she said, turning her attention to the now restless youngsters, "Rory and Rachael, and Jenny and J.J., after all. It isn't about Renee Parker's sexuality or Millie Gordon's personal feelings about it." She turned back to the judge to continue. "One of the most difficult aspects of our jobs as spokespersons and decision-makers for children is to be able to make that separation. What is it that the children need to flourish and grow and to be happy, not what I, as an adult somewhat removed, want for them? If the ideal of two loving, healthy, financially capable parents totally devoted to these children were possible, would I want that for them? Of course I would. But should I deny them the same chance to flourish and grow and be happy because they have a guardian that deviates from my ideal?"

Shayna took another look at the children and shook her head.

"No. Doing so would stand in the face of every important social advancement our society has made. At one time the ideal in this country, the accepted and practiced norm, was for women to be stay-at-home mothers. Society decided that that was their proper contribution, and they were denied a voice in politics and religion, and severely limited in career choices. If that ideal had not been challenged and changed, I daresay that none of us would be in this courtroom today."

Judge Botsworth, stoic until now, lifted her eyebrows in acknowledgment.

"And as recently as my parents' courtship, the accepted norm vehemently opposed their marriage. Not because they weren't mentally capable or of legal age, but because my father's skin was dark and my mother's white. 'What about the children you'd be bringing into the world?' they were asked, even by those closest to them. 'What about the prejudice and discrimination you'd be subjecting them to? The alienation, the exclusion by both races? Forego your own questionable happiness and think about the children.' And, thankfully, they did. They thought about them, brought them into the world, and loved them. Loved us, each of us, as if we were the most precious gift ever given. There is no father on this earth who could have loved us more, no mother who could have nurtured us better. We grew and squabbled and learned and loved, and went out into the world to be a doctor and a lawyer and a teacher and a business owner ... and parents. And the values we learned from those would-be-denied parents we are passing on to our children, and using those values to be the best we can be in our chosen careers. So, when *I* look into the faces of Rory and Rachael, and Jenny and J.J., I see how much richer this world is because the ideal, society's accepted norm, was challenged ... And that's what I'm asking of the court today. I'm asking you to believe the statistics that bear out the fact that no greater percentage of children of gay parents turn out gay than those of heterosexual parents, and in the studies that show most children of gays are well-adjusted and happy, and then to look into the faces of these children and let them stay where they are most loved."

And that was it, the last word of defense, the last chance to convince. Shayna sat with an air of confidence that Olivia could only envy. No one could have presented a better case. If it is to be lost today, Olivia decided, there will be no blame placed, no if-only's to second guess. She saw the hope in Renee's eyes as they met Shayna's and it caught her breath. More than anything, more than holding Renee in her arms, she wanted to be able to hold up that hope.

Judge Botsworth relaxed against the high back of her chair and removed her glasses. "I remember something that Gloria Steinem said years ago about how young the woman's movement was because any significant movement takes a hundred years to effect change. And I remember thinking at the time no wonder change seems so painfully slow—it *is*. Maybe, as you've pointed out, Ms. Bradley, we need to look behind us when we get frustrated, so that we can appreciate how far we've come." She pressed forward again to rest her forearms on the bench. "It didn't occur to me at the time to ask Ms. Steinem why she thought change took so long. My own theory is that time is a natural safeguard for assuring the merit of the change. Without the persistent conviction to carry the struggle to the next generation, the movement will die ..." Her gaze moved across the room, touching only briefly on those trying to follow her logic, waiting on her decision. "So, am I convinced, at this very early stage of the gay rights movement, that the changes it seeks will be good for our society? Not entirely; I'm afraid I need more time ... More specifically, am I convinced that Renee Parker's sexuality will not negatively impact the raising of her brothers and sisters?"

Olivia closed her eyes and pressed her lips to Rachael's head as it nestled against her chest. The sound of her own heartbeat promised to obscure the words she couldn't bear to hear. She held her breath.

"Of this," Judge Botsworth stated, "I am entirely convinced. It is in the best interest of the minor Parker children to remain in the home of Renee Parker. And it is so ordered."

Her gasp of relief muffled the thwack of the gavel and startled Rachael and Jenny. "It's okay," she said, her eyes beginning to blur. "Come on, we have to stand now."

"But you're crying," Jenny replied.

"We get to go home, don't we?" asked J.J.

"You bet we do," Renee said, squeezing through to grab Olivia in a tight embrace. "We're all going home."

"I was so scared," Olivia whispered. "So scared I'd lost you, and the kids."

Little arms hugged around them, little bodies jumped anxiously up and down. "I know. I know. It's over now." Renee broke the embrace in order to deal with the children's growing restlessness and, excusing herself, ushered them toward the door. "Come to the apartment?"

Olivia wiped her eyes and nodded. Then, as soon as she was able, made her way to Shayna. She hugged her graciously. "*Is* it over this time?" she asked.

Shayna hesitated as Millie Gordon walked quietly past them. There was no exchange, not even professional courtesy. Millie's face was unreadable, a featureless shroud of conviction. Misplaced. Injurious. "For now it is," Shayna replied. "And if Judge Botsworth's conviction becomes contagious around here, maybe for long enough."

"I don't know how we can thank you, you've done so much. I want to pay you, Shayna. Renee doesn't need to know."

"And why would you do that?"

"Those are my kids now, too. They are partly my responsibility."

"Well, I won't accept your money. Giving back is one of those values that my parents made sure we understood. You just make sure those four kids get it and we'll be even."

"That's a deal made in heaven."

"I have another one for you. Get the keys to the van for me, and Jean and I'll take the kids to Chuck E Cheese while you and Renee get things right. I'll call when we run out of tokens or we start hallucinating about giant mice."

Little was said on the trip across town—an awed re-cap, numbed reactions spoken in quiet tones. Renee held Olivia's hand tightly and stared at city blocks as they turned from commercial to residential. She'd thought it out on the drive back, how she would explain it to Olivia, why she ran, why she came back. She'd chosen just the right words to explain it, but now, she just couldn't put them back in order. Her mind refused to focus; like a tired eye, it wandered weakly.

Even as they stepped into Olivia's apartment, free of distraction and blessed with precious time alone, the words wouldn't come. Even as they wrapped their arms around one another, she could only offer a wholly inadequate whisper of, "I'm so sorry, Olivia."

"No ... no." Olivia touched both hands to Renee's face, held it as she would a priceless gem. "You have nothing to apologize for."

"I want you to understand ..."

"But I do."

"I was so afraid, so—"

"Shh." She drew warm lips over Renee's cheek and touched them lightly to the tip of her nose and her lips.

The need to make things clear, to be sure Olivia understood, was challenged by the need to make love with her. She wanted to lose herself in the feel of her and trust in forgiveness. But she couldn't. She needed to be sure.

"Olivia," she said, taking the hands from her face and clasping them to her chest, "I thought I was doing what was best for the kids. I thought that staying together and getting free of the system would let us start over."

"Honey, I *do* understand."

"I don't want you to pretend that what I did didn't hurt you. I know it did, and we have to talk about it. The most important thing I learned from what happened to my parents is that not talking about it will come back to haunt us. I've got the second chance that they never had and I'm not letting that happen."

"Come here," Olivia said, taking Renee's hand and pulling her toward the couch. "I know this is important to you, and as much as I want to celebrate us right now, I want to be sure that we get things right, too. So, tell me," she said as she sat to face Renee, "what is it you want me to know?"

"I don't want to keep anything from you, anything, even things that might be hurtful or make you worry. Not telling you is as bad as lying ... And I won't lie to you anymore either."

Olivia's expression was hard to watch—brows twitching twice with disbelief prompted an immediate explanation. "I knew the moment that Shayna told me the complaint was going to court that I would take the kids and leave. I lied to her and I lied to you. I even lied to the kids ... I want you to be honest. I want the kids to be honest. And look at me. Lying, doing the wrong thing for what I tell myself is the right reason—just like my parents. But you know what the scariest part was?"

Olivia waited, brows relaxed, her eyes wide with the empathy Renee was counting on.

"I don't think I could have stopped the cycle on my own. It was what I knew—not what I knew was right in my reasoning mind—but something imprinted in my brain that allows me to react like my parents did in a panic."

"When I was sitting in that courtroom for those few moments when *I* was the one under scrutiny," Olivia began, "I realized that I had no control over their judgment of me. In those strange, uncomfortable few moments, I began to understand what you must have been feeling for years. I wanted to leave. I would have left much earlier if I'd been through what you have. So I understand why you left, Renee. But what I don't understand is what made you risk everything to come back?"

"You ... tearing at my heart. And the kids, demanding to know why you weren't coming, asking when they could see you ... After John, after my mother, I thought I understood loss, but ..." She dropped her head, tried to find the words she needed. "... this was different. I wasn't losing you, I was leaving you, forcing you out of my life and out of the kids' lives," she said, looking up again. "I decided what *I* thought was best for everyone; I didn't listen to what everyone else needed, or even to what I needed, and I almost did the wrong thing for what I really thought was the right reason. It took the kids asking why you couldn't come with us and why you couldn't live with us, and my realizing that they saw nothing wrong with loving you for me to realize what running was going to teach them."

Olivia's eyes closed lightly. Fine lines of relief softened her face, making it irresistible to Renee's touch. She gently grasped the nape of Olivia's neck and brought her close to brush lips over the tender skin of her eyelids. "I love you," Renee whispered. "We all do. And the right to keep loving is worth fighting for."

Voice breaking slightly, Olivia said, "I was ready to accept that this wasn't possible."

"I was, too," Renee said as Olivia moved in against her and nestled her head into the hollow of her neck. "Can you forgive me?"

Tightening her arms around Renee, Olivia spoke intimately low. "For trying to protect your family? You don't have to ask ... Can you make the same promise to me that you made to the kids?"

Renee pressed her lips into the fine dark hair, and closed her eyes. "I can *make* it," she whispered softly.

"That's all I ask."